ON ROUGH SEAS

ON ROUGH SEAS

BY NANCY L. HULL

Clarion Books
New York

Clarion Books
a Houghton Mifflin Company imprint
215 Park Avenue South, New York, NY 10003
Copyright © 2008 by Nancy L. Hull

The text was set in 13-point Dante.

www.clarionbooks.com

Printed in the U.S.A.

Library of Congress Cataloging-in-Publication Data

Hull, Nancy L.
On rough seas / by Nancy L. Hull.
p. cm.
Summary: In Dover, England in 1940, fourteen-year-old Alex Curtis
wants nothing more than to go to sea, to absolve himself of the guilt
he feels over the earlier drowning of his cousin and to help the war effort,
but when he sneaks aboard a small boat going across the English Channel
to Dunkirk, his experience changes him forever.
ISBN 978-0-618-89743-8
[1. World War, 1939–1945—England—Dover—Juvenile fiction. 2. Dunkirk,
Battle of, Dunkerque, France, 1940—Juvenile fiction. 3. World War,
1939–1945—England—Dover—Fiction. 4. Dunkirk, Battle of, Dunkerque,
France, 1940—Fiction. 5. Coming of age—Fiction. 6. Great Britain—
History—1936–1945—Fiction.] I. Title.

PZ7.H88437 On 2008
[Fic] —dc22

2007037933

MP   10   9   8   7   6   5   4   3   2   1

*Every good and perfect gift
cometh down from above—*

*Thanks, Bruce, for helping me
to believe in miracles.*

Contents

1
THE CHANNEL

HE HAD BEEN CLINGING TO THE BOAT FOR HOURS. Salty spray pelted his face as the churning water pushed him tight against the overturned skiff. His fingers ached— but he couldn't let go. He had Georgie to think about.

"Georgie," he called. "You hanging on with both hands, like I told you? You keeping your head up, lad?" He listened for his cousin's reply. But the darkness brought no answer, only the smacking of waves against the hull.

At first, Alec had not been alarmed when Georgie upset the *Wayfarer* and dumped them both into the Channel. He figured they would flip the little fishing skiff over and climb back in. But the swells knocked them around so that within minutes they were too weak to do anything but keep holding on. With every wave, they drifted farther into the churning sea. By nightfall, Alec knew their only hope was for someone to find them.

"Georgie, you hearing me? You hanging on tight?"

"Alec," Georgie answered. "My arms hurt. I'm cold."

Alec heard the weakness in his cousin's voice, and the

panic he had fought to keep down rose again. Hand over hand, he edged toward the tow rope that dangled from the bow. If he could get the rope loose, he could tie it around Georgie's waist—keep him from drifting away. But Alec was cold, too, and it was hard going against the waves. When he reached the rope, it was wet and knotted. He couldn't work it free.

"Georgie, I'm coming back around to help you," he called, trying to sound calm. "We'll try again to lift you up and set you on the hull. Let's do that. What do ya say, mate?" Alec chattered as he worked his way toward the far side. The waves kept coming. One moment, he would be looking down on Georgie and the skiff, and the next, he was below his cousin, watching Georgie rise above him.

The cold water was wearing him out. It had to be well past midnight. Surely their families were looking for them, but would they know where to search? Would they realize Alec had ignored his father's orders to stay out of the Channel when the wind was whipping so? Would they guess that Georgie had come along?

"Alec. Alec, are you still . . . ?" The little voice choked.

"Aye, Georgie. I'm here. I'm coming to you. Right now. I'm coming." Alec inched his swollen fingers along the gunwale and rounded the end of the boat. As he grew closer, he saw the little lad bobbing like a buoy in the dark. Gripping the skiff with one hand, Georgie dug helplessly at the water with the other. His body flapped against the side.

"I'm here, Georgie," Alec shouted, and the boy turned

toward him. It was so dark, and the waves were fiercer now. Alec strained to see Georgie's eyes.

"I'm scared, Alec. You said they'd be coming for us. Where are they?"

"They're out there, Georgie. I'm sure they're looking for us right now."

"Can they find us in the dark?"

"It will be light soon," Alec lied. "We'll spy the white cliffs and the castle—then we'll get help. Once they discover we went fishing in the Channel, they'll come, mate." But now, he doubted his own words, and the gradual numbing of his arms and legs made him realize that he could not hold on much longer himself.

"Stay with me, Alec. Don't—don't go back—back where I can't see you."

"Aye, Georgie. I'll stay with you." Alec wondered if the overturned boat would be unsteady with both of them on the same side. He thought again about the tow rope. Georgie's voice worried him. His tongue sounded thick, and his words came slowly, as if they were struggling to get out. Something inside Alec stirred.

"Hang on, Georgie. It can't be long now," Alec said. He stretched toward the tow rope.

"I'm so . . . tired, Alec. I don't think . . . I don't think. I want to . . . rest."

"Georgie, don't sleep!" Alec turned away from the rope. "If you sleep, you'll forget to hang on. So don't sleep, Georgie, don't sleep. Do you hear me? We can't sl—"

But his words were swallowed up by the roar of a monstrous wave that rose from beyond the skiff and poured down on them, knocking Alec free of the boat. His head dipped below the surface as he clawed at the water, searching for a hold. Then his fingers caught the edge, and he drew himself up against the skiff. He reached for Georgie. He wasn't there.

"Georgie! Georgie! Where are you?" Alec screamed. "Georgie, do you hear me?" He listened in the darkness. Nothing. Nothing but the waves cutting in, smothering his words.

"Please, Georgie. Please be here!" he begged, turning first in one direction and then in the other. "Georgie! Georgie, answer me. You can't leave me!" He tried to lift himself higher to see over the boat.

"Where are you? Oh, Georgie, just answer—please answer!" His chest burned within his numbing body.

"Georgie," Alec groaned. "Georgie."

But the Channel didn't care. It threw wave after wave against the skiff, against Alec. His fingers ached, and he waited for them to simply let go and allow him to follow Georgie to his grave. He dropped his head back into the water and closed his eyes. He remembered how Georgie had looked, expecting Alec to save him. Now Georgie was gone. And Alec was alone.

He thought again about what he'd done. *What will our families think when we don't return? Will they know we've drowned?* He didn't deserve to survive. He had ignored his parents' words, and it had cost Georgie his life.

He felt his arms sag lower into the Channel. His tongue

was swollen; he tasted the salt seeping into his mouth. He had little strength to push the water away. *How . . . how could I have been so selfish . . . to bring . . . to bring Georgie with me.* Angry now, he raised himself halfway out of the water and pounded the useless skiff. *Whump!* "It should be me! I . . . I . . . should be gone!" he shouted. "It . . . it should be me . . . not Georgie!"

Far away, he heard a faint noise. He listened, certain that the wind and his body were playing tricks on him. But then he heard it again. *Wheet, wheet,* the sound rang out. *Wheet, wheet.* Alec knew the sound. It came from a fisherman's whistle. *Wheet, wheet, wheet.* The sound was louder now—it was almost upon him.

"Alec. Alec. Are you out there?" a voice called. *Wheet, wheet,* the whistle blasted. "Alec! Alec!"

"Georgie, do you have Georgie?" Alec answered. But he knew it was no use. He was too weak to be heard above the waves. Still, he tried again.

"Here. I'm here," he whispered. "Over here. Please. Please save Georgie." He slipped farther into the water.

"Alec? Georgie?" the voice called louder.

Alec wanted to answer. He knew the voice—a strong, rough voice—a voice he'd heard his whole life.

"Here, Father," Alec answered, resting his head against the boat. "I'm over here." But the wind spit the words back to him. He let go with his right hand and slammed his fist again on the boat. *Whump, whump, whump!* The sound carried above the waves. "Over here, Father," he said. "Here. This way."

"Alec, Alec! We're almost there. Hang on. We see you!" his father called.

The waves rolled on, drenching his head and forcing the boat away from his chest. He pulled himself close again and pressed his cheek against his curled fingers. It was too late; he knew the Channel would take him, too. Then the skiff jumped, bumping him from the opposite direction as his father's boat pressed up against his. He heard the boats scrape together, and then something touched his head, his shoulder. His father was reaching for him, bending far over the stern, placing a rope over Alec's head and beneath his arms.

Alec felt the rope tighten as his father tugged on its end. With each rolling wave, the boats smacked together and then drifted apart. Alec wanted to help, but his arms and legs were too numb to move. He felt himself being pulled from the dark water, his legs dangling beneath him. He heard the rope groan as it stretched over the gunwale. Then he felt hands reaching under his arms, dragging him over the side and onto the ship's deck. His father slipped the rope from around him. It was then that Alec heard his uncle Jack.

"Where's Georgie, Alec? Was Georgie with you?" Jack shouted. "What's happened to Georgie?"

Alec, his body shaking, whispered, "Gone—he's gone. Georgie's gone. He couldn't hang on . . . drifted away."

His father turned to Jack. "We'll find him. We just have to keep searching."

Thinking his father had not heard him, Alec said again, "He's gone. I tried to help him, but the waves. . . .

He couldn't stay with the skiff. I tried to get the rope. I couldn't—"

Alec's father did not answer. His gaze moved sadly from Alec to Georgie's father, who stood—even in the rough sea—and called out.

"Georgie! Georgie! Where are you, lad? Answer, Georgie; it's me, Da. Answer us, lad!"

Their cries were hopeless. Alec knew Georgie was gone, but he had no strength to argue. Curling up in the blanket his father had placed over his shoulders, he wanted to hide from the men. He had been found and Georgie was lost. Now he could do nothing but cower in the boat and listen as his father and Uncle Jack called again and again for the drowned boy.

"Georgie! Georgie! We're here. Georgie?"

He fought to stay awake, but soon he settled deeper into the blanket and fell asleep to the rhythm of the desperate cries and the rolling swells. He slept fitfully, rousing to hear the men calling, then drifting off, worn out from his fight with the sea. When he awoke, the early hint of dawn was creeping over the horizon. They were nearing shore. Alec looked aft to see the *Wayfarer* tied up and trailing behind. He heard the ship scrape against the planks of the wooden dock, and he lifted his head to peer above the gunwale. His father and Uncle Jack were making ready to haul up. He thought about Georgie and scooted back into the bow, where he could see the shore but stay out of view. People hurried toward the dock, lanterns dangling from their hands. They were anxious to hear what the fathers had found. The first voices he recognized were those of Mr. Walter, the baker, and Mrs. Tanner from the Fifty Shilling Tailor Shoppe.

"They've come. Frank and Jack. They're home," Mr. Walter called.

"Fetch their women," Mrs. Tanner shouted.

Alec saw the crowd gather, many holding their lanterns high, trying to peer into the ship. He spotted Farley Woodhams, owner of the town dairy. Next to Farley, Alec recognized Captain Cairns, skipper of the *Britannia*. Familiar faces should have comforted him. Instead, he hid again beneath the ship's gunwale, out of sight of those who called for news.

Mr. Walter spoke again. "Frank, you've been out most of the night. Did ye have any luck?"

"Aye," Alec's father called. "Some." And he nodded toward Alec, who rose high enough for people to see him.

The crowd cheered, then hushed as they saw Jack turn away and look out into the Channel.

"Oh my . . . no!" Mrs. Tanner cried as she realized Georgie was not with them.

Someone reached in and hoisted Alec from the boat. His legs buckled as Mr. Woodhams grabbed for him, and he crumpled into the dairyman's strong arms. More people were rushing toward the boat now, but Alec only wanted to hide.

Just then, two women scurried down the docks, arms wrapped tightly around each other. They pushed through the crowd as people moved aside. Alec's aunt Lucy broke away and ran to him. Her eyes searched his face, and then she rushed to the ship and looked over its edge. Grabbing the crumpled blanket, she tossed it aside. Her Georgie was not there. In an instant, her cry pierced the darkness, and with her wail, the town felt the loss of one of its youngest members.

"Where's Georgie, Alec?" his aunt demanded, turning toward him. "Where's me boy?" she screamed, grabbing his slicker.

Alec tried to pull away, but she was mad with fear. "What have ye done with me son?"

Before he could answer, he felt his father's grip on his shoulder. At the same moment, Uncle Jack's arms surrounded Lucy and pried her fingers from Alec's slicker. Thomas, Georgie's older brother, stepped up and took her other hand.

"But, Jack . . . Thomas . . ." Aunt Lucy looked from one to the other. "He's out there, ye know. What if he's alive? We've left him all alone! Ye didn't stay out long enough!"

"Lucy." Her husband turned her toward him. "The boy's gone. We looked, and called, and trolled for hours. The lad is lost to us, Lucy. We can't be thinkin' otherwise. He can't be helped."

Lucy looked up, her eyes searching her husband's face. But Jack shook his head and said again, "He's gone, love."

She started to speak, then covered her mouth and leaned into Jack. Alec could hear others in the crowd sniffling and whispering as Aunt Lucy, Uncle Jack, and Thomas turned and shuffled along the dock to their auto, parked near the shore.

Watching her sister move away, Alec's mum pressed her face against his wet hair. "Oh, Alec," she whispered into his ear. "Thank God you're home." But his father forced them apart and then nodded toward Farley Woodhams, who took Alec by the arm and led him along the dock to the lorry. Farley opened the door and let Alec climb in, and then he slid behind the wheel and waited.

From inside the lorry, Alec watched as his uncle prodded Aunt Lucy toward their auto. Thomas stood nearby. Aunt Lucy was shaking her head and pointing to the Channel. Then Thomas stepped over, whispered something to his mum, and opened the door. After settling her in the seat, he closed the door and walked around to the driver's side.

Alec's mum had seen it all as well. She looked his way and then turned toward her sister. For a moment, Alec sensed her struggle and wanted to call out, "Stay with me, Mum." But his shame kept him quiet, and he tried to understand when his mum moved away from Farley's lorry. She spoke to Thomas, who opened the door and helped her climb inside. Then Alec watched as his aunt rested her head on his mum's shoulder for the sober ride to the family home.

Alec's father climbed into the seat next to him and closed the door. Through the rear window, Alec saw the people from town dispersing, each of them off to do the business of a new day.

The lorry rumbled through the city streets. Alec looked up toward the white cliffs and saw the sun as its rays touched the walls of Dover Castle. The castle stood like a royal guard, keeping watch over the city. Gazing at it, Alec remembered the times he and Georgie had scrambled together among the rocky hills, tossing stones into the Channel far below. *Georgie.* Alec shook his head and leaned back against the seat. He thought about reaching across his father, flinging open the door, and jumping from the moving truck. He wanted to run as far from home as he could. But he knew he could not.

He shivered in his wet clothes as Mr. Woodhams and his father talked about the night before. Alec longed to have someone tell him that he was just a lad who was still learning, that he hadn't meant for such a thing to happen. He wanted to feel his father's arm around his shoulders and hear him say that everything would be all right. He wished his mum was sitting next to him, soothing his fears and keeping him warm. But no one spoke to him; their avoidance screamed his guilt. It was his fault; he knew it, and so did everyone else. Georgie had died, and he was to blame.

The lorry pulled up outside the Shaftbury Inn. Still stiff from the cold water, Alec waited for his father to get out and then lifted himself from the seat. His father paused only a moment, then stepped onto the stoop and through the doorway. Alec followed.

The Tiffany lamp on the desk lit the small lobby. The guest ledger was still open to the day before—June 29, 1939—the day he and Georgie had sneaked out to go fishing. A coal fire glowed in the grate, chasing away the early-morning chill, and the smell of bacon wafted into the room. Alec thought about their cook, Aga, who no doubt was flustered, worrying about Alec but needing to carry on with breakfast for the few guests at the inn.

Standing by the desk, Alec waited for his father to blast him with his words. He had felt their sting before, but today . . . today he deserved them. No punishment would be too severe.

Just then, the dining room door swung open, and Aga rushed past Alec's father to scoop Alec up in her chubby arms. "Oh, lad, oh, Alec boy, I'm so glad to see you safe," she sputtered, kissing him roughly on his cheek. He pressed his face into her apron. She smelled of bacon and fresh bread.

But just as quickly as she'd come, Aga stepped back. "The boy's wet and cold," his father snapped. "He needs dry clothes and some rest." With that, Aga scurried off to fetch fresh clothing and hot tea as Alec and his father walked down the back hallway to Alec's room.

Standing outside the bedroom door, his father turned to face him. "I'm going to take the lorry and join your mother at Lucy and Jack's. You stay here with Aga and don't leave the inn." Then he was gone.

In his room, Alec found things as he'd left them. His bed was rumpled, unmade in his hurry to meet Georgie and take the *Wayfarer* fishing. Though he usually kept his journal hidden in his nightstand, it lay opened to yesterday's entry. *Georgie and I will land a big one today,* he'd penned. His parents must have read it when he and

Georgie had come up missing. *It doesn't matter,* Alec thought. *What I've done is far worse than stealing a look at someone's journal.*

He sat on his bed and covered his face with his hands. He was sure to be an outcast now; the whole town would know. Why couldn't it have been him? Why had he let Georgie come along? Like the waves in the Channel, the questions kept coming. What would he do now? How would he ever face Georgie's family? Where would he go to escape what he had done?

"Alec," Aga whispered, rapping lightly on his door. "Here's some clothes, laddie. And some tea and toast. I'll just leave it all here. We'll talk in a bit. Get some rest, Alec boy."

He listened to her steps as she went back toward the scullery. Cracking open his door, he lifted the food and clothes from the hallway, closed the door, and peeled off his wet shirt and trousers.

The damp morning air surrounded him. His fireplace, untended since he'd been gone, stood cold and dark before him. He opened the flue, gathered some paper and kindling from the hearth, and reached for the match tin on the mantel. The tinder caught quickly and flared, casting a warm glow in his room. When the embers signaled it was time for the coal, he reached into the nearby bin and scooped a load of the black lumps onto the fire. Being careful not to add too many at a time, he formed a deep bed that soon glowed with a blue flame. Then he adjusted the flue and settled near the fire, waiting for its heat to warm him. The hot tea burned as it slipped down his throat. He didn't care. He thought about Georgie.

They had been best mates, even though Georgie was three years younger than Alec. Alec's father discouraged him from making many friends. "Living like we do, here in the inn," his father said, "it gives you no time or space to be with other lads. Keep with Georgie. He's family."

Alec remembered how Georgie loved to play hide-and-seek in the inn. He liked to hide in the larder among the tinned meats and jellies. He would tuck back under the bottom shelf, while Alec, knowing Georgie would be there, rattled about the scullery and drawing room before springing open the larder door.

Some days, they sneaked under the archway by the Church of St. Mary to make their way up the hill to the castle. Looming above Dover, the castle had sheltered the city for two thousand years. "As far back as the Romans," Aga told them, "the people of Dover would build big fires at the top of the tower so ships could find the opening near the cliffs."

Stone walls rose high above the farmlands to the north and west, and a drawbridge sealed tight the castle's main entrance. But Alec and Georgie spent their time on the side that overlooked the Channel. Holding hands, the boys peered over the edge and looked down at the chalky white cliffs that plunged many feet below them. From their perch, they saw the whole town of Dover, and on a clear day, they looked across the Channel at the coast of France.

To protect the castle, a small number of guards were posted inside its walls. "It looks like a playground for the king," Georgie said one day, glancing back at the stronghold. "I wish we could see inside of it."

"Maybe someday we will, Georgie," Alec said. "Maybe one day we can find a way to sneak in. But for now, we need to keep it a secret that we even come here. Father would not like it."

But his father had found out. One of the vicars at the Church of St. Mary had spotted the boys going up the hill and told Alec's mum the following Sunday.

"I don't want you wandering up Castle Hill Road, Alec," his father said. "That castle is off limits to the people of Dover. You've no reason to be climbing around there, annoying the guards."

Alec and Georgie had obeyed Alec's father and stayed away from the fortress. Instead, the Channel became their playground. On warm days, when the wind was quiet, they would load the little skiff with sandwiches and bait and shove off into the waters beyond the docks. Some days, they might catch a snapper or two, but most days were spent rowing around in circles or out and back to the shore. Alec's father didn't forbid their sea excursions, but he had warned Alec more than once to mind the weather and take no chances.

Now, with Georgie gone, Alec wished more than anything that they had obeyed about the Channel as well. But the truth loomed before him.

Sitting in his room, he felt the cold leave him while the

sadness lingered. He knew he couldn't stay at the inn much longer. He'd made a mess, and he had to do something. At thirteen, he was nearly done with school. Once that was finished, he would not stay. If he was to be shamed, he would be shamed alone.

2
FUNERALS AND FRIENDS

GEORGIE'S BODY WASHED UP ONSHORE TWO DAYS LATER.
Alec's father refused his pleas to attend the service. "You've no place upsetting your aunt and uncle again," his father said, "reminding them of your part in this mess. It's best you stay back."

"Georgie was my best friend. We were mates. How can I stay away? He would want me to come."

"Do you think Uncle Jack and Aunt Lucy could bear to see your face yet? Mates, Alec? Rubbish! Disobeying like you did and taking that poor lad to the Channel on such a nasty day! What were you thinking, boy? No, your place is here with Aga—for some time."

"But I tr—" Alec stopped. He wasn't ready to tell anyone about his pleading with Georgie that day.

"Tried what? What did you try, Alec?" his father asked.

"Nothing," Alec said. "I meant nothing."

"Do as I say and stay here. Aga will need you to fetch things for tea. You'll keep busy, but you are not to leave. Understand, Alec?"

"Yes, Father, I understand." Alec watched as his father opened the door and started down the steps.

He caught the door before it closed and followed his father out onto the stoop. He started to call out to ask if he could at least go down to the water but stopped himself. His father had said he could not leave; he would not argue. Instead, he sat down on the stoop and looked far down the street to where it ended. He knew his father was right; his aunt and uncle would do better without him. He was almost relieved to miss the service. He had been to a funeral only once—when Margaret Woodhams, Farley's wife, had passed away. She had been as good a mate as Georgie. Alec's parents had tried to prepare him for his last look at his friend Margaret, but when he saw her lying there in the coffin, surrounded by roses and greenery, she didn't remind him of anyone he had known. Certainly not the Margaret Woodhams he had loved.

Margaret would settle Alec on the flapper bracket of her motorbike, and together they would rumble down to the Channel. Many days, the air was thick with the smell of fish and brine. In the mornings, heavy fog often surrounded the Dover port, hiding the pubs nearby. But by afternoon, when Alec and Margaret picked their way along the water's edge, the fog would have lifted. Ships came in to the wharf to drop their loads, and Margaret and Alec listened as fishermen up and down the wooden planks reported their news.

"Aye, it was a good day to toss out a line near Folkestone, mate," old Charlie bragged to a nearby sailor.

"We snared big flounder and snapper and 'ad our fill by midmorning." Then, turning to his dockhand, he called, "Come 'elp me tie up and we'll sort 'em."

"Your fill by midmorning?" Margaret teased. "If that's the truth, Charlie, what are you doing getting back well past afternoon tea?"

"Aye, midmorning—as I say it, I mean it. We spent the rest of the time repairing that petrol engine in me boat."

"Don't listen to him, Margaret," another seaman answered. "He's daft to think he did better than this crew. I'll wager the middle of the Channel's got the best fish today."

Alec, caught up in the banter, would often move too close to the ships, forcing sailors to stop and back him out of their way. But Captain Cairns, skipper of the *Britannia*, took a special interest in Alec. "You remind me of a young soldier I knew in the Great War," Cairns told Alec one day. "I called that lad 'sonny,' because he was so young—young enough to be my own boy. And he was eager. Aye, like you—had big dreams, he did."

Alec liked the captain. Captain Cairns had the respect of all the workers at the dockyard. A short man with a face that suggested years of sun and wind, he commanded attention. Often, he strolled the docks in the evening, pipe stuck between his teeth, and stopped to speak to everyone along the way. Sometimes, it was just a word about their catch or cargo. Other times, he offered advice about dockhands who tried to pinch a shilling or two.

"Are they good workers?" Cairns asked. "Or can you do without them? If they're good, then it's worth your trouble to thump them into shape. Aye, they'll come around. If they're good mates, I'd keep them," the captain recommended. And his advice was never ignored.

"Cap'n Cairns," the dockhands would say, "now, there's a bloke what knows the sea. 'e's a good man, 'e is. And smart. So proper in 'is speech. 'e won't steer you wrong."

Cairns was rarely wrong about fishing, either. "I've sailed the Channel for thirty years. The best spot? Near Calais. The current's always pulling the snapper in from the lower Channel."

As the men squabbled and bragged, Margaret and Alec would settle on a bench and share the scones and sugared milk they'd brought with them. The smell of fish filled the air. Knives thudded and scraped across wooden tables as the bounty was divided up for supper. Fish heads and tails were tossed into nearby buckets. Alec would watch every movement, thinking only of his dream to join the men one day.

Once the commotion died down, Margaret and Alec would be left to the sound of waves lapping against the dock. Then Alec would watch as Margaret tilted her head back and let the fading sunlight warm her face. He always wanted to ask her what she was thinking, but he couldn't interrupt her moment. So he would sit in silence, letting his legs swing back and forth beneath the bench. Then one day, Margaret surprised him with a question.

"So what's a lad like you doing hanging around with an old tomato like me?"

"You're not old," Alec said.

"I am old, Mr. Alec Curtis. But I'm glad you come to the boats. It would be dreary coming alone. You make my days go faster when Farley's always working."

"Someday I'm going to work on the boats," Alec said. "Then you can come and watch *me* pull into port and listen to *my* stories. I'll be earning my wage on the water as soon as I'm done with school."

"That's showing cheek, Alec. Big dreams for a lad of ten." Margaret looked out across the port. "But I think you're going to do just that. You're quick to learn, and a good worker. You'll make a fine seaman."

Alec grinned. Margaret was like that—always telling him what a good lad he was and how proud she was of him. And she had time for him. Some days, when the fog lingered and the ships couldn't sail, Margaret and Alec would work in her garden behind the dairy.

"You have to get the soil soft, Alec," Margaret had once said. "The seeds will do best if the ground is not hard and rocky. Sift through the dirt and throw out the stones so when you dig the furrows and then plant the seeds, they'll have smooth ground to take root."

After he'd prepared the garden plot, Margaret would empty seed packets into his hand. And he would place each seed in the row, careful to cover it with soil.

Margaret trusted him to do the planting right. She didn't have to come along behind him and "fix" what he'd done. She just patted him on the shoulder and said, "Good job, lad. Summer's end, we'll have vegetables for supper."

Alec liked the way Margaret let him be. But his father

was not so easygoing. Swiping at the stair rail after Alec's dusting, Alec's father would call him back to repeat the entire task. Or after Alec had built a fire in the grate, his father would come along and scold him for smothering the flames with too much coal. Though Alec could not see his mistakes when straightening the larder or carrying out the rubbish, he did the jobs again and again until his father left him alone.

Margaret was different. If the rows were not planted perfectly straight, she didn't care. "Vegetables grow with love and water; they don't need perfect rows," she would say. Or if the biscuits he'd helped make turned out a bit brittle, Margaret would pop one in her mouth and smile. "Warm and crispy—just the way I like them!" She never sent him back to the market if he forgot something. "I can get it another day," she'd say. "No need to bother with it now."

So in spring, he and Margaret planted her vegetable patch. In late summer, they harvested the bounty, and Alec returned to the inn with armloads of potatoes, carrots, and onions.

Then one day, working in the vegetable patch, Margaret looked pale and went in early.

The next day, she didn't answer his knocking.

"Have you heard?" Alec's father asked his mother that night at supper. "Margaret's not doing well. Farley's with her, but things look grim."

"What's wrong with her?" Alec asked. "I want to see her."

"Not now, Alec," his father answered. "She needs her rest. You can see her in a few days."

But things grew worse, and days turned into a week. The next time he saw her, she looked old and weary. Stretched out in a box at the Church of St. Mary, her hands folded and resting on her stomach, Margaret showed no hint of her familiar smile.

Alec backed away from the coffin and sat down next to his mum at the far end of the church pew. Soon he heard the vicar step to the front and begin his talk. "We're here today to say good-bye to Margaret Woodhams, a dear woman and wife of Farley. Margaret lived well . . . ," the vicar continued, but Alec was no longer listening. He turned toward the windows and watched the rain streaming down the glass.

A few moments later, he heard the rustling of skirts and shuffling of feet as people prepared to leave the church. Not waiting for his parents, Alec darted through the crowd and pushed open the door. He looked back to see a queue of people forming near Farley Woodhams. Alec didn't want to talk to anyone. He closed the door behind him, moved off to the side, and turned his collar against the rain. In a few minutes, Mrs. Tanner and her friends stepped out.

"At least she didn't suffer long. She wouldn't have wanted that," one old woman said, snapping open her umbrella.

"No, Margaret was not one to waste away in her bed," another joined in.

"Well, I think she brought this on herself," Mrs. Tanner argued, ignoring the rain. "Acting like she was always on holiday, riding that motorbike all over Dover and then running down to the shore and throwing rocks into the water. Was she daft? You'd think she would have been more proper, considering that Farley was a respectable businessman and such. But she didn't seem to care; she just carried on like a young lass. No, this was sure to happen. People are supposed to act their age. It isn't natural to expect we can do such foolishness and not pay the price."

Alec could barely hold his tongue. He ran from the church toward home, far away from the gossip. When his parents returned later, he didn't tell them about the women and their words. He wouldn't talk about Margaret.

In the months that followed, he tried to visit Margaret's grave, but he couldn't bear to see her name on the stone. Then one day, Georgie had agreed to go along, and together they hiked up the hill and placed a flower on her marker. After that, the first of every month, Georgie and Alec went to the market and bought one flower for Margaret.

Now, sitting on the stoop, Alec knew he would be visiting the cemetery alone, and he would have to take two flowers. He wondered if his parents had talked to Mrs. Tanner at Georgie's funeral. Nosey parker that she was, she would blast him for his reckless ways. Alec didn't care, because Mrs. Tanner had been wrong about Margaret. Margaret *did* act her age. She acted the age of her heart, and her heart was young. Mr. Woodhams knew that. Her heart wasn't shriveled and dry like Mrs. Tanner's. She just used it up sharing it with others—sharing Alec's dream.

When he visited her grave, he sometimes imagined he could hear Margaret nudging him on . . . "Big dreams for a lad. You'll make a fine seaman." Alec wished he could hear her now. She would know what to say about Georgie.

"Alec boy." The voice startled him. He hadn't heard Aga step outside. "What are you doing out here, lad? It's the sadness pulling you here, isn't it? I remember what it was like—when I lost me husband. I should have kept him home. The Channel was rough then, too. But me husband wouldn't have it; he was a plucky old johnny. Not one to listen to anyone once his mind was made up."

"How did you go on, Aga?" Alec whispered.

"That's where your father saved me. When me husband didn't come home, I thought I would stay billeted in me flat forever. But then I knew I had to do something. Would he have wanted me to waste away in some grotty pub, feeling sorry for meself? He would not. Mr. Frank, he dropped in at the pub one day when some bloke was demanding another pint—though he'd already had too many. Your father, he stopped that bloke right then, sent him on his way, and offered me work here at the inn. Aye, Mr. Frank was a bit gruff even then, he was." Alec watched as Aga spread her feet apart, placed her hands on her hips, and mimicked his father: "Mrs. Greshem, if you'll help with our lad, you can have your own room near the kitchen."

She smiled at the memory. "And as you know, Alec boy, I've been doing the work ever since."

And a good worker she was. From the time he could

read, Alec had called her Aga—after the nameplate on their Swedish cooker stove. "She's *our* Aga," Alec had announced. "*Our* cooker. She's warm and big."

Her body showed her fine cooking. Plump and stocky, Aga waddled more than walked. She was the comfort Alec needed when his parents were busy with guests and cleaning, as they so often were. Even now, she soothed Alec's sadness, leading him inside for biscuits and tea.

Later, when he had finished helping Aga clear the dishes, he took his journal and settled into the big horsehair chair in the drawing room. Looking out the window, he saw the chaps from the dock heading home from their work. *Georgie is gone, and I am here. It was my mistake and it should have been me,* Alec wrote in his journal. Then he thought about the weeks following Margaret's death. People had gone back to their jobs as if nothing had happened. As if Margaret had never been alive. *As long as I live,* Alec wrote, after brushing a hand across his eyes, *I will be remembering Georgie, and I'm going to make up for what I did. Margaret would say that I'm right to try. She would say that what I decide to do, I'll do.*

I will make things right.

Alec closed his journal and leaned back, watching as the first drops of rain crept down the window glass.

3
GALLEY BOY

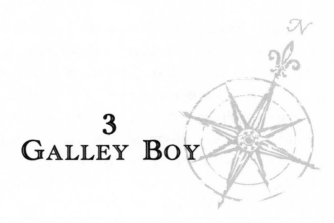

OVER THE NEXT FEW WEEKS, ALEC DID HIS BEST TO please his father. He stayed close to Aga, helping in the kitchen and running errands to the market. He thought often of Georgie—especially when he had to fetch guests from the train at Dover Priory and escort them to the inn. Georgie had always loved going to the trains, watching the people scuttle about, wondering where they'd come from, what led them to Dover.

Although June had been cold and dreary, July and August brought sunshine and warmth. Alec had turned fourteen and had spent his last day in school. He thought often about the future and his plan to leave. In spite of the warmer weather, the cloud of despair that had settled over the inn after Georgie's drowning brought a coldness he couldn't avoid. He never mentioned Georgie, nor did his father, but he knew the memory was always lurking, threatening to erupt and put more distance between them. And other fears troubled his parents. When Germany had invaded Czechoslovakia months earlier, in March, the trouble seemed far away. Now the guests at the hotel were full of stories of Germany and the evil Hitler, who had vowed to conquer all of Europe—and then England.

The first blackouts came near the end of August. Every business, ship, home, and auto was required to cover its windows or seal off any spot where light might penetrate the darkness and betray a city's location to enemy planes flying at night. Those who smoked cigarettes were forced inside. Air-raid drills worried people who had been through the Great War, and rumors circulated about the rationing of food.

Alec was not concerned. He rather liked the tension of the conversations around the table. But he had not seen a war. Those who had—like his father and Aga—were troubled by the news from the continent.

Gas masks were issued to every Dover resident, and at first, people toted them everywhere. Then days passed, and residents began leaving them behind when they went to the market or church. Some, like Alec, even found them a bit amusing.

"I think they're dandy," Alec said to Aga one day.

"That's because you've had no need to use them, Alec," Aga argued. "Things like gas masks, they stir memories that haunt you. Believe me, anything connected with war is sad."

A few days later, Alec got his first twinge of what Aga was feeling. People at the market that morning had been buzzing about Germany and its relentless chanting: "Today Germany is ours, and tomorrow the whole world!" In the evening, Aga, Alec, and his parents turned on the radio just in time to hear the report from the British Broadcasting Corporation: "On this day, the first of September, 1939, German forces have invaded Poland and its planes have bombed Polish cities, including the capital, Warsaw."

Two days after that, England and France declared war on Germany. Still, Dover seemed safe. After all, the war was across the Channel. Then Alec saw groups of soldiers arriving by train at the Dover Priory station. Soon after, a military encampment began to take shape up on the hill. Slowly, more and more troops arrived and set up their bases on the white cliffs above Dover. The encampment was off limits to civilians, but that didn't stop Alec from being curious about the military plans. The activity brought more business to Dover and to the docks, so he was sure to learn some news as he rambled about the city.

"Hitler says he will not stop until he's taken England," one traveler announced at supper. Alec smirked at Hitler's threat. Dover had felt such threats before in its history, but no one had ever succeeded in marching through her port and on to all of England. Alec was sure that Hitler was no different from the others.

But even if he had been allowed to go up to the cliffs, Alec didn't want to go without his mate. Every day, he helped out at the inn, fetching guests from the Dover Priory or running to Shannon's Grocery for Aga. Then, with his chores finished, he would head for the dockyard.

His path would always be the same. He'd scoot out the back door, jump down the steps, and run down the High

Street, past the little shops. Mr. Walter's FRESH BREAD sign would be hanging above the biscuits in the window, tempting seamen on their way home from the docks. Dr. Henchley would be reaching into his auto to arrange his kit of medicines. And Mrs. Tanner would be pretending to sweep her stoop while really trying not to miss the latest gossip. Alec was careful to walk on the other side of the street.

At the docks, Alec found his place. He wandered along the pier, waiting for someone to toss him a line. Looping the rope under and over the mooring hook, he would wave and call out.

"Any luck today, mates? Will there be fare for supper?"

One day, Captain Cairns smiled at him. "Aye, Alec. The fishing is good."

"I'm sorry, Captain. But I think you're blowin' wind," a young sailor argued. "The fish across the Channel are all off to a party, if you ask me. Nothing's nippin'."

"Well, here's the proof," the captain answered, tossing a hefty flounder into Alec's hands. "Tell your mum you've brought fare for supper, lad. It's fish and chips you'll be having."

Later, sharing the story with Aga, Alec dropped the fish into the scullery basket and sat down. His father surprised them both as he charged into the room.

"Father, look—" Alec stood up.

"We've no time to be gazing at fish. Supper's due, and you've been mucking about on those docks all afternoon. We've got business to do and a name to protect. Help Aga with supper." He pushed his way through the swinging door.

"He's . . . he's . . ." Aga tried to explain his father's harshness. "He's worried about business, Alec. The BBC is reporting more and more of the trouble in Europe. He's afraid we won't have guests if the news gets any worse."

"He's always worried about business," Alec said. "About the Curtis name. Well, I can't change him. And I can't keep away from the docks. My future's there."

"Alec, I know your heart's there. But can your mind be here? Can you help set the dining room for supper?"

"Aye, Aga. I want to do what helps you. But he makes me batty. Always telling me to 'do the Curtis name honor.' I'm not like him." But in one way, Alec was just like his father: they both knew what they wanted, and neither would give in.

In the dining room, Alec's mum helped him with the table. "He wasn't always like this," she said. "I know your father. You can't see it, but he's proud of us—of you. In the war, when he fought—in the Dardanelles—something happened. Something horrible. He won't speak of it. But it changed him, took away his spirit, and made him hard. I wish you could have known him before then."

Alec wanted to understand. For his mum's sake, he wanted to get along with his father. But each day brought arguments and pushed him more often to the docks.

One afternoon, Captain Cairns called him over to his ship. "Alec. Would it suit you to spend some time with me on the old boat—scrubbing the deck, brewing the tea, loading and hauling cargo to Folkestone or Ramsgate? And when we don't have any cargo, well, then, we'll cast off for the other side to do some fishing. The pay wouldn't be much, but I'd offer a fair wage. How about it, sonny? You think your mum and dad would go for such an arrangement?"

Trying to tie the *Britannia*'s rope to the dock stake, Alec struggled to control his trembling hands. Was he imagining Cairns's words, or had the captain really asked him to work on his ship? Could there be a better day than this? A better moment than now—his first chance to be a true seaman? He wanted to jump on the boat right then and be carried away. He didn't care if he had to scrub decks or clean fish—he just wanted a chance. But would his father allow it? Alec had his daily chores at the Shaftbury. But he could get up early and set the table for breakfast. And most days, he wouldn't be out past supper, so he would have time to help Aga in the evening.

"Speak up, sonny. You know I'm an old bloke; I don't hear so well anymore. What do you say?" the captain asked.

"Yes. I say yes. I'll ship out on the *Britannia,*" Alec said.

"And your folks?"

"They'll be glad I've got something to do during the day. Sometimes the inn doesn't keep me all that busy," Alec fibbed. Actually, Aga could find plenty of jobs for him, but he was a sea lover; someday, he would be a real seaman. How could he let this chance slip by? He would beg for his father's approval. "Tomorrow's Wednesday, Captain. I promised Aga I'd go to market in the morning. But I'll come by in the afternoon when you've docked. You can tell me then what I need to do."

On his way back to the inn, Alec realized that, maybe

for the first time since Georgie's death, he could get beyond the past. Being a hand on the *Britannia* would help him prove himself. He could not live forever under the dark cloud that hovered over the inn. He had to do something to break from his father. He also had to convince his father that this job was right for him. He was determined not to lose his courage.

Fog was moving in over the city, and the streets were growing dark. It wouldn't go well with his father if Alec came home late and then asked about Captain Cairns. So to save time, he cut through the pub section and raced across Market Street. Turning the corner, he glanced back a moment; then he thought he heard someone call out. Before he could turn back around, Alec collided with a bloke just leaving the White Horse Pub. The man was scruffy-looking, big, with a strong smell of ale and tobacco lingering about him.

"My fault, mate," Alec volunteered. "Sorry to have rammed you like that."

But the man was not interested in apologies; his anger erupted. "Why don't ye watch where ye be goin'? What do ye think yer doin'? If ye were my lad, aah'd smack ye for being so careless. Where's yer 'ome, boy? What's yer father's name?"

Alec fumbled for the lie that would get him on his way. "I'm just a mate on one of the ship's crews, sir. Don't have a home here. Sorry for the trouble. I'll be more careful."

"Those words don't help much, laddie. Ye nearly

broke me leg, and yer captain needs to know about such foolishness. Come now. Show me which ship ye tend."

Terrified, Alec looked around for help. Then he did the only thing he could think of. He ran. He heard the slapping of feet on the brick street as the man chased him. Alec darted between two nearby pubs and slid through a lattice opening into an alley. Turning left, he raced along the base of the hill that held the military encampment. He stopped and listened for the man. Nothing. Circling around Mr. Woodhams's dairy, Alec hurried down York Street toward the back gate of the inn. Taking the steps two at a time, he flung open the door to find Aga standing in the scullery looking quite muddled.

"Alec. Your father's been pacing in and out of here asking what's become of you. What's happened? You're dripping sweat."

"Shh, Aga," Alec whispered. "Tell Father . . . tell him I was out on an errand for you," he pleaded.

"I've already told him half a dozen times that I didn't know what had become of you. How can I suddenly remember an errand?"

"Please, Aga. Father knows you to be forgetful sometimes. Please tell him you forgot that you needed some bacon for breakfast, and you sent me for it. He won't question your word."

Just then, his father pushed open the swinging door to find Alec standing there.

"We've been searching the whole street for you, Alec."

"It's my fault, Mr. Frank," Aga said. "I forgot—I sent

Alec on a run to the butcher's for bacon for tomorrow's breakfast. It isn't an English breakfast without bacon. I told Alec this morning I needed it, and he stopped to get it on his way home from the docks. Don't blame him, sir. I asked him to go."

His father hesitated, but Aga and Alec stood together, and Alec's father seemed too tired to press the matter. He left the kitchen, calling over his shoulder, "Supper needs to be ready by half past, Aga. See to it that the guests are fed on time."

"Of course, Mr. Frank, we'll be ready," Aga answered as she shot a threatening look at him.

"Thanks, Aga." Alec relaxed. "I can't be found out or Father will be angry, and I've an important question to ask him. He won't say yes if he thinks I was careless again."

"It had best be a life-or-death question, Alec boy, for me to lie so to your father. I've never felt so ashamed as I do now. You'd better have a good reason for asking me to do such a sinful thing."

"It's the beginning of my new life, Aga. Is that important enough?" Alec grinned.

Aga cocked her head and looked at him. "Lad, sometimes I don't know whether to smack you or hug you. Now wash your hands and then put this Yorkshire pudding in the cooker before you go to the dining room."

After supper, Alec took his time doing his chores. He didn't want to give his father any reason to say no to Captain Cairns's offer. So as soon as the guests had retired, Alec set about clearing the dishes and sweeping the dining room floor. Carefully moving every chair, Alec pushed the broom under the table, cleaning out any dust or crumbs that might have settled in the cracks. Then, even after Aga had dismissed him, he set out the plates and cups for the next morning's breakfast.

He nagged Aga for more jobs, but she grew weary of his pestering and finally pushed him into the dining room. His father was not there.

Alec heard voices coming from somewhere in the inn. He stepped across the dining room and through the lobby and peeked into the drawing room. "German forces now control all of Poland," the radio announced. His father was sitting alone at his desk, his ledger resting before him.

Alec quickly lost his nerve. His father hated interruptions when he was working on the ledger. The chore always agitated him, and combined with the news from the BBC, the ledger work would be even more dreadful. Alec tried to back away from the door, but his father heard him.

"What is it, Alec?"

At first, Alec's mouth wouldn't form the words. He feared that the moment he spoke, his father would hush him and send him away. Yet he also knew he had to ask now. He had given the captain his word. He stepped into the room.

"Father," Alec began. "There is something I need to ask."

His father didn't look up.

Alec tried again. "Father . . . it's . . . it's very important to me."

"Can't it wait?"

"No, no, it can't. Captain Cairns has asked me to hire on as a galley boy for the *Britannia,* and I told him I would." Alec hurried on. "Please, Father, please let me work with Captain Cairns. I love the sea, and I won't let it interfere with my chores for Aga. I can do both; I know I can. And it's time for me to make my own way."

"Alec, Aga needs you here. Besides, how could you even consider that you're ready for such work? Does Cairns know what happened to Georgie?"

"He was there, Father. The day we came back. He saw it all. He wants me anyway. He'll teach me what I need to know. And I'll do anything he asks. It's not as if we're going out for weeks at a time. He's a local skipper; we'll be back before supper most days. Please, Father, let me do this!"

Alec watched as his father made a note and then closed the ledger. He could only guess what his father was thinking. But he had gotten this far; he was not going to back down now. "Father," Alec pleaded, "don't keep me from this. Please."

His father turned to speak. Then he slumped in his chair, resting his head in his hands. "It's not my wish, Alec, but you've shown already that you're going to do what you're going to do. You ignore the rules. Georgie's accident is proof of that. Would you really stay away from the docks if I told you to? No, your head is set. I am not pleased with Cairns's offer, but I can't hold you here."

Alec stood for a minute, hoping his father would soften and give him some bit of encouragement. None came.

Instead, his father picked up his pencil and turned back to his ledger. Alec backed out the door to the lobby and walked down the hallway to his own room.

I don't care if he doesn't like the idea. I'm going with Captain Cairns first chance I get. How many times do I have to be reminded about Georgie? Doesn't Father know that I think about Georgie every day? Doesn't he know that the less I'm around, the better everyone else will be? My world is not going to be ledgers and cleaning and catering to the needs of every guest who passes through the Shaftbury. My world is the sea. I will move on with or without Father's blessing.

As Alec wrote in his journal, he considered every detail. He would not abandon his post at the inn; Aga depended on him. He would get up early, do what he needed to do, and each day be at the *Britannia* before it shipped out.

Later, he got dressed to go out. He slipped a note into his pocket and pulled his cap over his eyes. Tiptoeing across the floor, he turned the doorknob and surveyed the hallway. Then, forcing his legs to move, he made his way to the kitchen and down the back steps, into the alley.

He crept through the darkness toward the docks and the *Britannia*, feeling guilty for his stubborn ways. But if he did not follow through that night, he would lose his nerve and forfeit his best chance to get on with his life. He hurried to the docks before he changed his mind.

Moving quietly among the ships moored near the

Britannia, he took a deep breath and smelled the salt of the sea. Alec knew the port well. Two lengthy docks pushed out into the Channel. Surrounding the dock to the south were dinghies, rowboats, fishing smacks, and drifters tied up for fishing near the shore. Along the other dock, the larger vessels like the *Britannia*—tugboats and trawlers, barges, and even some paddle steamers—bobbed up and down on the rolling tide. Another port farther along harbored the ferries that shuttled people and autos across the Channel to France.

Before the blackout, Alec used to see small lanterns glowing from within the wheelhouses on some ships. Now, lights were doused and windows were covered. He was relieved that he knew the docks so well. He could find the *Britannia* in the dark.

He stepped over the gunwale and onto the deck, looking for the right spot to post his message. He settled on the wheelhouse, walked over and opened the door, and slipped inside. Reaching into his pocket, he pulled out the note. He didn't need the light to see; he'd rewritten the words so many times, he had them memorized:

Dear Captain Cairns,

　　My father has granted me permission to work on the Britannia. *As promised, I will stop by in the afternoon to get more details about my duties and our first trip. Until then, I am respectfully yours,*

　　　　　　　　　　　　　　　　Alec Curtis

The captain's clipboard hung from a nail above the wheel, so he took it down and snapped the note under the catch. *He can't miss it,* Alec thought.

He strode back across the deck, jumped to the docks, and ran up the ramp toward York Street and his bed. More confident with each step, he told himself over and over that he was doing the right thing, that he was on his own path.

By the time he was in front of the Shaftbury, he was nearly skipping, happy that he had left the note. Then something caught his attention. A man wearing a white cap was walking in front of him. Alec passed the Shaftbury, keeping his eyes on what was ahead. Darkness hid the man's face, but Alec followed the white cap as the man zigzagged back and forth along the walk. He wondered where the bloke was headed at that time of night. Then the man turned onto Castle Hill Road, and Alec lost sight of him.

Alec shrugged and told himself the man was not his business. And in a few minutes, he was climbing the steps to home. He'd taken care of his own business that night, and he wouldn't turn back. The next day, he would be a seaman.

In his room, he changed his clothes and stirred the fire. The thick drapes covering his window held in the light that rose from the burning embers. Too excited to sleep, he sat on his bed and thought about the next day. His mind couldn't settle on one image. He thought about the Shaftbury and all the years he'd helped Aga with her work. He thought about his days in school. From his bed, he could see the short pants and jackets still hanging in his closet—the uniforms he'd worn until, at age thirteen, he was allowed to wear trousers like the other boys his age. It seemed so long ago. He had grown up since then, since Georgie.

Georgie. The thought of the boy's name caused Alec to reach for the small airplane on his dresser. The plane had come unassembled in a kit. He and Georgie had spent hours looking through Alec's plane spotter cards, trying to decide which kit to buy. They finally settled on the Spitfire, after the real thing launched in 1936. A single-seater fighter plane, the Spitfire could zip through the clouds with cracking speed. Georgie had later gotten his own kit—a Hawker Hurricane. They would battle each other in the skies above Alec's bed. But one day, the Spitfire's propeller had snapped off when Georgie's Hurricane came soaring toward it. Alec told Georgie it was okay, that they could fix the plane, but Georgie still cried.

Other things in the room made him realize how much he had changed. The *Beano* comics with Lord Snooty, who lived with his guardian, Aunt Matilda, in Bunkerton Castle. *The Magnet,* a weekly paper carrying stories of schoolboy Billy Bunter. All of these things had once been so important to him. What had happened? When had he stopped wanting them?

He imagined Margaret Woodhams shaking her head and smiling her crooked smile. "Well, Alec, lad, you gave them up as most lads do when they move on to bigger dreams. If you don't give them up, you can never get beyond those boyhood fancies. Most boys want to be men, to discover new things and new paths. You've gone and done it, too. You've discovered the sea. Now walk your path."

He smiled. That was what he would do. Travel that path to the sea.

He lay down and tried to sleep. But too many memories kept rolling back to him: Captain Cairns and his offer, his father's hardness about his new job, . . . and the odd man in the white cap.

4
CRUSTY BADGER

ALEC HEARD THE SHOUTING AS SOON AS HE STEPPED onto the dock. It was late afternoon, and most of the other ships were already in port, tied up for the night. The argument was coming from the *Britannia*.

"We've no need for a boy on this ship!" the man bellowed. "'e'll be in the way, makin' more work for us. We can manage without 'im."

Alec slowed his pace and then hid behind the *Tamzine*, which was moored next to the *Britannia*. Captain Cairns was speaking.

"He'll do the jobs we can't be wasting our time doing, Badger," the captain said. "Scrubbing the decks and reeling in the lines once we've loaded the hold. He'll free us to collect our pay and settle accounts. Besides, with Alec along at the end of the day, you can start early on your pints in Snargate Street. You'll see—the boy'll work hard. He's been raised to carry his load. Give him a chance . . . and treat him better than you do the barmaid at the White Horse."

"I'll be treatin' 'im the way I care to treat 'im, and if 'e gets in my way, I'll give him a thrashin' 'e won't soon forget. I've got no time to be trainin' babies 'ow to be seamen.'"

Alec didn't wait for more. He stepped out from his hiding place and cleared his throat.

Captain Cairns turned toward him and smiled. Alec could tell by the wet deck and loose ropes that they'd just come into port. "Alec. We were just speaking of you, lad. I was telling Badger that you're coming on as galley boy. . . . Badger," the captain said, "this is Alec Curtis. Alec, Badger's my first mate. Been with me for some time."

"Aye, good to meet you, Mr. Badger," Alec said.

"Not Mr. Badger. Just Badger," the first mate replied.

"We've had a long day, Alec," Captain Cairns went on. "A bit tired we are. Let me show you the ship, and we'll make plans for tomorrow morning."

Alec could see that the *Britannia* was an old ship, sitting low in the water, three feet high from deck to gunwale. Its beam was about ten feet, allowing room for working with cargo. Near the stern were two doors that swung open to the hold below. In the middle was the wheelhouse, where the captain stood as he guided the boat through the Channel waters. Atop that, the boom extended upward at an angle, ready to be used for loading and unloading cargo and catch. Just in front of the wheelhouse, doors lifted up to reveal a few steps that led to the small galley.

"You'll help with casting off the ship, and then I'll need you to clean up any mess on deck," the captain said. "Once that's done, we'll want some strong tea brewed, and then, if

Badger has nothing else, you're to wait atop the locker on deck until we make port. Badger tends to the mechanics—making sure the engine is running and the petrol is stocked."

The *Britannia* wasn't a big ship—about forty feet bow to stern—but what with keeping the ship running, and loading and hauling cargo, and cleaning up after, Alec could see that they were all needed. He would prove that to Badger.

"That's it, lad," Captain Cairns said, climbing up from the galley and moving past Alec toward the stern. "We're a small business, hauling light cargo—wire, scrap metal, steel posts—up and down between the smaller coastal towns. And when the weather's good and we've no loads to deliver, we'll cast some nets for fish to sell at the pubs. It can be a hard life. But it puts money in our pockets. And it usually gets us out to sea six days a week."

"Aye, and it'll get you 'urt if you don't stay awake and keep out of my way," Badger snarled. "So be sharp. This is no life for a reckless bloke."

"Aye, Mr. B—," Alec began. "Aye, Badger. I'll do my job. You can believe that."

"Alec," Captain Cairns said. "Depending on how thick the fog is, we leave at seven. Don't be late, lad."

"Aye, Captain." Alec answered. "I'll be up early to do my work for Aga. I'll be on time."

"Until tomorrow, then, sonny. Get your rest. You'll need it."

Alec nodded and stepped over the gunwale and onto the dock. He heard Badger grumbling to the captain, but he didn't care. Captain Cairns owned the *Britannia*. Badger worked for the captain. And now, so did Alec. Badger would not change that.

The next morning, Alec was up early as planned. He had the breakfast table set and hot water boiling on the cooker by the time Aga came into the kitchen.

"I'm off, Aga. Wish me well on my first day."

"Aye, Alec. I wish you good sense and good weather. I just stepped out to bring in the milk, and the clouds are thrashing about. Take your slicker."

"Already have it here." Alec pointed to his pack. "I'll be back before supper."

The streets were wet and dim as Alec made his way to the docks. Though he couldn't see the dairyman because of the fog, he could hear the clopping of horses' hooves on the brick streets and the clinking of bottles as the man placed the milk on the back steps and waited to collect the ration stamps from his customers.

Mrs. Tanner was sweeping the sidewalk in front of her tailoring shop. Alec didn't see her until he was nearly past. He tried to ignore her.

"Young man," she said. "Where are you off to this early in the morning?"

"To the docks. I've a job on the *Britannia*. A galley job."

"Well, you've got a dreary morning to be shoving off. Rain will come before you're back."

"A little rain won't scuttle us," Alec said.

"Who's your skipper?" Mrs. Tanner asked.

"Cairns," Alec answered. "Captain Cairns."

"Cairns, is it? Aye, I know him. Older chap. Too quiet. Always wonder what he's thinking."

Alec didn't answer her. He was not going to be late—especially not because of Mrs. Tanner. So he sprinted off before she could question him further.

Old Mrs. Tanner, Alec thought. *She's nothing but a gossip. She might run a good tailoring business—at least, that's what Mum says—but I'm not wasting words with her.*

On the corner, he looked up to see that the fog had begun to clear. He could barely make out the gargoyle perched menacingly on top of the old shoe factory. *Wouldn't Dover be surprised if that gargoyle suddenly swooped down and snatched Mrs. Tanner right off her front stoop?* He smiled as he imagined Mrs. Tanner on the gargoyle's back, rising up to the heavens, spewing gossip to the folks below.

His thoughts soon shifted to Captain Cairns and the boat. *One day I'll be a full shipmate,* he imagined. *Then I'll buy my own boat, something small for odd jobs along the Channel. Like Captain Cairns, I'll run my own business until I'm old, and be free of anyone telling me what's good and what's not.*

Past the Tea Shoppe and then the Snargate pubs, Alec continued down the hill to the docks. The town rested peacefully by the Channel. Most Dover merchants had not yet opened for business. Only the greengrocer was out, filling the bins in front of his store with asparagus, potatoes, and the few oranges he could get. Across the street, the haberdashery stood silent, its windows displaying the latest hats and trousers. A charwoman, her apron starched white against her black dress, greeted Alec on her way to work. And just as Alec passed the newsstand, the agent stepped outside and bellowed, "Alec! Alec Curtis. Where have ye been, boy? I haven't seen ye at me stand for weeks now. What—are ye too old for them *Beano* comics? I've the latest issue right here."

"No, no thank you, Mr. Kelly. I'm in a bit of a hurry. I've got a job now. I'm the galley boy on the *Britannia*. I've not much time for reading anymore, with helping Aga and then tending ship."

"The *Britannia,* ye say? Can't picture it. Who's the captain?" Mr. Kelly continued.

Worried that he'd be late, Alec edged away from the stand. He knew Mr. Kelly would want to find out more than he had time to tell.

"Captain Cairns," Alec answered. "It's an old oyster smack—with a Kelvin forty-four engine. Runs on petrol. Used for fishing and carrying light cargo." Alec paused. "I'll stop another morning, Mr. Kelly. Maybe I'll grab that *Beano* comic then."

"Aye, Alec. You do that—if I've any left. Watch for the weather today. The clouds are hanging low."

Alec scurried on past the post office and Lawton's Jewelry and emerged from between the buildings. He crossed the High Street and sprinted along the dock to where the *Britannia* waited. Captain Cairns was winding up the ropes as Alec came down the planks.

"Hey, sonny. Ready for some rough waters today?"

"Doesn't look too awful, Captain. But Aga was worried, too. Think we'll get in our trip before it hits?"

"Aye, sonny. I wouldn't risk going to Folkestone if I thought the old ship couldn't handle the water. We've started out in worse. Now help me with these cargo doors so we can be on our way."

"Where's Badger? Isn't he coming?" Alec closed the doors and slipped the board through the handles.

"Aye, I'm wondering the same. He's a smart first mate. He's also a crusty one. Likes the pubs most nights. I've waited for him before. He'll be here, but my patience is getting short."

"What's our cargo to Folkestone, Captain?"

"Fencing. The council there wants to yard up the area between the beach and the town. We've got posts and fencing for them. Loaded it last night with Badger."

"A neat job," Alec said. "Should be a quick jaunt, right, Captain?"

"If the weather cooperates, we'll be back in a shake. But keep your eyes on those clouds rolling in from the south; storms usually kick up pretty quickly with clouds like those."

"Aye, I know." Alec nodded. He remembered the *Wayfarer* and Georgie. It had been such a morning. He hadn't seen it coming. How could he have missed the signs? How could he have thought they'd be okay in a little fishing skiff? If he was to be a seaman, he must learn to see the signs.

Alec scanned the dock for Badger. He couldn't decide

whether to be disappointed or happy with the man's absence.

But before he had a chance to make up his mind, Badger staggered down the dock, looking hung-over and ornery. He squinted through the fog with his bloodshot eyes and tangled with the mooring rope of the *Tamzine* before stopping at the *Britannia*.

"Thought we were going to have to shove off without you, Badger." Captain Cairns looked him over and wrinkled his nose at the smell. "Have you been stumbling around all night?"

"'ad meself a row last evenin', Cap'n, and I feel it this mornin'. I'm a bit sore. Though I fared better than the other bloke, I can tell you that. Where we off to?"

"To Folkestone. Remember? That fencing we loaded? Have to get it to the docks there. Those blokes think it'll keep the Jerries off their beaches. . . . Soon we'll see the fencing up here as well."

"Now, Cap'n, we've nothin' to worry about, don't you think?" Badger watched as Alec untied the ropes from the dock stakes and stepped onboard. "We've got the Royal Navy and the British Expeditionary Force. Aye, those boys in the BEF, they'll be after the Jerries soon as they get the word. And a bloke at the White Horse? He says there's special troops comin' into Dover. Those Jerries—they cannit take British soil."

"You weren't old enough for the Great War, Badger, but I can tell you, those Germans are still upset at their disgrace. They've been building up arms, just waiting for another chance to storm Europe. And Hitler—the news-reels are filled with him and his propaganda. Says his air power—his Luftwaffe—is something to be feared."

"Well, they've been scrappin' over in Europe for months now, and nothin's 'appened 'ere but a few air-raid sirens and the blackouts. I'm not worried—though I'm glad for the work. Carryin' fencin' gives us business."

Alec felt the *Britannia* shudder as the captain started the engine and steered the ship out of port.

"Take a seat on the locker, Alec, until we get into open water." The captain turned the wheel and pushed forward on the throttle. The rumbling of the engine gave Alec chills. Just the way Margaret had told him. Here he was—on a ship.

Leaning back on the locker, he closed his eyes and felt the wind brush his face as the boat cut through the choppy water. Surrounded by sea and whitecaps, Alec felt content. What Aga feared about the Channel, Alec loved—the uncertainty, the wide expanse of water, the mysteries beneath.

Sometimes, when he had been out rowing with Georgie, Alec would tell stories about sea creatures and giant fish. Though they never lost sight of land, Georgie would stare at the shore, planning his escape yet quivering with excitement as Alec spun his tales. It took some time for Alec to convince Georgie they were only seamen's tales with no truth to them.

Now, relaxing on the locker box, Alec smiled, remembering how Georgie would slip his hand into Alec's—just to feel safe. Alec felt a twinge of guilt about not missing Georgie as much lately. But he'd been so busy. Could it be that easy to forget a friend?

"You haven't forgotten him, Alec," Margaret's voice said in his head. "Why, you're thinking about him right now. You're just remembering the good times. You've started to move past the bad. He'll always be your friend."

The ship pitched left and jolted Alec out of his daydream. Rolling waves beat against the hull as the wind picked up speed. The gray-blue sky and water came together, causing Alec to think the ship was floating free. His hands gripped the side of the locker.

It took most of the morning for the *Britannia* to cut through the water to Folkestone. By the time they reached port, they were weary from fighting the waves. Badger released the boom and swung it around to the hold while Alec opened the cargo doors. He stepped back as the captain snapped the hook onto the first roll of wire. Then the captain and Badger swung the boom around and lowered the wire to the dock. A crew of dockhands unclipped the load and carried each bundle up to shore. The whole business took only an hour.

"It's looking ugly out there, mate," one of the dockhands called. "Can you get home, or should you tie up and wait it out?"

Alec felt his chest tighten. He didn't want to risk a disaster—but he also didn't want to be home late on his first day. Father would never let it go.

"Aye, it is a bit nasty. But I've sailed enough to know

we'll be okay if we don't dawdle," the captain answered.

After closing the hold and securing the boom, they were ready to leave Folkestone and turn north to Dover. Though the wind had picked up even more while they were docked, Alec was hopeful they could make it to Dover well before supper. Settling into his spot behind the wheel, Captain Cairns beckoned Alec.

"Lad, go below and secure anything that could come loose and bounce around the galley. We've got some foul weather coming—rain for sure."

"And tea?" Alec inquired. "Will you be wanting tea?"

"Too much pitching for a flame today, lad. No, just snug things up and then stay below until we're done with this wind. Those clouds over there tell me that the *Britannia* will soon be tossed around a bit. I don't want to take any chances of you flipping overboard."

"Yes, sir," Alec answered, disappointed. He descended the short stairway to the galley. He tried to steady himself when the ship heaved fiercely to one side. Bracing his foot against the wall, he checked the galley cupboards. Then he felt the ship lurch to the other side, tilt back to the center, and stop with a jolt that sent him banging into the cupboard behind him.

Racing up the steps, Alec made it to the wheelhouse just as Badger ran in. He pushed Alec aside.

"What's the bloody matter?"

"I shut her down. She won't turn," the captain answered.

"What is it?" Badger shouted.

"The rudder, I think. Something's tying it up."

"Someone's got to go over." Badger shot a look at Alec. "The boy's not strong enough. It'll have to be me." Alec felt the sting of his words.

The captain continued. "Alec, get a rope from the hold. . . . Badger, we'll tie one end around you and the other to the post near the wheelhouse—pull you back up after you've gotten a look." Badger nodded.

Within minutes, Alec and Captain Cairns had knotted the rope around the post. They watched as Badger tightened the other end at his waist. Above the wind, Badger barked orders to Alec. "Once I've checked it over, I'll call back up. It's no time for larkin' about, so pay attention."

By now, the waves were tossing the ship like a toy. Alec planted one foot against the side and clung to the railing as Badger checked his rope.

"You've got to hurry, Badger!" the captain hollered. "Water's too rough and cold. If you can't see it right away, leave it. We'll ride out the storm. . . . Did you hear me, Badger? No need for foolishness."

"Aye, I'll take no chances," Badger shouted as he held to the side of the ship. Captain Cairns went back into the wheelhouse, and Alec stood by Badger, who put one leg over the edge, swung the second around, and then dropped into the sea.

Alec watched him disappear beneath the foam and then bob up again, moving toward the stern. Grabbing the railing, Alec squeezed his eyes shut. The water was rolling just as it had been with Georgie. He saw again Georgie smothered by the waves and felt as helpless as he had then. He thought it was useless to try to make repairs. Badger would drown.

But then his eyes sprang open. Badger had said to pay attention. Alec would prove he could do it.

So he moved to the stern, leaned over the rail, and waited for Badger's signal. As the waves beat against the ship, Alec wondered if he and the captain would be able to hoist Badger in when he was done. But then he saw the first mate with his hand in the air, signaling for Alec to lean toward him. Alec felt his heart pounding. The water was close, the waves so loud. He thought he would fall in.

"A wrench! Get me a wrench!" Badger called. "Some scrap metal—it's caught up in the rudder. Got to work it free."

Alec turned and skidded toward the locker. He put his knee against the front and flung open the lid. His hands dug deep into the box, and he shoved other tools aside until he found the wrench Badger needed. Grabbing a short piece of rope, he tied it to the wrench and then staggered back across the rolling deck and lowered the tool to Badger.

The wrench flopped against the hull, bouncing off the side and swinging out into the sea before it settled into Badger's hand. He loosened the rope and disappeared again beneath the water.

Alec stared at the spot where Badger had been. Nothing. He looked again, thinking Badger needed to come up. He turned toward the captain and threw up his hands, wondering what he should do. Then he turned back to the sea. There was Badger, tossing his head free of water and holding the wrench above him.

"Tell the captain it's free. The rudder's free. Have him turn the wheel."

"He's got it, Captain!" Alec shouted. "Try to turn the wheel."

The captain started the engine and spun the wheel just enough to feel the boat list slightly to starboard.

"It's working! Tell Badger to get to the side. We'll heft him in."

Alec leaned over and called into the wind, "Badger, Captain says the rudder's working. Come back. We'll help you in."

Badger nodded and flung the wrench up and over the gunwale and onto the deck. Working hand over hand, he dragged himself through the water and back to starboard. He coughed as waves washed over him

Badger wasn't far below him; still, Alec wondered if he could hoist the big man up. Then the captain joined him, and together they began pulling on the rope. The Channel fought them, but Alec and the captain kept on. Alec felt the burn through his gloves as he and Captain Cairns reached farther down the rope. At first, their pulling seemed to make no difference. Then Badger's body rose out of the water. Grunting now in rhythm, they leaned away, heaving on the rope. With each tug, the captain stepped farther back from the edge. Alec stayed near the side, heaving and pulling, until Badger's head appeared over the gunwale.

"We're almost there, Badger," the captain called. Then,

without warning, the ship rolled as a towering wave pounded it, knocking both Alec and the captain to the deck.

Alec clung to the rope. He shook off the blow and raised himself to his knees. Just behind him, the captain was getting up. Alec felt the cold spray seeping into his trousers. Using the rope as support, he got to his feet and worked his way back to the side. Peering over the edge, he saw Badger dangling from the rope, his legs dragging in the surf. He looked dead.

"Badger! Badger!" Alec called. "Are you okay?"

Badger didn't answer. His body bounced against the ship with each rolling wave. Then Alec heard a cry. The first mate stirred.

"Badger!" Alec screamed again. "Badger!"

"Me leg!" Badger howled. "Me leg! I've snapped me leg!"

Alec leaned farther over the edge and gasped. Badger's trousers were slit; his bloody leg stuck out through the hole.

"Captain!" Alec screamed as he turned to Cairns. "Badger's hurt!"

Without waiting, Alec grabbed the rope again and pulled hard, straining to lift Badger. The captain was soon at his side, tugging along with him.

"Me leg!" Badger cried again. "Get me in!"

The rope stretched taut against the railing. Above the wind, Alec heard Badger moan with every jerk of the line. Still they pulled. He was dead weight for them to lift. The going was slow, but finally Badger's hand slapped atop the gunwale. Alec and the captain reached over the side.

"Try to hold his leg, Alec. Keep it steady. I'll lift him under the arms and pull him in."

As the captain turned sideways and supported Badger from behind, Alec cradled the mangled leg in his arms and lifted it the last few inches over the side. They carefully set the first mate on the deck.

"It's a bad break, Badger," the captain said. "We'll get you back to Dover." He motioned for Alec to come nearer. "He'll not be thinking well with that wound, Alec. Try to keep him calm."

"I can keep him still, Captain. Just help me get him over by the wheelhouse, where we can rest his back against the wall. Then I'll get some blankets from the galley."

They went to work and made Badger as comfortable as possible before the captain resumed his post in the wheelhouse and restarted the ship's engine. The motor sputtered a bit and then chugged to life, moving the boat through the waves. The captain turned the ship north and headed toward Dover. Waves beat against the ship's stern.

Badger felt every roll. "Ahhh! It's broken, isn't it? You saw it. It's snapped, isn't it?"

Alec wrapped the blankets tightly around Badger's body, and then he knelt at Badger's side, placing his hand firmly on the first mate's chest to keep him quiet. He was unable to see where they were. The time passed slowly. Badger rolled his head back and forth against the wheelhouse wall. One moment, he was awake and asking Alec if they had far to go, and the next, he was deathly still, passed out from pain. Alec prayed for the storm to subside.

At last he heard the captain yell, and he spotted the Dover cliffs. Within minutes, they were sliding into the docks as the captain called out to a man onshore. "Ring for help! My first mate's been hurt."

The dockhand turned and ran, calling to those near-by to give the captain a hand. A dozen men lined the dock and grabbed for the ropes the captain had thrown to them. Alec stayed with Badger.

"You're going to be all right, mate," Alec whispered. "Aye, it's a nasty wound, but you'll find yourself at the pubs before you know it. We'll see you here on the *Britannia* again."

An ambulance was moving down the High Street. When the men boarded the ship to lift Badger off, Alec shouted out orders. "He's got a bad break there. Watch his leg. Hold his head up, too. Give him some room!"

Badger winced as they picked him up to place him in the back of the waiting ambulance. After it had left, Alec stepped up next to Captain Cairns.

"You did well today, lad." Cairns patted Alec's shoulder. "You kept your head and proved your worth."

"What about Badger?" Alec said. "He'll be okay?"

"His sailing days are over for some time. I can tell you that. I've never seen such a nasty break."

"What'll you do, Captain? You can't move about the Channel without another hand."

"No, you're right, lad. We need three for loading and unloading. We may be docked for a bit. But I don't mind taking some time off. This petrol rationing has started to pinch us. We soon won't be charging off to any port we want, as we have in the past. So far, we've been able to get extra rations, since we're hauling the barbed wire and other wartime freight. But even those loads are slowing down. No, a holiday won't hurt us."

"I'm ready to do whatever you need," Alec said. "I'll be checking in the morning to see how Badger's feeling. The three of us will be going again, you'll see."

"I hope you're right, lad. Now, you head on home as soon as you've cleaned up the deck. And be careful what you tell your dad and mum. Don't make the story too good or they may just decide *your* sailing days are over as well."

"No worry there, Captain. I'll save this story for Aga."

Alec coiled the rope and swabbed the deck. As he was leaving, a crowd was still waiting to hear the captain's tale of bent rudders and broken bones. Alec didn't need to stay and listen; he'd lived it.

On his way to the Shaftbury, he thought about the minutes after Badger had gotten hurt. Alec hadn't done anything foolish. Even the captain had said he'd proved himself. Maybe with Badger injured, the captain would make Alec first mate. Then wouldn't his father be surprised—that he had done his job well, that he had earned his place.

5
COMING AND GOING

AS HE PASSED THE SHAFTBURY AND TURNED THE CORNER
to go up the back stairs, Alec heard the front door of the inn
open and saw Mrs. Tanner step out onto the stoop. His heart
sank. The only reason for her to visit would be to spread the
news about Badger's accident. She had probably bothered
every dockworker coming up from the port until she'd found
one who would pass on what he knew about the *Britannia*.
Alec shook his head and hurried up the back steps.

In the kitchen, he saw Aga first. "Alec," she began. "Are
you okay, lad? Are you hurt?"

"Aye, Aga. I'm more than okay. I'm an able seaman. Even
Captain Cairns said so."

"Your father knows all about Captain Cairns and the
Britannia's mishap. Aye, Mrs. Tanner—she told your father
and mum the whole story. They're looking for you. So keep
your words to yourself when your father shows up."

He didn't have long to wait. He had barely begun cutting onions for stew when his father and mother came
into the kitchen.

"Alec, is it true what we've heard? About the storm and the first mate? Is Cairns daft to go out like he did?" his father demanded.

"It wasn't so bad at first," Alec said. "And we would have made it fine if not for the stuck rudder. Nasty luck for Badger, it was. But the captain says he'll be around again soon."

"It's just what we feared, Alec," his father continued. "You won't be able to manage working for Cairns and for the Shaftbury."

"It's only my first day! And it was not normal. Captain Cairns said he's never seen such a bad break as Badger had. Just one of those rotten times, the captain said. It can't happen again."

"You must tell him you're finished, Alec. You need to wait a few more years and give yourself some time to grow into the sea life. You're too—"

"Too what, Father? Too foolish? Too irresponsible? What is it you think I am?"

His father avoided his questions. "I told you before, this is not the work for you. But you insist on charging on."

"I know you don't think I can do it," Alec said. "But the captain does, and until he fires me, I want to be his galley boy. I'll prove I'm the right one for the job."

Before his father had come into the kitchen, Alec had decided he would stand up to him. He was done ignoring his own feelings and following his father's plans. He had weathered one storm today. But this storm brewing in the Shaftbury was a different challenge.

"Supper is due in one hour, Alec," his father said, moving toward the door. "I haven't time to argue with you now. But we will talk again. This matter is not settled." With that, he left Alec and the two women in the kitchen.

Alec's mum followed him into the scullery, where he went back to slicing onions.

"It's hard on us, Alec, these times when you're away and we can't help you if you need us. You've got to understand how it wears us down."

"But it's not as though I've left home and joined the BEF, Mum. I'm a galley boy, working on a good boat. Captain Cairns has been around longer than most men at the docks. He knows what he's doing. It was just some bad luck."

"I know that now, Alec. And I know you're not going to join the British Expeditionary Force. But hearing the news from Mrs. Tanner—well, she made it out to be worse than you say."

"And you're surprised by that, Mum? She's a wretched woman."

"I know. She's got to have her nose in all the business. But between her report and a telegram that came today, your father's in a flap."

"What telegram? What did it say? Can I read it?"

"Your father has it. It's from a Vice Admiral Ramsey, asking for rooms to be saved for a group of soldiers who are to arrive next month. Your father's grateful for some guests, but he's also afraid of what it might mean for the war—soldiers at the Shaftbury instead of up by the castle. It's very odd."

Alec could feel his stomach muscles tighten. And though his mum kept talking, he heard nothing beyond the telegram news.

Later, helping Aga after supper, he imagined what it could mean. "They must be British spies," he said.

Aga smiled. "What makes you think so, lad?"

"Regular infantrymen would billet with the others up on the hill. But these chaps—they must be the Special Forces Badger was talking about. He said some bloke at the White Horse was telling about Special Forces who are going to be posted in Dover. I think these men who'll be staying at the Shaftbury are spies."

Alec was unsure what to make of it. For several months, British troops had been leaving England for France; the radio said that the British were there to help protect France from a German invasion. But special troops in Dover? Did the army think the Germans would get across the Channel?

"No need to get all excited, Alec boy," Aga said. "You know we've been seeing soldiers move through southern England for months now. Just because a few of them are staying at the inn doesn't mean they're spies. Maybe they're part of the medical corps headed off to France to tend the wounded. We've no reason to think anything more than that."

Aga motioned for Alec to help her with the ashes in the fireplace. He grabbed the brush and swept up the cool ashes, then knelt down to pile the sticks and kindling and set the coal bin nearby for the evening fire.

"No matter," Alec replied. "I can't wait until they come. I want to know all about Hitler and the Jerries. We'll blast them out of Europe—that's what the men on the docks are saying. Hitler's no match for England."

The next morning, Alec went to the docks after breakfast, looking for Captain Cairns and word on Badger. It was late enough that the fog had cleared, and the skies showed bits of blue mingled with clouds. Alec had just reached the shore when he heard a loud roar overhead. The ground shook, and he looked around for a place to take cover. But the planes were already over him. He started to run and then turned to look up. He stopped when he saw the Royal Air Force crest with the king's crown painted on the side of the fighters. The roar followed them as they soared over the ocean. Alec kept his eyes on them until they were out of sight, and then he sprinted the remaining distance to the *Britannia*.

"Did you see that, Captain?" he shouted. "Captain, are you here? Did you see the planes?"

"Aye, sonny. I saw *and* heard them. A menacing sight, I fear. It means the war is pulling us closer."

Alec sat down on the locker. "Do you really think so, Captain? Are we in danger?"

"When there's war, Alec, everyone's in danger. For now, it's stayed on the mainland—in Europe. But every day I see evidence of our getting sucked into the mess."

"Aga will go batty," Alec said. "She's always talking about the Great War and how this feels like it did then."

"She's not far from the truth, Alec. We fought with Germany then, and it looks like we're in for it again. Aga is right to be worried."

"And Badger?" Alec asked. "Have you heard any news?"

"Aye, I was by the hospital this morning. They had to do surgery, set the bone and all that. As I feared, he'll be out for a while—maybe as long as four months."

"Four months? What will you do?"

"Well, I'm going to take enough time to think it through, Alec. Seeing those planes, I'm not sure how much I can plan ahead."

Alec was disappointed at the news. But the captain had said Badger was a loyal and smart first mate. He would not be in a hurry to replace him. And Captain Cairns had been sailing long enough that he could afford some time ashore. "I'm here, Captain. Ready to go when you are." He thought back to his argument with his father. He hoped Captain Cairns would not ask him how his parents had taken the news. He wanted to tell him about the telegram but decided against it. "I've got to run." Alec rose from the locker and crossed the deck. "I'll still visit the docks. And you'll be checking on the *Britannia*. I'll see you then."

The captain nodded, and Alec waved and set off for the inn, still a little shaky from the planes and from his dashed hopes about the *Britannia*. He had a long time to wait before sailing again. But when he was ready, he would screw up his courage and ask the captain to train him as first mate.

Back at the inn, he had just settled down with his journal when he heard a knock on his door.

"Alec," a familiar voice said. "Can I come in? It's Thomas."

"Thomas. Yes, come in. Sit if you want," Alec said, opening the door to Georgie's brother. Standing next to Thomas, Alec realized that he had forgotten how tall his cousin was. He'd seen him only once since the accident—at the post office with Aunt Lucy. They hadn't talked.

"I'll stand. I'll only stay a bit," Thomas said. "I've got something to say."

Alec felt his body stiffen. *What will I do if he starts to blast me?* he wondered. Thomas was between him and the door; he had no escape. *I just don't want to feel more anger,* he thought, rubbing his damp palms on his trousers.

"Alec," Thomas began, "I want you to know I hold nothing against you for Georgie's death. I know he was your friend, and he loved being with you. He would not have stayed behind that afternoon."

Alec thought back to that day. When they had gotten to the shore and seen the wind picking up, he had tried to talk Georgie into going another time. But Georgie had begged—

"I'll be going away soon," Thomas continued, "and I want nothing between us, no anger, no hate. Our family's too small to be at odds. We'll need each other in the days to come."

Alec sighed, relieved. Then suddenly, he understood. "Going away?" he asked. "Where are you going?"

"I've enlisted," Thomas said proudly. "I'll leave for London tomorrow, and from there I'll go to Aldershot for training before heading off to France."

"Enlisted? But Aunt Lucy—"

"Aye, she won't speak of it," Thomas interrupted. "But all my mates are going. I can't stay behind. England needs me. And I'll be back. You'll see."

Thomas's words seemed to settle in the room like fog on a dreary day.

"I don't want you to forget that we're still cousins . . . and friends. Maybe when I get back, we can do something together. Maybe we'll go fishing." Thomas smiled.

"I'll never forget Georgie," Alec blurted. "I always think about him."

"I'm sure you won't, Alec. You and Georgie were always larking about, acting a bit daft. He wanted to be with you—even that day. But we have to move on or this thing will drive us apart, make us bitter. Georgie wouldn't have that."

Alec was close to tears—the first tears since Georgie's funeral. For a moment, neither boy spoke.

"Well, old chap," Thomas said, ruffling Alec's hair. "I mean it about the fishing. Soon. Very soon." Then he offered a quick salute and was out the door.

It wasn't until later that night, after supper, that Alec discovered his parents had known about Thomas's enlistment but had not told Alec.

"They didn't want you to worry. They were trying to keep you from the war," Aga said. But Alec knew that it was because his parents didn't want him visiting Thomas and upsetting Uncle Jack and Aunt Lucy.

The next morning, Alec went to the railway station on his own. He went early to find a spot to hide, wanting only to catch a glimpse of Thomas as he boarded the train for London.

Alec stood there in the damp air, watching Aunt Lucy clinging to Thomas's arm. Surrounded by his mates, Thomas looked almost joyful—ready to go. In contrast, Aunt Lucy and Uncle Jack were sober and quiet.

Then Alec saw Aunt Lucy pull Thomas to her and hug him tight. Uncle Jack patted him on the back, hesitated, and then stepped up and wrapped his strong arms around Thomas's shoulders.

The young soldiers boarded the train. Alec looked on as the steam engine puffed its way out of the station. Still, he would not leave until Uncle Jack and Aunt Lucy were gone. Hidden behind rolls of fencing, he heard his aunt speak.

"How can we let him go? What will become of him?"

"The lad will do what he needs to do, and he'll come home," Uncle Jack answered, taking her arm and turning her away from the platform. "There's no keeping Thomas here if he thinks he's got to go. We need to let him be. The boy's old enough to go, but he'll sit at our table again. I am sure of that."

Alec didn't move until Uncle Jack and Aunt Lucy had pulled away in their auto for the lonely drive back to their home. He wanted to believe that Uncle Jack was right about Thomas. But Captain Cairns's words haunted him now: "When there's war, Alec, everyone's in danger."

6
SNOOPING

"ALEC! ALEC! LAD, WHAT ARE YOU DOING IN THERE? You're needed at the station. Have you forgotten you're to be at the Priory first thing?" Aga called from outside his door. Alec stirred, trying to see through the dark morning. It had been a month since Badger's accident. He was still exhausted from the work his father had assigned him.

He'd spent the first full week scraping chipped paint from the moldings and doors in the guest rooms on the third floor. The following weeks, he had worked into the night putting a fresh coat of paint on the walls. Then his mother had found another job for him.

"Frank," Alec's mother said. "What are we to do if the inn is bombed? What about Alec? We need to think about Alec."

So Alec's father had followed many other fathers in Dover and brought home an Anderson shelter to set up behind the inn. He and Alec had spent a silent afternoon digging a deep hole near the garden; then they had bent the metal of the shelter to fit into the space. By the time they'd finished bracing it with the dirt dug from the hole, it was suppertime. Alec found the whole matter quite foolish. And the extra work had worn him down. He knew the captain needed time to think about when he would go out to sea again, but Alec wasn't sure how long he could manage under the load at the Shaftbury. He was sleeping soundly when Aga woke him.

"What time is it?"

"Lad," Aga pleaded through the crack in his door. "Alec boy, get up and come. The soldier guests are due to arrive at the Dover Priory by half past. Don't let your father think you've overslept and missed them."

Alec's covers tumbled to the floor as he shot out of bed and grabbed his trousers and shirt, strewn on a nearby chair.

"Coming, Aga," he answered. "I'll be right there. Don't bother Father. I'll be on the run in a minute."

How could he have slept so long? Since the day the telegram had arrived, he had carried on endless chatter with Aga about the men and their purpose for coming to the Shaftbury.

In a few minutes, he was hurrying toward the railway station, hoping he was not too late. He owed Aga another favor. Not only had she wakened him when he'd overslept, but she had kept his father busy in the kitchen while Alec dressed and sneaked out the front door. He arrived just as the train was pulling into the station. As passengers stepped onto the platform, Alec realized that today, unlike other days, the train carried only soldiers. They poured from the cars, collected their kits, and congregated near the corner of the Dover Priory station.

They looked young even to Alec. They also looked tired. Yet watching the crowd swell before him, he felt compelled to join it. He was not old enough to sign up and fight with the BEF, but he still wished he could do something to help England stand with the French. The swarm of soldiers in their uniforms made his heart pound.

The men milled about and waited for orders from their leaders. An officer—Alec recognized a lieutenant's patch—stepped onto the platform and called to the mass of men. Alec was far back in the crowd and couldn't hear what the lieutenant said, but in minutes the platform was cleared as groups splintered off, making their way toward the encampment on the cliffs above Dover.

Then only four men remained. Alec stepped up just in time to hear the lieutenant speak.

"Men, as you know, we've been asked to stop here for a bit to wait for orders from Vice Admiral Ramsey himself. We're to be billeted at the Shaftbury Inn. Someone should be here soon to meet us."

Upon hearing the lieutenant mention the inn, Alec called out, "Alec Curtis, sir. I'm here to take you to the Shaftbury." With that, Alec waited while the men gathered their kits and joined him to walk the few blocks to the inn.

Alec looked at each soldier. Except for their leader, they were dressed alike. Each carried a brown canvas haversack. They were clothed in brown—trousers and shirts. Gray wool socks peeked out above heavy black boots, while brown berets hung low over one eye. Patches designating rank adorned the left sleeves of their shirts. But something else caught Alec's attention. A small red badge, not more than two inches long, was stitched just below the patch that indicated each one's rank. Glancing at the badge, Alec could barely make out the word *Foresters*. He wondered what the deuce Foresters were, but he didn't ask.

Walking to the inn, with the soldiers trailing behind, Alec recalled Aunt Lucy and Uncle Jack saying their good-byes and waving as Thomas left the station, promising he would return. Alec thought about the soldiers who now followed him. Were they so sure about going? He would soon be adding their names to the list of events he had been entering in his journal: Badger's accident, the telegram from the vice admiral, the RAF planes, the day Thomas left. Alec wanted to be a part of the adventure; he wanted to meet new people and listen to fresh stories. These soldiers offered both.

Then they were at the steps to the Shaftbury. Alec glanced again at the small group of men and wondered what he might learn from them about Thomas. Though young like Thomas, they had something that set them apart, even from the other men at the Dover Priory. For one thing, they seemed to know each other well. While the other soldiers at the station had stood quietly, waiting for orders, these blokes had made a good show of it, bantering and joking from the time Alec had spotted them. No, they were not new friends just meeting on the train.

What was it that had brought them together, that had led them to Dover?

"This is it, mates," Alec said. "My mum will help you check in, and then I'll show you to your rooms."

Holding the door, Alec watched as the soldiers stepped into the lobby one by one. They grew quiet, their eyes scanning the surroundings. A hat stand with a rack of pegs stood to the left. Just beyond that was the drawing room with its large, padded chairs. To the right of the lobby was the dining room. A heavy table, surrounded by a dozen chairs, sat in the center of the room. Against one wall was the sideboard for serving tea. Beyond the dining room, through the swinging door, Alec could hear Aga moving about in the kitchen as she prepared the noon meal for him and his folks.

The lobby was dark but for the lamp on the desk.

"We haven't had time to open the blackout drapes today," Alec explained. "We've plenty of paraffin lamps to light your rooms. And in spite of the rationing, Aga manages to keep us well fed."

"We're not concerned about the inn, Alec," the lieutenant answered. "It suits us well. And the military will help with our food rations. We're not sure how long our stay will be, but we're grateful to be billeted with you rather than up the hill."

"Aye," Alec started to say, "I've—I've wondered why—"

"Well, men," the lieutenant interrupted, "let's check in and get our kits to the rooms. We've got some time to catch up before supper."

At the back of the lobby, Alec's mother stood behind the large oak desk, waiting for the soldiers to step up. Shifting from one foot to the other, the young soldier in front moved aside to make room for the lieutenant.

"Good morning, Mrs. Curtis," the lieutenant said. "We've a special detachment here. We're going to need a few beds for a little while until we get our orders. I understand you have room."

"Yes," Alec's mum said. "We've been expecting you, though the vice admiral's telegram didn't say how many of you there would be."

"Only four. If you have a room for each of us, we'd like that. We'll be sharing pretty close quarters soon enough, so a little space now would be welcome," the lieutenant replied.

"We've only six rooms total," she said. "But we've no other guests at present, so your men can each have a room on the third floor. Freshly painted by my son, Alec. And for you, Lieutenant," she continued, "we've a nice room on the second floor. Would you sign our registry?"

The lieutenant nodded and took the pen to print his name. Behind his mother now, Alec stood peering over her shoulder at the entry: Lieutenant Joseph Courtright, Kent, England. *Courtright,* Alec thought. The name suited the man. He was courtly and proper, and a Joseph, not a Joe or Joey. Standing over six feet tall, Lieutenant Courtright commanded attention. His light brown uniform was identical to the others' except for the yellow braiding that encircled his right shoulder. The black patch and stripes on his left arm set him apart as an officer. He had smiled politely at Alec's mother, but he was interested in getting his men settled to await further orders.

"The rooms are small but clean." Alec's mother spoke softly. "Divide yourselves up as you please, but you'll have to share lavatories. We've got only two. Supper is at half past six; breakfast at seven sharp. Aga serves a fine English breakfast of eggs, bacon, toast, and tea, but she doesn't take kindly to latecomers, so please be prompt."

"Thank you, Mrs. Curtis," the lieutenant replied. "We'll be quiet guests, I assure you. And we're used to being punctual, so breakfast at seven will be fine." Then, turning to his men, he called, "Grab your gear and follow the lad. We'll not be here long, so rest while you can."

Alec paused as the soliders gathered up their kits and waited, expecting the lieutenant to go first. Instead, Courtright held back to let Alec take the lead. As the soliders made their way to the stairs, no one spoke until they reached the second-floor landing, and then the lead man called back to the lieutenant.

"How shall we split up, sir?"

"As you like. Store your gear where Alec says and meet me in the drawing room at half past. We'll go over what to expect the next few days."

"Your room is the first on the left, Lieutenant." Alec pointed down the hallway. "You have your own lav. The door's open."

At first, the lieutenant only nodded and moved toward his room. Then he stopped and snapped a command.

"Remember, men. No loose talk. Our training, our mission—no chatter about that, even among yourselves."

"Yes, sir," a soldier who wore glasses answered. "We've no desire to wrinkle our plans now."

The lieutenant strode toward his room. Alec heard the door close. He wondered what was important enough to take these men from the others. And what about the Forester patch? He'd not seen it on the others at the railway station.

"Rooms four through six," he said, nodding toward the next floor.

The soldiers hurried up the stairway, and he could hear each of them taking a room. He decided that if they were spies, they couldn't have trained long. None of them looked older than Thomas. He moved toward the servants' stairs at the end of the hallway and had gone only a few feet when he thought he heard footsteps on the main stairway. Then the floor creaked behind him, and he hurried along to the back stairs, pausing to listen as the footsteps continued and then stopped. A door opened and closed. He listened a moment longer but could hear only the muffled sound of someone talking. Alec realized that the soldiers' mission had begun.

That night, only Aga and Alec were at supper with the men. His folks had gone off to Uncle Jack and Aunt Lucy's. Supper with the guests was one of Alec's favorite times of the day. At an early age, he'd been trained to share the table with their visitors. Between his parents and Aga, he had been well instructed in proper etiquette. He had learned to listen and not speak.

The soldiers quickly made friends with Aga, praising her pot roast and boiled potatoes.

"I'm Will Sweeney," the smallest soldier volunteered. "And this, Aga, is just as good as me mum's pot roast."

"And do I detect an accent, Will? Irish, perhaps?" Aga asked.

"Indeed, Aga," Will answered. "My folks are from Ireland; they moved to London before I was born. I've picked up a bit of their Irish brogue."

"A wee bit of Irish for a wee bit of a man," the soldier with the thick glasses teased. "They call me Specs," he said, waving his glasses in the air. "And this pot roast is enough to make a bloke desert—better than we'll be having in the next few weeks, I'm thinking."

"Aye, I wish we could take some of this with us," Will piped up again. "To fill our spirits and our stomachs."

"And he's Harry," Specs said, nodding toward the third solider.

Harry shook his head. "I can see us now," he said. "Surrounded by the Jerries, guns blasting away, and for what at the end of the day? A few tins of jelly and some smoked beef."

"So we'll blow those Jerries back to Germany and come home," Specs declared. "But it won't be easy. The Great War. It was an embarrassment to the Germans. And they blame us for their money problems now. They're ready to recover their name, and we're in for a battle before we're through, I can tell you that." The others nodded, not wanting to admit that Specs was probably right—they were walking into the fight of their lives.

"They'll be sorry they left home," Harry chimed in.

"Lieutenant," Aga interjected, "what about you? Are you married?"

"Yes, ten years. When I got called up, my wife was beside herself. So she turned her flowerbeds into a victory garden, believing that those very vegetables would end up on my tin plate. She hates that we're at war. 'It's foolish,' she says. 'Slopping about in muck up to your neck and then, when it's over, wondering what took you there.'"

"Well, I was a young lass during the Great War, and I've seen all the war I can stand," Aga said. "So no more talk of it at my table; I want to know nothing about the German army or about France. Now, everybody tuck in and eat your fill. Though we're a bit strapped for some staples, we can still get pork and potatoes. Beef, flour, and sugar— they're harder to gather. But with the stamps on the ration cards you gave me for each of you, Lieutenant, together with those we have for the family, we'll manage nicely."

Alec was disappointed when Aga stopped the war talk. He liked the newness of war, the chance for excitement. He sat quietly, hoping that any minute one of the soldiers would slip and give away their orders.

Alec could see Aga soften as each man lauded her work, and when she served the bread pudding, she gave Will a double portion for his compliment on her pot roast. Aga smiled as she scooped out a large helping and poured on the thick cream.

Later, with supper over, the lieutenant whispered

something to Harry and then disappeared up the stairs. In a minute, he was back, signaling for the men to join him in the drawing room. Alec followed, pretending he had work to do in the lobby. Ducking behind the desk, he tried to look busy, but all the time he was straining to hear the conversation in the next room. "You've been specially selected," he heard the lieutenant begin, "to be part of a unit . . ." Then the lieutenant stopped, glancing at the open drawing-room door. He took two quick steps and closed it. Alec waited a minute and returned to the dining room. Secrets were filling the inn. The war had settled into the Shaftbury.

Back in the kitchen with Aga, Alec told her what he had overheard.

"Specially selected," Alec said. "The lieutenant said they had been specially selected for something—I told you they were spies."

"Lad, the only spy I know in this inn is standing in front of me, and he should be keeping his eyes and ears away from those soldier boys. You have enough trouble without snooping about looking for more. What would your father say? Now, away with you. We've both got our work to do."

Alec was responsible for the guest rooms. Every evening, his routine was the same: after supper, while the guests lingered at the table or had a smoke on the stoop, he entered each room and turned down the covers, laying out blankets if the evening was brisk. When Aga could get enough flour and sugar, she baked small biscuits, and Alec left plates of them on the nightstands.

Normally, he was careful to do his duties without disturbing the guests' belongings. But sometimes, if a guest had left an open letter or a photograph on a dresser, he could not resist taking a peek. All in all, the nightly routine in each room was fun for Alec; he sometimes uncovered bits of news without doing any harm. What could be wrong with that if he kept his findings to himself?

His father would be furious if he knew Alec had been snooping in the guest rooms. Alec never told anyone what he found. But he would record his discoveries on the pages of his journal.

Stepping into the soldiers' rooms, he went right to work. Because the men had hurried to make an afternoon meeting and be on time for supper, they had stopped in the middle of their unpacking and left their belongings scattered about their rooms.

In Lieutenant Courtright's room, Alec found a large photograph of the lieutenant and his family. In the photo, Courtright had his arm stretched around his wife's shoulders while his children, a boy and a girl, clung to his legs. The boy was rugged-looking, much like his father, and the girl had long, wavy hair and a playful look. The lieutenant stood tall and solemn in his uniform, and his wife looked sad in her fitted jacket and slender skirt. Behind the family, other soldiers mingled on a platform, almost hidden by the steam billowing from a nearby train. And a poster just to the left of the lieutenant reminded people: *Watch Out in the Blackout*.

Looking at the photograph, Alec saw that the lieutenant had something to fight for, and something to come home to.

Setting the photo back on the nightstand, Alec reached toward the bed and flipped the covers back to fluff the pillow. He didn't notice the folder barely sticking out beneath the mattress until the blanket snagged it and scattered its contents on the floor. Scrambling to clean up the mess, he tried to stack the papers together. But they were in a heap, some facing up, some turned sideways. His hands fumbled to get them straight. He was suddenly aware that the laughter below had stopped. "Oh, no," Alec moaned, "the men are coming up. I'll be caught for sure."

His breathing was choppy now as with quivering hands he worked quickly to put the papers in order. Scanning each page for a number—for anything that would help him to organize the mess—he found nothing. Then he heard chatter outside. The men were on the stoop having a smoke. So he calmed himself and slowed a bit.

As he worked, his eyes caught a word stamped in red on several sheets: *Restricted,* the papers proclaimed. He couldn't help himself; he had to look. But as he read, his hands began to shake again. He gripped the papers tighter, nearly bending them in half as he scanned each line. He had been right. These men were not common soldiers; their mission, their training left Alec numb. Demolitions experts? Follow their own troops? To do what?

He did his best to collect the special documents and return them to their hiding place, being careful to leave one corner peeking out as it had been. Then he placed Aga's biscuits next to the photograph, fluffed the pillow a bit more, and left the room.

He shut the door, leaned against the wall, and closed his eyes. He felt as if he had been running for miles; his blood was pounding in his ears. He told himself he had to stay calm. He couldn't let anyone suspect what he'd done. He wanted to stop right then, go downstairs, and forget the other soldiers' rooms, but he couldn't. Aga would ask him if he had taken care of the biscuits. He had to finish.

In a few minutes, he was on the third floor, in Will's room. There, Alec moved quickly to the bed and started again on the covers and pillow. Next to his bed, Will had left a family photo as well. The young soldier was surrounded by his mother, father, and a sister who looked to be about ten. Standing proudly in his uniform, Will looked ready to begin his adventure, while his parents stood soberly next to him. In the corner of the photo was a small bit of writing: *God Go with You, Will.*

Troubled by his discovery in the lieutenant's quarters, Alec couldn't snoop further in Will's room. Besides, Will had his belongings stashed in the corner.

Specs had not left photos or papers lying about, but he was a reader. A copy of *The History of Germany* lay open on his bed, and a prayer book rested on the nightstand. As Alec worked in Specs's room, he began to feel even more uncomfortable. Specs's book only reminded Alec of the soldiers' talk about Germany. Although at first he had been excited at the prospect of a real war, now that he knew the men, he did not want to think about it. He did not want them facing what Specs was predicting. He hurried to finish up.

In the last room, Alec spotted Harry's journal. *Harry,* Alec thought, *the one with the jaunty step and a bit of cheek; he keeps a journal.* Knowing the privacy he demanded for his own diary, Alec would not have opened the journal on his own. But, again, in the rush to be on time for supper, the solder had left the book open to an entry dated three days earlier. *We're set to leave for Dover,* Harry had written. *This special detachment is only four blokes, including the lieutenant. Don't know what that means, but I'm glad I'm not staying behind. When I get to France, those Jerries will all turn tail and go home for fear of the likes of me.*

A crazy bloke, Alec thought. *He'll be good for the others. Help them to keep their spirits up.*

Finishing in Harry's room, Alec placed the biscuits on the nightstand, turned down the covers, and checked the drapes on the window overlooking the street. As he did so, he saw Harry and Specs down below, finishing their cigarettes. He wondered if they knew the secrets tucked away in the papers downstairs. If they had the choice now to go or stay, would they go? He thought about himself. *I know I would go if I could.*

Glancing out the window again, Alec saw that the stoop was empty. He opened the door and scrambled down the back way just as the soldiers reached the second-floor landing.

"I'll catch you in the morning, mate," Harry called to Specs.

"Right. See you at oh-seven hundred," Specs replied.

Back in the kitchen, Aga was just finishing her cleanup and hanging the tea towels to dry on the rack above the cooker.

"Everything in good order, Alec boy?"

"Covers turned down and biscuits served," Alec answered. "I think these blokes are going to be easy guests. They're tidy and they don't fuss."

"Indeed, Alec boy, they're good lodgers. And they like my cooking. They can stay as long as they want." Aga laughed, turning toward her room. "But as for me, I'm done for the day." Then she paused and came back toward him. Taking him by the shoulders, she looked at him and spoke. "Oh, Alec, I'm glad it's not you we're sending off to fight. Aye, I couldn't see you go. You're the life of this inn, you know. When you're on that ship, I worry you'll not return. You'll be here in the morning, won't you?"

"Aye. I'll be around. I've been checking with the captain, and he still needs time to think about the *Britannia* and what he'll do without Badger. I'll be here to help with suppers, too. And don't worry about the sea, Aga," Alec said on his way out the door. "Captain Cairns is a good skipper; he'll keep me safe."

As he headed to his room, he couldn't help thinking that Aga would be worried about those papers stuffed under the lieutenant's mattress. She'd not sleep tonight if she knew that news.

I can't just sit here and let Thomas get lost with the others in France, Alec wrote in his journal. *And we can't just all sit back and wait for Hitler to land on our shores. What would become of all of us then? Those lads upstairs—they're on a mission that makes no sense. What is England thinking?*

Questions flowed onto the pages. His strokes were thick and scattered. He could barely read his own lines. He told himself to stop thinking about the folder. That there was nothing he could do for now. But the *Restricted* pages kept floating through his mind.

7
BREAKING AWAY

OVER THE NEXT WEEK, THE QUESTIONS NEVER LEFT HIM. He found himself daydreaming, wondering when the soldiers would begin their dark mission.

"Alec," Aga said. "What is wrong with you, lad? You've set the breakfast plates for supper, and the teapot is about to sail right off the cooker. Are you daft, boy? What's keeping you in such a state? Come here and let me look at you. What's wrong?"

"Nowt—nothing, Aga, nothing is wrong. I'm just not sleeping, you know. I can't seem to get the sleep I need."

"Well, don't be letting your father hear that, lad," Aga warned. "Mr. Frank is just looking for a chance to keep you here in the inn all day—wants you to help me. So don't be telling your father that you're worn out. He won't allow you to go back when the captain decides to go out again."

"Aye," Alec said, "I'm not about to tell Father how nasty I feel. I'll just go to my room right after supper."

But he didn't rest much. He worried instead—about the soldiers, about France and what was waiting for

Courtright and his men. *Specially selected*—the words still lingered in his head. He now knew that demolition was part of their mission.

Could anyone sleep, knowing what I've discovered? And Thomas—what will happen to him? Alec's journal held a dozen questions he wished he could ask the lieutenant. But since he wasn't supposed to know anything about the soldiers' mission, he was forced to live with the fear that kept him awake.

He left his light burning late into the night, writing down other thoughts. Then, still unable to settle down, he put out the lamp and stood by his window, the drapes drawn back. Nothing stirred. Everything was black but for the moon that reflected off the Anderson shelter below him. Gazing at the metal roof, he knew the shelter wouldn't begin to save them from a bomb. Why, it couldn't even keep water from seeping in. He closed the drapes and lay back down on his bed.

He wished he could talk to Margaret. He could tell *her* the news, and she wouldn't betray him. Though he was not a soldier and was barely a seaman, he knew when something was wrong. And Lieutenant Courtright's secret mission was wrong for England. Alec hated knowing it alone. But for now, he had to hide it in his mind and not let it out.

Sometime during the night, sleep finally came.

"I know it's your dream to be on a boat, Alec boy," Aga said the next morning when Alec appeared, looking worse than the day before. "But I'm beginning to think your father's right. You're too young—not yet strong enough for a seaman's life. You'd be much better off here at the Shaftbury, taking over for your mum and dad someday. That's a life with more promise than to be a shipmate on the Channel. The sea holds too many surprises. I'm hoping Captain Cairns's ship stays docked for a good long while."

"We'll be safe, Aga, you'll see. Besides, a full shipmate, well, that's a long time off. I'm only a galley boy. I have to earn my place." He yawned as he reached for the tins on the larder shelf.

"Oh, Alec," his mother said, joining them in the kitchen. "You look awful. You're worn ragged from your work here. How could you manage the Shaftbury *and* the *Britannia?* How do you expect to keep up? Why not do as your father asks and give up these silly notions of owning a boat and working on the docks?"

Alec was silenced by his mother's harsh words. In recent days, although she had not taken his side in front of her husband, she had not criticized Alec, either. Instead, she was usually silent during his father's tirades, waiting until she was alone with Alec to talk. She had never been so strong against him as now.

"I mean it, Alec," she continued. "You can no longer expect us to agree with this galley boy job. It's a ghastly life for a boy your age. You could have been lost that day; it was more than a small Channel storm."

"You don't understand." Alec held out his hands. "We had some bad luck, but we were not in danger. And I'm not asking you to agree with my choice. Please, Mum, I'm only asking you to let me have a chance. I'll be responsible for what happens. I want to be a seaman, and I'm not afraid of what that demands. You'll see; I can make it to first mate and then to owning my own boat. You'll see."

His mother looked at him. Her words seemed to have made him more determined.

"I've got to be off now," Alec told her. "I told Specs I'd run for supplies." Then, turning to Aga, he said, "I'll be back in a bit." He touched his mother's arm and scooted out the back door.

Alec was disappointed in his mother's betrayal. She had always been loyal to him. How could she turn against him now? He thought about the soldiers in the inn and wondered if they had ever argued with their folks. Or had their parents sent them off with good wishes? It seemed that the older Alec got, the harder it was for him to get along at home. Before Georgie's death, he had gotten into a row now and then with his father, but never anything with his mum.

Since the soldiers had arrived at the Shaftbury, Alec had made a few trips to the store for them. Normally restricted to military personnel, the supply store stocked goods for the troops. Because Lieutenant Courtright and his men were at the inn, Alec was allowed to go to the store to buy their supplies. Sometimes he picked up cigarettes for Specs and Harry. Other times he stopped at the post office to get their stamps. And occasionally he even posted a telegram for Specs to his girlfriend up in Leeds.

The army staff had gotten used to seeing Alec at the store, and they didn't ask him for identification anymore. At times, they even forgot he was around as they talked military business among themselves.

"Too many men shoving off for France, I think. We've got trouble there," one old sergeant growled now to the young clerk at the counter.

"Do ye think so? Or do ye think we're just gettin' ready to wipe out those Jerries in France? Methinks we're too many for the likes of them."

"You mark my words, laddie," the sergeant said. "We're not through with this mess by any means; we've a nasty fight in front of us. Heed my words."

"What?" the other man replied. "What are ye sayin', man? What do ye know?"

The sergeant leaned closer and spoke slowly. "There are rumors about that we'll soon see trouble—big trouble—in France. Those French, they can't hold back the Germans forever. The radio isn't sayin' it yet, but one bloke from up the hill let it slip. Said our troops will be under fire. Said like Poland, France will soon be runnin' from those German panzers. Terrible stuff, those panzers. I've heard they can roll right over a lorry without stoppin'. Crushin' everythin' in their path."

Alec lingered in the aisle. The old sergeant's words had cut through his thoughts. It was just as he feared. Thomas? The trouble in France? The old sergeant was worried as well. As he left, Alec wondered even more about the men at the inn. Maybe the sergeant was just an old blowhard, but his words chilled Alec. Too many pieces in this war were pointing to a disaster.

Will was sitting on the stoop when Alec returned from the store.

"Got some smokes for Specs," Alec said. "And some notepaper for you. Have you heard any more about your orders?"

"No. But we should hear soon. We've already been here longer than we expected."

"Well, I wouldn't mind if you stayed for weeks. Your stories and your banter—they brighten the inn. And Father fusses at me less when you chaps are around."

"Parents don't mean to get in the way," Will said. "They've just lived so long deciding what's best for us that when it's time to let go and keep quiet, they can't do it."

Alec looked puzzled, wondering why Will was saying this to him.

"I heard your mum talking about the inn and your ship—the *Britannia,* is it? I'm not surprised you're upset. It's hard to grow up, especially as the only lad in a small family."

"This isn't the life I want. But my father . . . he won't hear of my doing anything else. He's not being fair. When he was old enough to choose his own way, he bought the Shaftbury. Why can't he give me a choice?"

The air was thick with moisture, and Alec could smell the heavier rain as it moved in from across the Channel. A slight mist settled on their faces. It was still early in the day, and Alec and Will had the street to themselves.

"I know what you're feeling, Alec. Struggled a bit with me folks as well. They don't mean to be harsh; they've had trouble letting go."

"I don't know," Alec shot back. "No matter what I do, it never seems to be good enough for my father. And then—and then something happened, and now I can't do anything to get his respect, either. I'm spent on trying. I can't waste my whole life hoping to please him. He'll never be proud of me. I need my own path."

"Aye, you feel that way now, but over time, you'll come to understand your father's ways. I joined the army against me own dad's wishes. Lied about me age. Me dad—he's a stubborn Irishman. He didn't want me to leave, but I did anyway." Will turned away and continued speaking. "Sure, I want to go with me mates and do what I can to stop the Jerries. But I'd like it more if me mum and dad were behind me. . . . *'Teaghlach,'* my Irish grand-da used to say, *'teaghlach*—family—is the best gift. Value it above all.'"

"I know what you're saying," Alec said, "but I'm not going to war. It's a seaman I want to be. And I've a job. I'm old enough to choose that for myself."

Fingering the cross hanging about his neck, Will spoke again. "And is what you want worth losing what you already have?"

"But you're doing what you want."

"Aye. And I'm ready to go on with it. It's just a bit lonely sometimes."

Alec hesitated. "So why *are* you and Specs and Harry

and the lieutenant here? At the inn? Why aren't you with the others at the encampment above the cliffs?"

Will didn't seem to mind Alec's question. "Well, mate, we've orders not to say anything about our assignment, but two weeks ago, each of us got a post telling us to meet at Victoria Station for a train to Dover. We'd just finished demolitions training."

"Demolitions?" Alec echoed, not letting on about the papers he'd seen in the lieutenant's room.

"Aye. Powerful stuff, mind you. Strong enough to dig a nasty hole even in rock."

"I knew it!" Alec said excitedly. "I told Aga that soldiers wouldn't stay at the Shaftbury unless they were under special orders. Specs and the rest of you, you're going to do big things for England, aren't you? You'll be heroes!" He hoped Will would tell him something that would help him make sense of the lieutenant's papers.

"No, Alec. We're just men like the others. I don't feel like a hero." Will stood to go back inside. "The vicar always said it is the duty of children to honor their parents. But when does that duty end? When do we find our own life? That's the mystery, Alec."

Will lingered a moment more, then nodded to Alec and stepped through the door. Alec stayed behind. He was even more confused than before. Will had done what he wanted, but he was no more settled than Alec.

Too many thoughts tumbled around in his head. He liked Will; he admired his honesty. He also liked working on the *Britannia*. What could be so wrong with that? Was it his duty to give up his dream of owning a boat simply to please his father? Could he even do that? And if he chose the sea, could he live with the sadness Will spoke of? The questions had no answers. He would need time to sort them out. But he was certain that the *Britannia* was to be part of his life. He picked up his packages and stepped into the inn.

Lieutenant Courtright and his men were sitting down to Aga's special English breakfast. With ration cards, Aga was still able to get bacon, and its aroma filled the room as the hungry men devoured it along with fried eggs and toast. Aga stood in the doorway, watching them. "Never know, lads, when you'll be called or when our food supplies will dwindle, so eat what you can now," she advised.

Alec waited nearby, waiting to fetch more food or drink. He wondered where the soldiers' orders would take them. He wondered if they would be with Thomas. He felt uneasy about Will's words.

Now watching them enjoying breakfast as they talked and laughed, he wanted to go with them. They were ready to defend England against the Jerries, and they were proud. But the army would never accept a lad as young as he was. Still, he wished he could be a part of their mission. Will had lied about his age; could he do the same? He had no mates like they did, no one to tell about his dreams.

"Have you rung your wife and family since we've been in Dover?" Specs asked Lieutenant Courtright as Aga placed another rack of toast on the table.

"Not since leaving London. There's nothing really to

tell, and she'd just worry more if she knew our orders had not come. I'd like to ring her, though. Tell her how I miss her and the children and all their fussing about. . . ." He paused a moment. "It's the small things I miss. Seeing her work in her victory garden, nursing those vegetable sprouts and such. She'll be worrying about the children and their friends—saying she can't do it all on her own. But she can," he said sadly, lowering his head. "She'll have to."

The men left, but the lieutenant's words had brought the war into the room. Alec saw Aga wipe her eyes with her apron. She picked up a few empty plates and went through the door into the kitchen. Alec gathered more dishes and followed right behind her, bumping the door as it swung his way. He didn't think she would be returning so soon to the dining room—and he rammed into her as she started through. She fell backward, and Alec grabbed for her with his free hand, but missed. Aga went down in a heap.

"Aga, Aga, I'm so sorry. Are you hurt? Can you get up?" Alec put the dishes on the table and lifted her to her feet.

"No bother, Alec boy. You just knocked the wind out of me, I think. If you help me to that chair over there, I can rest and get meself back together."

Alec put his arm around her thick waist and helped her shuffle to the chair. Just then, his father came through the back door and saw Aga's flushed face.

"Is something wrong? What's happened here?"

"It was a wee accident, Mr. Curtis," Aga responded.

"No harm done. Just took the wind out of me sails for a minute. I'm nearly back to normal now. We were just coming through the door at the same time, and we collided."

Alec's father shot him a look and turned toward the lobby, leaving Aga and Alec to stare after him.

"Oh, Alec. I've gotten you in more trouble. I would never do anything to hurt you," Aga said.

"Aga, this was not your fault. It was mine. I'm just so distracted that I overlooked the first rule about the dining room: check first before barging through the swinging door. Are you sure you're all right?"

"Aye. I'm fixed and ready to stand. I just wish we could fix you and your father. I hate to see you both so unhappy."

"I'm almost used to it, though at times, I still wish for a chance to turn things around. But I'm beginning to think nothing will change his mind. Ever since Georgie, I've felt a space between Father and me. And it gets worse after he visits Aunt Lucy and Uncle Jack. He comes home and doesn't say anything. I want him to see that I'm trying hard to do better, but I don't know what else I can do. Now with Thomas gone, and Aunt Lucy and Uncle Jack grieving once again, the sadness will never leave this inn."

He felt discouraged as he finished his chores and went to his room. He needed to write in his journal. He wouldn't write about his father. He'd done that too many times already, and each entry was the same: *Father is angry with me again.* It was time to make a decision to do something new— both with his journal and with his life.

Perhaps if he wrote it all down—the news from the

lieutenant's room, the words from the old sergeant, the advice from Will—he could see the whole problem clearly. One thing was certain: he would not, could not, live like this much longer. Something would have to change. The inn would have to go on without him. He would soon break away.

8
SHIPPING OUT

"ALEC, ALEC, STOP A MINUTE, BOY," THE SCREECHY voice of Mrs. Tanner demanded. "I need to speak with you."

Alec couldn't believe it. Old Mrs. Tanner had seen him returning from the docks. He had gone there after tea, needing some time away from the inn to think.

"Alec. Alec Curtis. Stop this minute and talk to me!" she called again.

At first, Alec pretended he had not heard her—had even taken a couple more steps along the sidewalk. But then she called a third time, and he turned and walked back toward her. He stopped in front of her shop.

"Yes, Mrs. Tanner. What do you need?"

"I don't *need* anything, boy. Rumor has it things are jumping in the military encampment up there on the cliffs. Someone said it looks like the whole lot is preparing to ship out. I thought maybe there was talk on the docks and you might have heard it."

"No, Mrs. Tanner. It's Sunday. Nobody's at the docks today. I was just on my own, skimming rocks off the pier."

"The man who delivers my milk says the pubs are humming with rumors about troops leaving and more destroyers heading to France. Seems to me that you would hear all sorts of talk and bits of news at the docks. He says there are tunnels beneath the castle, running for miles, and that some of the BEF are billeted there."

Alec knew she was looking for gossip from him. Though he'd never heard anything about tunnels under the castle, he resisted the urge to ask about them. She was not going to trap him into being her messenger.

"Maybe you've even been in those tunnels beneath the castle? With your cousin?" she said.

"No, Mrs. Tanner, that tunnel business is news to me, too," he said, controlling the excitement he felt rising within him. "Can't say as I've ever heard anything about any tunnels up on the cliffs. I haven't been up there in months." He thought of Georgie.

"Well, I am puzzled," Mrs. Tanner persisted. "I would have wagered a few shillings that you, Alec Curtis, would know more about this war than just about anyone in Dover. With those soldiers living at your parents' inn, I just imagined you would know it all."

"Sorry, Mrs. Tanner." Alec shifted his weight from one foot to the other, letting her know he was anxious to move on. "Well, I've got to go. Aga will be looking for me to help her." He hurried on down the street.

He was glad, in a way, that Mrs. Tanner's questions had been so specific; he had been able to answer without actually lying. On Friday, when he was fetching a letter for Specs, the blokes sorting the post had said the mail would be slowing down soon. More of the troops on the hill were shipping out to France, they'd said. But Mrs. Tanner had asked about the docks, not about the post office, so he *hadn't* lied, though he felt a twinge of guilt at being so deceptive. At the same time, he remembered Mrs. Tanner's cruel words at his friend Margaret's funeral. *Margaret would understand,* he thought.

Aga's face was blotchy and red when he came in the back door of the inn. She wiped her eyes with a tea towel.

"What's wrong, Aga? Has Father been in here looking for me again?"

"No, Alec boy, your father's in the drawing room. I've just heard the news about our guests. They've got their orders; they'll be leaving Dover tonight. Going over to France on some mission. Oh, those poor young lads. God help them." She sighed and then buried her face in her apron.

"Tonight?" Alec said. "Are you sure? Why tonight?"

"No other details—at least from the lieutenant. The message came from Vice Admiral Ramsey himself, delivered by army courier about an hour ago. They're all upstairs packing their kits and getting orders from the lieutenant. Oh, Alec boy, I can barely stand to send tham off. Especially that young lad, that Will. He doesn't even look old enough to go. What's to happen to him? What's to happen to all of us?" Aga sighed again and settled into a chair to collect herself. "No one's ever ready for war, Alec lad. But eventually, people just charge on through."

"It's what they've been trained to do, Aga. It's why they all came. They've been waiting for this."

"Aye, you're right. I just remember the Great War, and I don't want to see that again; I don't want to lose any of those boys. But you and I—we need to be about fixing the best supper they're ever had. At least we can send them off with full stomachs. God only knows when they'll eat well again once they leave."

Rising from her chair, Aga moved toward the vegetable bin and began chopping and stirring. Alec stayed with her, forgetting about Mrs. Tanner and scrambling around to fetch what she needed. Then, when she had calmed herself, Alec left and went up the back stairway to room four and knocked on the door.

Will flung open the door and then seemed disappointed to see Alec standing there. "Oh, it's you, Alec. How are you, mate?"

"I'm sorry if I'm bothering you, Will."

"No, it's just . . . the lieutenant said he'd let us know if there was further news on our orders. I thought maybe you were him."

"Aga told me about the courier's message. She says you're to go tonight. Is that true?"

"'Tis true. You must keep it to yourself, but we're to be ready to shove off at twenty-two hundred hours. We'll be going out of Dover on a minesweeper called the *Gossamer*. Headed over to France, but I'm not sure what port. The lieutenant says he'll tell us once we're under way."

Alec looked around Will's room. He had gotten used to seeing each soldier's nightstand holding his few belongings. The men's stories were hidden among the items. But now, as Alec scanned Will's room, he was saddened to see Will collecting his things. The family photograph remained near his bed. Alec found himself staring at the faces.

"I couldn't pack the photo just yet," Will said, noticing Alec's attention to it. "I'll wait until we're ready to leave to put it away. Me family's going to wonder now about me. I won't be able to post a letter for some time, I expect. I hope me mum will understand."

"She'll know that you would write if you could," Alec reassured him. "Besides, you'll be back soon. Why, you may go over there and rout the Jerries before a letter could be posted."

Will was sitting on the bed now, looking like a child waiting for his first day of school—wanting to get on with it but afraid all the same. Staring out the window, he touched the cross hanging around his neck.

"That's a fine cross," Alec said, trying to ease Will's mind.

"It was a gift from me grandda when I finished me first catechism class. It's a Celtic cross—with a circle for Christ's death, but also for hope. Me grandda told me to think of it as forever *dóchas*—forever hope. I never take it off."

Alec nodded. He admired Will. And the faith he carried in the cross made him even more likable. Alec knew this moment was difficult for Will, who was torn between his devotion to his fellow soldiers and his duty as an only son. Yet Alec also imagined that if Will had been sitting at home right now on his own bed, he would feel even worse. He was a soldier; he wanted to help England.

Aga's right, Alec thought. *No one is ever ready for war. Eventually, people just charge on through.*

For a few minutes, they sat quietly on the bed. Alec wanted to say something, but he felt that anything he said would sound weak to a young man facing a war bigger than either of them could imagine. Then Will broke the silence. "We've been taught to set explosives that can be detonated from a hundred yards or more," he volunteered. "Sometimes the loads are packed with only enough power to upset a lorry, but some charges can blow huge craters in the roads or demolish a bridge. We're prepared to take out everything—from the smallest pillbox to a German tank or a French bridge."

Alec listened. He knew that Will was probably telling him things he should not be hearing. But he also knew that Will needed to talk, needed to pass the dreadful minutes that were dragging by as he waited to board the ship that would soon take him to the war.

"It's turned out to be one of the most important times of me life," Will continued. "I wasn't supposed to be much more than an infantryman, but the lieutenant spotted me hustling about the training camp. Said he needed someone small and quick. He got me orders changed and brought me to Specs and Harry. We're part of the Foresters regiment, trained to come behind the ground troops. We'd do anything to save each other.

That's what makes all the training worthwhile; we know we're guarding each man like we'd guard a brother."

"To be going out tonight, after dark, you must be needed badly," Alec said.

"Aye, but we're late getting into France. Thousands have gone ahead of us. I don't know why we're shipping out like this. The lieutenant knows more, but he's not saying just yet. I'm not sure where we fit in, but given what Hitler has already done in Czechoslovakia and Poland, France could be next. Even with our troops in Europe, the Jerries haven't been slowed. No turning back now."

Alec smiled as Will stood up, looking taller, a bit more sure. He played nervously with the cross around his neck, brushed at his shirt and trousers, then adjusted his beret to hang just so over one eye. He stuffed his things into his rucksack—maps, his mess kit, a few tools, and the photograph—and swung the sack over his shoulder. A round steel helmet, reserved for combat, hung from a strap and banged silently against him. Alec found himself hoping that Will would never need the helmet, but the soldier standing before him seemed ready now for what lay ahead.

They faced each other, Alec shuffling his feet, not knowing what else to say, and Will still tugging at his uniform. Then Will stretched out his hand to Alec, who shook it.

"Make the Jerries sorry they left home, Private Sweeney," Alec said, recalling Harry's words from their first supper at the inn.

Will smiled and whispered, "Aye, Alec. That we will."

9
TUNNEL TALK

"DON'T YOU BE THINKING THAT WHERE THOSE BOYS are going is anywhere you'd want to be, Alec boy," Aga scolded. "I saw you admiring them and their gear as they fetched it down the stairs. Where they're headed is no place for lads. I'd be beside meself with fear. Those poor boys."

Alec poked the fading fire and then went about preparing the table for supper. Tonight, he and Aga and his folks would eat with the soldiers. Aga had again gathered all the ration stamps and then haggled with the manager at the market for enough pork to feed them all one last time. That, together with the potatoes and cabbage Alec had bought from the greengrocer, made for a fine evening meal and set the lieutenant and the others to joking about army rations.

"From here on, it'll be sausages and potatoes packed in a tin," Harry said.

"Aye, and rolling our own tobacco," Specs growled. "You'd think the royal family could keep us in smokes while we're saving the country."

"Everything's rationed, Specs. You know that," the lieutenant said. "Besides, maybe you should think about giving up the smokes."

"Crikey, Lieutenant, I've had to give up me bed and me lass. Don't ask me to give up me smokes, too. We need some comforts to get us through."

Alec smiled at Specs's bluntness. He was right. They were willing to give up what they must, but they were eager to hang on to whatever they could.

"But this pork and cabbage, Aga," Specs continued, "this is a meal fit for the royal family itself." Then, turning toward Alec's mother, he said, "Mrs. Curtis, be careful. They'll enlist Aga in the ranks as well and move her to London."

Alec's mother nodded. "You're not the first guest to think Aga's cooking is the best in all of England."

"Aye," Will agreed. "This is a good sendoff for all of us."

"Just a few meals together and you lads have become like my own," Aga said. "I can't understand why you have to be dropped into the middle of that mess—and in the dark of night, at that. It makes no sense to me. But then when does war ever make sense?"

Alec's father spoke up. "Lieutenant, Aga's memories of the Great War have made her fearful."

"As they should, I believe," the lieutenant answered. "War has all kinds of casualties. Those who lose their lives, and those who sometimes lose their hope."

Aga motioned for Alec to help her get the dessert. "I don't want to rush them," she said in the kitchen. "But those men have never been late for a meal; I know they'll not be late to their muster."

As she was dishing out the custard, Aga could barely hold her hands still. "Lad." She turned to Alec. "Give me a hand here. I've got meself so upset, I cannot scoop a serving."

Alec obeyed and finished spooning out the custard, then picked up the tray. He heard loud voices as he entered the dining room. Lieutenant Courtright was standing and Aunt Lucy had ahold of his arm, her face flushed. Uncle Jack stood back a couple of steps, but he, too, was red-cheeked and winded.

Alec stood off to the side, surprised by his aunt's appearance and sudden outburst.

"Jack, Lucy," Alec's father said. "Join us for some custard."

But Lucy had not come for dessert. "Lieutenant," she said, "I've come for a desperate word with you. I've heard the talk about troops emptying out of the encampment up on the cliffs. I need to know what you know—about the events in France. Please, sir. Our son, Thomas Spencer, he's there. I need to know if our Thomas is safe. Are the Germans mustering to move into France, like we heard today?" Aunt Lucy's eyes darted from the lieutenant to Alec.

Uncle Jack removed Aunt Lucy's hand from Lieutenant Courtright's arm. "I'm sorry. For the intrusion. But she was at the post office today to mail some letters to Thomas, and the bloke there said no mail's leaving England now. Said the men on the hill were moving out to France soon. Wouldn't even take her letter, the rotter. Said they couldn't be sure the mail would arrive. And ever since, she's been like this." He glanced at Alec as he put his arm around his wife.

The lieutenant spoke softly. "Mrs. Spencer, I wish I could help you. But the truth is—I don't know much more than you do, and I am under orders to share what I do know with only my men. I'm sorry."

Alec watched his aunt. She stared intently at the lieutenant, her lips pinched together. Her arms hung down, pinned to her sides by her husband, who held her lovingly but firmly away from the others. Alec thought she looked like a madwoman. He remembered the morning he'd returned without Georgie.

"But we won't tell anyone, Lieutenant," Lucy begged. "We promise we won't say a word. We just need to know what's happening with our Thomas. Please, sir, please help us."

Lieutenant Courtright sighed. "I'm sorry, but an officer in the BEF is under oath to protect the information he has. I hope you understand."

For a moment, Alec heard only the labored breathing of his aunt. Then she erupted. "No, I don't understand. You don't know what it's like to wonder about your child. To think he's been hurt and you can't help him. To think he's calling for you as you've always told him to do and to know you can't go to him. He's all we've got now, and this ghastly war has taken him. What do you expect us to do?"

The lieutenant stepped closer to her. "I expect that you will go home and continue what you've been doing for Thomas. Keep writing letters even if you can't post them.

Tell him what you're thinking, how much you miss him. Hold him in your hearts and minds as you've always done. Pray for him and for England. No one could expect more of you," he said, reaching out to touch Lucy on the shoulder. But when she backed away from him, he let his hand fall to his side. "Please understand, I do know what it's like to wonder if he needs you. Indeed, I know what that feels like every day. It's a burden we share."

Lucy stood a moment and scanned the faces in the room. She was out of words. Then she looked at Alec. "Do you see what it's like, Alec? How it's been for me and your Uncle Jack? Your life has gone on, but our home is empty." She turned to Uncle Jack, who wrapped his arm around her shoulders and steered her toward the hotel lobby.

Alec's father lowered his chin to his chest. His mum looked at him. The whole scene had torn at Alec. He was the reason Lucy and Jack had come. His mistake had left them desperate to have Thomas back. Now everyone knew. They all sat waiting for someone to speak.

The silence was broken by Aga's raspy voice. "I certainly didn't make this custard dessert to have it go to waste. Who wants a large helping?" No one spoke at first, and then Specs cleared his throat and said, "Yes, a large helping for me—and I'll take Harry's, too." Harry laughed. The lieutenant shook his head and grinned.

Unable to eat his dessert, Alec rose to help Aga clear the dishes away.

Once in the kitchen, Aga pulled Alec aside. "Now, you listen to me, Alec boy," she demanded. "I saw your face in there. Don't be thinking that Thomas's predicament is any fault of yours. Thomas joined the army because he wanted to. It had nothing to do with you and Georgie, and *you* have nothing to do with this horrible war. You are not to blame."

"I am the reason they have only one son," Alec said. "And as long as I live, I will never forget that. Every time I look up at the castle or head to the shore, I imagine him tagging along beside me. And for Aunt Lucy it's worse. If Georgie were still here, Aunt Lucy would be better. I— I can't blame her."

"Nor can I, Alec," Aga agreed. "I know that she thought the lieutenant would tell her something. But she also knows he can't risk telling anything that could hurt the war effort. She has upset everyone. That was a nasty row."

"It's been nearly six months, Aga, and sometimes I think I'm no farther from that day than when it happened. Neither is Father."

Aga wanted to say more, but it was time to serve the tea. So she collected cups and spoons and hurried into the dining room.

The soldiers lingered longer than usual after tea. They spoke again of their families and what they missed. Then the lieutenant checked his watch and stood up. "It's nearly time to leave. Why don't we finish our packing and meet down in the lobby in fifteen minutes? Bring only what you need. Specs, that means one box of smokes, not three. Be sure your papers are in order. And any mail you need posted home can be left with Alec. He can take it to the post office tomorrow."

Alec nodded and watched as the men rose slowly and pushed in their chairs for the last time. They had known this moment would come. All through their training up north and their short stay in Dover, they had known that, one day, they would move across the Channel.

By twenty-one hundred hours, the men had assembled in the inn's lobby. Alec stood nearby. His father shook hands with each soldier while Aga hugged the men and dabbed at her eyes with her apron. Alec's mum stood quietly off to the side, having already said her good-byes. Then the lieutenant picked up his rucksack, and the others followed his lead. Alec grabbed his slicker to go with them to the docks. When his father started to object, the lieutenant interrupted. "We could use Alec's services one last time, if you don't mind, Mr. Curtis. We'll be sure to send him on back as soon as he's left us."

Alec's father nodded and disappeared into the drawing room. Aga held the door as the men passed through, touching each soldier lightly on his shoulder. "God be with you," she whispered, and watched as they moved down the street.

Alec kept up with the men stride for stride, carrying the lieutenant's rucksack while the officer checked his papers again. Alec was proud to be accompanying them to their ship. He hoped Mrs. Tanner was out so she could see how important he had become. But if she saw him, he never knew, since the men clipped right on past her business as they made their way to the docks. The city was silent and dark, but the clear sky and a bright, full moon lit their way to the shore.

Alec wondered if Captain Cairns had been to his boat lately. Alec had been so busy with the soldiers, he hadn't visited for a few days. Hearing the foghorns calling through the blackness, he realized again how much he wanted a seaman's life.

The men moved quickly down the dock toward the small boat that would shuttle them out to the Royal Navy ship waiting for them. Though they could not see it from shore, the *Gossamer* was anchored out in the Channel, a half mile from where the *Britannia* was generally moored. The *Gossamer* was a minesweeper that crossed the Channel in search of mines the Jerries had planted. Tonight, it would also carry the lieutenant, Specs, Harry, and Will to the French coast. Cloaked in darkness, they hoped to slip through the Channel waters and arrive on the French coast well before dawn. Only the lieutenant knew their destination.

At the edge of the dock, the lieutenant offered his hand to Alec. "You've been quite the good soldier, Alec, rambling about and fetching our supplies. It's been a pleasure to be billeted at the Shaftbury. Watch yourself on the *Britannia*."

Alec smiled. "You keep yourself safe as well, sir. Push those Jerries back and come home."

"We hope to do just that," the lieutenant said.

Alec watched as Lieutenant Courtright handed the waiting oarsman a small slip of paper. The sailor saluted, read the paper, and took the rucksack from the lieutenant, who stepped down into the boat.

Specs and Harry stood near Alec. "You've been a good mate, Alec, running to the post and all that for us."

"Come back," Alec said, "and Aga and I will serve you up some custard and tea. Don't let Specs take your rations, Harry."

He shook their hands and watched them as they found seats near the lieutenant. Finally, only Will remained, standing next to Alec and shaking his head. "I don't know, Alec, which of us is cheekier—you or me. Let's hope me cheeky side serves me well when those Jerries come knocking at our door."

"You'll get it done, Will, and you'll do it right. The lieutenant will see to that," Alec assured him. "Write me when you're back home and let me know what your mum and dad say when they find out their son is a hero."

Will shook his head and smiled. "No hero, Alec. Just a bloke wanting to do his part." With that, Will shifted his kit to his other shoulder, slapped Alec on the back, and climbed into the boat next to Specs. The men waved to Alec until they were swallowed up in the blackness.

He kept looking where they should have been, listening for any sound that would tell him they had boarded the *Gossamer*. His eyes burned—from straining to see, he supposed. "God go with you, mates," Alec whispered into the darkness.

He lingered only a minute more and then started for home; his father expected him. But a noise on the dock caught his attention. It was coming from down by the *Britannia*. He walked quietly toward the ship—where he discovered the captain just leaving the wheelhouse.

"Captain Cairns?" Alec said. "It's late. I didn't expect to find you here."

"Alec? What are you doing out here, sonny?"

"The soldiers from the inn are just off. How's Badger?"

"Badger's healing. But he needs to get back to sea. He's driving his family mad. He won't be sailing soon, though. Needs a few more weeks for that leg."

"How about us?" Alec asked. He knew the captain wouldn't wait much longer to sail again. He'd need Alec to step up as first mate.

"Us?" the captain asked. "We'll be sailing next Tuesday, I expect. I was waiting for you to stop by so I could tell you."

"Then you'll need me here early to check the engines and rig the ship before we load the cargo?" Alec asked hopefully. He had watched the ships go out enough times that he knew the routine. He was certain he could do the work.

"Well, sonny, I hired me a first mate to fill in until Badger's back. He'll be going out with us. That is, if you're still willing to come along as galley boy?"

Alec couldn't answer. Fresh from seeing his friends off to France, and now hearing the captain's news, he felt the last piece of fight leave him. How could he have been foolish enough to think the captain would hire him, a mere boy, as first mate? He imagined his father saying the same:

"Do you think the captain would want you dashing about the ruddy ocean making a show, not knowing what you're doing?" Alec's eyes were fixed on the dock below him.

"Sonny?" the captain called. "Alec, are you hearing me? Can you work on Tuesday?"

"Aye. . . . I can. . . . Yes. Yes, sir," Alec said. "I'll be around to help you when you need me. Same time as before?" he asked, trying to sound eager.

"Aye," the captain continued. "I'm here tonight to meet the new chap. He's like Badger. Stays late at the pubs. He's done some work on tugs."

Just then, a gruff voice spoke from behind Alec. "This Cap'n Cairns's ship?"

"Aye, it is," Alec said, stepping out of the way so the man could climb aboard.

Something about the man was familiar, but Alec couldn't say what. Watching him move across the small ship, Alec tried to think where he might have met him. Then the man spoke again.

"We're agreed on me pay, right, Cap'n?" he demanded. "Aah'm not servin' one day aboard this ship if ye cannit agree to what we discussed."

"Aye, Mr. Douglas, I haven't changed my mind about the pay. But you understand it's only until my first mate is up and well. When he's strong enough to come back, I won't be needing your services."

"Agreed," the man said roughly, and at that moment Alec knew his voice. It had been almost dark when they'd met before, but he still knew him. He'd been coming out of the White Horse Pub when Alec bumped into him. Ready to give Alec a thrashing, he'd been.

I wonder if he'll recognize me, Alec thought. Just then, Captain Cairns turned to Alec. "And this is Alec, our galley boy. He goes out with us on day trips. Brews tea and scrubs the deck—just about anything we need done."

The man grunted and turned to Alec. "Name's Douglas, boy. Ye can call me that," he snapped.

"Did ye hear that a minesweeper just pulled out of the harbor?" Douglas asked, turning back to the captain.

"No, but Alec's just come from seeing some soldiers off."

"Aye, aah've just come from the White Horse," Douglas continued. "Not many in there tonight. Rumor has it all the blokes from up on the cliffs are leavin', goin' off to France. They're takin' every soldier we've got. Aah'm glad aah'm not goin'."

Alec said nothing. This was one of those times he chose to be quiet. The captain and Douglas talked on about the French and the Germans, angry that the Jerries had overrun Poland and were threatening France. Alec wanted to stay and listen, but he knew he should be on his way back. His father would be looking for him by now. Then Douglas's next words stopped him.

"This bloke, 'e comes into the White Horse some nights an' 'as a few pints too many. Always ramblin', 'e is, about the war and the tunnels that 'e says run under the Dover Castle. 'e says that the whole English operation is being ordered from inside those tunnels. Aah'd niver 'eard o' that before."

"I've heard those rumors," Captain Cairns said. "I've also

heard that those tunnels are caved in and useless; haven't been worth anything to anyone in years."

"The bloke says 'e stays there at night. 'e's hired by the BEF. Says 'e works in the kitchen inside the castle and collects food from the Dover Priory. 'e claims some of the big military brass 'ave come to live an' work in the tunnels. 'e talks like 'e means it, an' 'e says people in Dover will find out soon that 'e's tellin' the truth."

"I'd say he's blowing wind," Cairns responded. "Just wanting to bend somebody's ear. Now, let's see what we need to look at here before it gets too late." He turned to Alec. "You planning to stay around, lad?"

"No, no, sir. I've got to get back to the inn. I'll see you Tuesday. Is it a fishing cargo we've got, then?"

"Aye, we're headed to Ramsgate for the day. To haul from there to the pubs on Snargate. We'll see you then, sonny."

Alec ran up the dock toward the shore, grateful that Douglas had not recognized him. Making his way along the streets to the inn, Alec thought about Douglas's words. He recalled Mrs. Tanner's questions from earlier and wondered if there was something to the tunnel gossip. What if the military *was* getting its orders from Dover? That would explain the mustering of the soldiers and all the activity the past few days.

Until that moment, Alec had believed that the purpose of the encampment on the hill was to guard the closest port to France. But what if there was more to it than that? What if someone up in the castle was commanding Thomas's unit or Lieutenant Courtright's men?

As Alec climbed the steps to the inn, he realized that his disappointment about the first mate's job had almost disappeared. In its place loomed a new chance for adventure. Tunnels—under the castle. Could it be true?

He was out of breath, though he had not been running. He squeezed his hands tight, feeling the energy surging through his arms. His spirit had been revived; his body felt stronger. Stirred by this new information, he was eager for the days before him. Could Dover hold more promise for him than he had thought?

10
MISSING CHILDREN

ALEC'S PARENTS HAD NOT STOOD IN HIS WAY THIS TIME. He wondered if the row with Aunt Lucy had made them feel sorry for him. He decided, instead, that the soldiers' stay had softened all of them a bit. And he imagined his father was weary of challenging him. Besides, he had worked hard for his father, getting the inn ready for the soldiers and then helping Aga with every meal. He deserved to go back to being a galley boy.

From the first day, Alec could see that Douglas was even crustier than Badger. In the daylight, he looked as rough as he sounded—hair matted to his head and arms branded with unsightly tattoos. He always seemed angry, ready to strike out at the smallest blunder. Alec kept his distance, working hard to earn Douglas's trust by jumping at every command.

Their work on the *Britannia* was demanding. When they weren't carrying fish, they hauled barbed wire and posts up and down the Channel as coastal towns moved to protect themselves from a possible invasion from the sea.

As the *Britannia* glided past the towns and their beaches, Alec noticed how each community was beginning to look the same. Barbed wire fringed the sandy coasts, preventing not only enemies but also residents from using the shore.

Some towns even installed weapons. In Dover, civilians and military men built a hiding place at the end of the dock for an antiaircraft gun. Perched on a rotating platform so it could turn full circle and fire quickly at enemy planes, the gun was hidden in a small boatlike structure tied to the dock. From the air, the gun might be mistaken for just another ship in the harbor, but if necessary, a few bits of planking could be removed to clear the gun for firing.

Alec was fascinated by the army's tactics. He was fascinated by the feel of war. Large holes had been dug on the shore, and stacks of sandbags had been brought in to surround the holes. From the docks, Alec could see dozens of the sandbag huts that would hold soldiers and guns if needed. Oh, he knew he should listen to Aga and be more fearful, but he couldn't help himself. He wanted to be part of it.

Alec rarely missed the radio reports. Every evening, he, his father and mum, and Aga tuned in to hear the latest news. The broadcasts upset Aga. She feared the war was nearly upon them. And her fears increased as the people of Dover felt more pinched every day with rationing of petrol, food, and even clothing.

By early spring, the BBC was reporting that more than 250,000 British troops had landed in either France or Belgium.

Certain that Hitler and his army didn't have a chance against the entire BEF, people adjusted to rationed food and waited for news that their lads were coming home. Instead, the news turned worse. Blackouts were stricter, curfews kept people off the streets after ten o'clock, and air-raid sirens blasted forth nearly every day. Alec and his family tried to go on as before, but the signs of war were hurting their town and their business. They'd had only a few guests each week since the soldiers had left.

They were all surprised when the mayor called for an evacuation of the children. "Good thing you're the age you are, boy," Mrs. Tanner called to Alec as he walked past her on his way to the market.

"What's that, Mrs. Tanner? What is it you're saying?" Alec asked.

"You ought to be glad you're nearly grown. You don't have to worry about being sent off to live with some distant relative up north. That's what they're planning to do, you know, send the children away."

"Who is sending children away?"

"The mayor and the town council. They've decided the children will be safer if they're away from the coast. The council thinks we'll be bombed soon—too much of a risk to keep the children here. Schools are closing. Parents are ringing up relatives to take the children until the war's over. Should be no surprise. They've already done the same in London."

"But why now?" Alec asked. Though he spent no time with other children anymore, he could not imagine his

town without them skipping along sidewalks or crowding into candy stands. Dover was not a large town. But the many-storied flats rising side by side at the base of the chalky cliffs housed dozens of young families.

"I've heard no more than I've told you. But don't bother with me. Check at the market or the post office. See if they don't tell you the same news."

"No, I believe you, Mrs. Tanner. It's just that I hadn't heard," Alec said as he moved away from her tailor shop and on toward the market.

He tried to imagine what could have pushed the mayor and council to act now. He felt something nagging at his thoughts. Lieutenant Courtright's papers seemed to float before him. Could this all be connected with their mission?

He stopped at the post office, eager to confirm Mrs. Tanner's words. "Aye, heard the news this morning from the mayor himself," one man told Alec. "Parents are being told to find somewhere for their children to live for the next few months."

But why now? Sure, they'd had some false alarms and everyone was a bit edgier, but why now? Then he realized he was sounding just like Aunt Lucy—suspicious that the news in France was worse than they had been hearing.

Alec hurried out of the post office and turned toward the market. There, after collecting cabbage, onions, and what sugar he could get with one ration stamp, he hurried home, anxious to tell Aga about Mrs. Tanner's news.

Early warm weather had brought spring to Dover. Flowering trees held out their boughs as if to shake Alec's hand as he passed by. The newsboys were calling out the headlines—NAZIS INVADE DENMARK AND NORWAY—as they peddled the dailies to shops around the town. The warm weather usually made Alec feel good, but not this day. He barely took notice as he worried about the war looming just across the Channel.

He was certain the BEF was in control over there. After all, most of Britain's forces were settled in France. But now that piece didn't fit with the puzzle about the children. Maybe Aga would know more.

She wasn't there. Climbing up the back stairs, Alec called for her as he peeked into vacant guestrooms. Then, moving down the front stairway to the lobby, Alec heard her speaking to someone at the desk. He stopped and sat down on a step, close enough to eavesdrop.

"Whatever is going to happen, Mrs. Curtis?" Aga pleaded. "What are we going to do if the Germans start bombing? They're sure to aim for the business district, and this inn sits smack in the center of everything."

"I know as much as you do, Aga. It's true we're sitting in the middle of Dover, but we can't let fear beat us. If things get worse, then we'll worry. But we have to go on for now."

"But the children, Mrs. Curtis," Aga persisted. "They're sending the children away. What do you make of that?"

"Maybe the mayor is trying to save the children from the wailing of those horrible sirens." Alec could hear his mum fussing with some papers on the desk. "But you've said it yourself, Aga. War can quickly turn into something awful."

"It's just like the Great War, Mrs. Curtis. Things are happening just like before. We'll not get out of this easy. This corner of the country is what the Germans want. We're the gateway into England, Hitler says. No, this war—this war will give Dover a place in history."

"Perhaps you're right, Aga, but we cannot let it paralyze us."

Once his mum had gone, Alec stood up and continued down the steps. He approached Aga in the lobby. He thought she might be too upset to talk. But he had to know what she had heard about the children.

"Rumors are flying around town, Aga. Have you heard anything?" he asked.

"Oh, Alec," Aga sighed, sitting down on the chair behind the desk. "Children being sent away from their parents. What are we to think? And what about those children who have nowhere to go? What becomes of them?"

"What does the council think is going to happen?"

"I don't know what to think other than what we know already—that Dover has always been a target for invaders. But I've never known our town to send young ones away. Dover has always stood as one."

Alec tried to piece everything together. "Have I got some time before supper, Aga?"

"Sure, Alec boy," Aga replied. "We've got more than an hour before the guests will be down, and setup won't take but a bit this evening. I'll call when I need you."

In his room, Alec pulled out his journal and opened it to a blank page. When the soldiers first left, he had written in his journal every day, trying to keep a record for when they returned. Often, he wrote a message to Will, as if they were talking to each other as they used to do; other times he made notes about the *Britannia*. But lately, he had written nothing. Now he picked up his journal to make a list. He was certain that tucked within the news around Dover, he could find something that would bring him closer to the truth about the events in France.

Mrs. Tanner talked about the tunnels before the soldiers left.

If Mrs. Tanner is right about the tunnels under the cliffs, orders could have come for both groups on the same day—especially if the command post is under the castle.

Aunt Lucy was sure that the lieutenant knew more than he was saying.

If something big is about to happen in France, Lieutenant Courtright probably knew but couldn't say.

The news about the children from Dover means that danger is getting closer.

Once he had finished, Alec paused and looked at what he had before him. Something big was coming, but what could it be? Were Will and Thomas and the others in the middle of it now?

As soon as he asked himself the questions, he knew where he could find some answers: Douglas's man from the White Horse Pub. He could lead Alec to more details. But how could Alec even get close to him? At fourteen, Alec was much too young to be in a pub, especially at night. And Douglas had said the man came only after dark to the White Horse.

Maybe Alec could hang around outside the pub and follow the bloke on his way back to the castle. Aye, that was what he'd do. Catch up with him on his way back, after he'd had a few pints. Maybe he'd be so tipsy he wouldn't notice he was being followed. No matter. Somehow, Alec had to figure out what was about to happen. He had to find out for Aunt Lucy and for Thomas and for himself. And he was sure the answer was in the castle.

They were going out on the *Britannia* the next day. He would get up and help Aga, then go early to the ship to talk with Douglas about the bloke from the White Horse. He had many questions.

His plan set, Alec checked the time and realized Aga had forgotten to call him for setup. Poor Aga. He would have liked to tell her what he was plotting—he usually told her everything. But this time he couldn't. She was so upset about the war; she might slip and tell his mum and father, and then he'd be confined to the inn. Soon enough, if things worked as he hoped, he might have information about Thomas that could help Uncle Jack and Aunt Lucy— that could change how they felt about Alec.

Slipping his journal back into its hiding place, Alec nearly ran from his room. This secret was his alone.

11
THE MYSTERY MAN

"THOSE SQUALLY WINDS COMING FROM THE SOUTH ARE going to keep the *Britannia* in port today, lad," Captain Cairns said when Alec arrived the next morning. "I've got to ring up the mates near Folkestone and tell them we'll not be coming."

Alec watched as the captain gathered his rucksack and set off to make the call. He and Douglas were left to themselves on the boat.

"So, Douglas," Alec began, hanging over the cargo hold, where the first mate was untangling one of the fishing nets, "are you from Dover or did you move here from somewhere up north?"

He didn't look at Alec. "Raised in London," he snapped. "Got tired of the thrashin's from me dad. Soon as aah could, aah made me way to the coast to get work on the docks."

"So you've worked the docks for a long time? You like the sea?" Alec took one end of the net and stretched it out for Douglas.

"Aye, aah've been a seaman many years. But aah hate the sea. Can't swim, don't like the smell of fish. The sea is me work, not me love."

"And do you have family here in Dover?"

"Aah've no use for a family," Douglas growled. "Just take me money and give me trouble. The pub, now, that's me family."

Alec stirred at the mention of the pub. "The White Horse Pub, isn't it? You go there most nights, do you?"

"Me an' the White Horse, we're family. The blokes there, they understan' me an' the docks. Though aah finds plenty of drink and fightin' there, too. Aye, it's 'ome to me every night."

"And the man who talked about the tunnels, does he come often to the White Horse?" Alec asked, taking a chance that Douglas was still willing to talk.

"Most nights. As I told the captain, 'e meets the train and picks up supplies—but 'e's always there on Thursdays—payday. 'e blows in an' says 'e'll buy drinks for every bloke in the pub. Nobody believes 'im. 'e never has that many shillings. 'e just likes to look important an' thinks 'e's better than us because 'e doesn't work the docks."

"What did you say he did in the tunnels? Is he a cook or something?"

"So 'e says," Douglas replied. "But cripes, methinks 'e's just a loudmouth rotter without the brains or the strength to do the work on the docks. 'e's stout and not much taller than ye, an' always wearing a white seaman's cap. Too barmy to ever do a real seaman's job, though. Aah've seen 'is kind before. All blow an' no guts. 'e has to sneak out just to get a pint at the pub."

Just then, Douglas unraveled the last knot.

"There. Make it easier the next time we're out fishin'. Good thing, too. Aah was ready to drop the whole mess over the side."

Alec watched as Douglas stored the net and climbed up out of the hold. Captain Cairns returned at the same time.

"Sonny," the captain said. "Here's your wages for the week." He handed Alec an envelope. "Why don't you swab the deck and then go home? Douglas and I don't have much to do here, so we'll be leaving soon as well. No doubt your folks will be glad to see you home early."

Alec nodded and turned to his mop and bucket, thinking about what Douglas had just said.

"Always wearing a white seaman's cap." Alec remembered the night he'd sneaked out of the inn to bring his note down to the *Britannia*. The man in the white hat. It had been late, and the man had stumbled along ahead of him. He'd seen him going up Castle Hill Road. Maybe the bloke did stay at the castle.

"I'll be back tomorrow, Captain, if you think we'll sail." Alec put his mop and bucket in the wheelhouse.

"Aye, sonny. If the weather clears, we'll be shoving off at seven. We'll make a trip to Folkestone, so we'll leave early and be back by midday."

"I'll be here. We've only a couple of guests right now."

He couldn't hurry. His mind was filled with bits of news. Like a weathervane whipped by a squally wind, he felt himself spinning from one clue to another. The tunnels, the man in the white hat, the stories about the castle, the troops all leaving at once—somehow they fit together. But he wasn't sure how. Douglas didn't believe the man. But then where *was* he going the night Alec had seen him near Castle Hill Road? He had to have gone somewhere up that road. No, the scheme was too involved to be just pub talk. Something was happening up in the castle. Alec was going to find out what it was.

He would go to the pub. He couldn't wait another week; he was barely sleeping now. Besides, another week could be too late. No, it was payday. It had to be tonight. After his chores, he would sneak out and hide near the pub and follow the man. If he got lucky, maybe he would find out what he needed to know about the tunnels. He smiled as he pulled open the door. All this time he'd believed that Will was the spy. Now he could see Aga was right—Alec himself was the spy.

Inside, Aga was surprised to see him so early. "Alec boy. Just in time to help me with these potatoes. Do you mind, lad, peeling and cutting them up for supper? We've only two guests, but we've little meat tonight. They've cut our beef ration to one day a week. So potatoes and turnips will have to carry us for now. Can you help me out a bit?"

"Aye, Aga," Alec agreed. "I've come early to see what I could do. I'll start right now."

Working next to Aga, Alec let the knife slip and drop to the floor.

"Alec lad," Aga asked, "have ye forgotten how to peel potatoes?"

"No, Aga."

"It's early. No need to hurry," Aga assured him.

Alec was still trying to put the pieces of his plan in place. What if the man in the white hat spotted him? If he drank as much as Douglas said, he could get nasty. But if Alec didn't follow him, he might never know the truth. If there was bigger trouble in France, he needed to know.

It was settled. He was going that night. Just like Will, he'd made his decision; he'd see it through.

Later, while the guests finished supper, Alec climbed the rear staircase to prepare their rooms for the evening. Then he scrubbed the floors in the kitchen and stored everything in the larder before excusing himself.

Back in his room, Alec waited for Aga and the others to settle into their quarters. When he didn't hear any more activity in the kitchen, he opened his door just a crack to see that the kitchen was dark. Creeping past the cooker, he leaned over the hearth for a moment to warm his hands and listen for any movement. Then he held the door until it latched, and took off.

He passed the Fifty Shilling Tailor Shoppe and Cooper's Sweets before turning toward Snargate Street and the pubs. He strained to see in the pitch-black streets. Storefronts were dark, and silent flats stretched three floors above him, the buildings standing like sentries on guard.

He was glad that he often used the shortcut through the pub section. In the blackout, he would not have been able to tell one building from another if he had not seen them in daytime. But he was certain of where he was going, so the darkness worked in his favor.

"Hey—you there! Lad! What are you doing?" a voice bellowed. He didn't recognize it, but since the blackouts, people had been warned against robbers roaming the streets.

He took off on a run through the alleys behind the shops. The stranger's steps echoed behind him, but they grew quieter as Alec outran the man, darting around corners and sliding under fences. He slowed to a walk, heard nothing, and covered the next two blocks, ending up kneeling behind a rubbish bin across from the White Horse.

His breathing came in short puffs. He'd been tired before he left, and now the run from the stranger had drained him. He began to think he was wasting his time. But his chores had ended early; his parents thought he was safe in his room. No one would be looking for him. He would hunker down and wait. That was the plan.

He watched the pub doors swing open as sailors staggered out of the White Horse and down the street. He was grateful for Douglas's hint about the mystery man. Even in the darkness, Alec knew he could spot a white hat.

He wondered what time it was. Normally, he could hear the church bells chime, marking quarter hours, but since the war started, churches were forbidden to ring their bells unless signaling an air raid. Guessing it must be nearly curfew, he was ready to abandon his post and head home when the pub door swung open again, and out stepped a man wearing a white cap. Alec held his breath. How could he be sure it was him? But Alec was relieved to see the man turn to his right and make his way toward Castle Hill Road.

Alec swiped at his dusty clothes and hurried to fall in behind the man. He followed at a distance, this time keeping an eye out for anyone who might interfere. A couple was coming toward him. Alec pulled his hat lower—he mustn't be recognized. But they passed without looking at him. He crept along behind the man, ready to stop and turn aside if the man glanced his way. As they moved past York Street toward Castle Hill Road, Alec worried again about the time. If his mum or father checked his room and found him missing, he'd have a mess to explain. But he was too close now to give up and go back. He hurried along. They passed the Church of St. Mary at the foot of the hill, its cemetery standing silently nearby. The old tombstones spied on Alec as he followed his quarry.

Castle Hill Road turned sharply to the left, and Alec watched as the man took shorter strides up the steep section that led to Dover Castle. Suddenly, the man sat down on a rock near the side of the road. Alec supposed the man must be catching a bit of wind. He stepped behind a short hedge to keep from being spotted.

Short of breath himself, Alec turned his head and inhaled deeply, trying as much to calm himself as to recover his wind. Then, after a few moments, he felt better and peeked around the hedge. The man was not there! Jumping up, Alec sprinted toward the rock where the man had been sitting. He peered up the hill but saw no sign of the white cap. He looked in every direction. Then he spun around and strode quickly up the road, thinking maybe the man had turned another corner, but still Alec saw nothing. The mystery man had simply disappeared.

Alec couldn't believe it. The man had to have gone up that hill. Alec recalled his adventures with Georgie. There was only a tiny ledge on the other side. The man wouldn't have gone on that at night. So Alec crept farther along the path, certain that the man could not have outpaced him. But there was no sign of him. Puzzled, Alec stood in the night air and gazed once again up the hill. Nothing. One moment the man had been there; the next moment, he was gone. A wasted night, Alec decided as he started for home.

He made his way back down Castle Hill Road and across York Street to the Shaftbury Inn. He grabbed the back door handle and entered the kitchen. He stood a minute, listening again for anyone stirring about, but the only sound he heard was the deep snoring of Aga from her spot behind the kitchen. He made his way to his room and closed the door.

The cool night air on his sweaty body made him shiver. He stirred the embers in his fireplace and thought again of the man. How could he have been so stupid? If only he had kept his eyes on the white hat the entire time, he would have discovered how the man entered the tunnels. He felt like a fool. How could he ever be a seaman or a soldier like Will? He couldn't even follow a silly drunk in the dark.

Too discouraged to get up and change into his night clothes, Alec lay there in the dark, blaming himself for his carelessness. If he didn't get another chance to follow the man, he might never know what was happening with

Thomas and Will. What if commands were coming from the castle tunnels? How would he ever know?

Then he heard a sweet voice reminding him, "You found him once, lad. You'll find him again. You're no quitter, Alec Curtis."

And Margaret was right. He was not a quitter. He needed to believe in himself as much as she had believed in him.

He relaxed, but sleep did not come until well past midnight. It wasn't a restful sleep. He dreamed of bombs dropping and soldiers scrambling over one another, seeking a safe place. He woke in the night, wondering what it all meant. He even imagined he'd heard Will call his name. But that was silly; Will was in France. Nonetheless, the dream was so haunting, he sat up and wished for the darkness to end. That dream had made his next step even more important. If there were tunnels, he must find them—and soon.

12
PRIME MINISTER

ALEC ROSE EARLY THE NEXT MORNING TO HELP AGA before going to the *Britannia*. Exhausted from his venture the night before, he stumbled into the kitchen, expecting to see only Aga. Instead, his father sat hunched over a small table near the cooker, reading the *Daily Mail*. He turned as Alec entered.

"Alec," his father said. "Where have you been?"

Afraid that his father might have discovered his plans for the tunnels, Alec struggled for a quick answer.

"Your clothes? They're all rumpled."

Looking down, Alec saw that his clothes were covered with dust from his hiding place near the rubbish bin. He tugged at his trousers, smoothing the wrinkles. He could feel his face getting warm as he told the first of many lies. "I, uh, I stayed up too late writing in my journal and must have fallen asleep with my clothes on. Sorry. I forgot all about them. I'll change right after I set the dining room for breakfast."

"They look like you've been shuffling in dirt," his father said, unwilling to let the matter drop.

Alec wondered if his father had seen him leave the night before. He knew that if he'd been seen, his days on the *Britannia* were over. But he couldn't be sure his father knew. And he couldn't tell the truth; he was too close to a discovery for that. He scrambled for yet another lie. "When we stayed in port yesterday, the captain needed some fence posts—from up on that back lane, near the end of the docks. Awful dusty up there. Captain Cairns didn't want to go himself, so he sent me. I didn't know how dirty I got. I'll go change now." Alec darted through the swinging door and into the safety of his own room.

He changed his clothes, laced his boots, and checked his hair in the mirror. Until last night, he had honored his father's orders to stay away from the castle. But now it was different; he wasn't using it as a playground. Now he had a logical reason to climb the cliffs. He was on a mission, as Margaret would call it.

By the time Alec returned to the kitchen, Aga was there. Alec chatted with her, avoiding his father, who still sat at the table reading the newspaper.

Over his father's shoulder, Alec read the bold headline—WINSTON CHURCHILL TO BE NAMED PRIME MINISTER. Aga saw it too.

"Mr. Churchill," she began. "Now, he's the one that can get us out of this mess. He's been suspicious of Hitler from the start—even when Neville Chamberlain thought he could be trusted."

"Think that if you will," Alec's father argued, "but I've seen Churchill in other times. Served under him, if you must know, and I've no faith in him. He'll be our ruin, he will."

Though it was the first time Alec had heard his father speak of his time in the Great War, he ignored the debate. He had become hardened to his father's bitter remarks and weary of his storming out of the drawing room during the BBC updates, convinced that England was wrong to be in France. Now the dailies declared what Alec's father had dreaded: Winston Churchill was going to direct the war effort. No wonder his father had challenged him so early in the morning.

Alec finished his duties and turned to Aga. "The captain's looking for me to give him a hand on a short trip to Folkestone. Says we'll be out and back by midday. I could run to the market if you need me to on my way back."

"Aye, lad. I'll ring Mr. Walter at the bakery. Why don't you stop by his place before you come home? I'll ask him to have the order ready."

Alec nodded and turned to collect his gear hanging near the cooker. As he did so, his father grabbed his arm.

"You won't be working with Cairns much longer, Alec. It looks like the war could take a nasty turn, and with Churchill stepping in, God only knows what we're in for. If things get too messy, your mum and I will be keeping you home."

Alec looked down at the hand that gripped his arm. Without speaking, he turned his wrist and released himself from his father's grasp.

"I mean what I'm saying, Alec," his father called after him as Alec continued toward the door. "You won't be deciding what's safe and what's not if we think you need to stay home."

"I'll hear what you have to say," Alec shot back, "but I won't like it."

This time he let the door slam as he jumped down the steps and entered the alley. He did not want to argue. If his father made him quit the dock work, he would not stay at the inn.

On York Street, Alec heard the *clop, clop* of the milk-wagon horses being nudged along by a lad no older than himself. He watched the boy hold the reins as the dairyman collected the ration stamps from each stoop. At one time, Alec's father, too, had done those very jobs. But he had left the dairy business to make his own path. Alec tried to imagine how different his life would be if his father had stayed with Mr. Woodhams.

He knew his father well. He would not have been happy working for someone else. He was too stubborn to take orders forever. And Alec was the same way. For now, he would take orders on the *Britannia,* but in the end, he would have his own ship. Why couldn't his father see that? Alec shook his head and scooted on toward his job.

Cloudy skies hung overhead as Alec turned the corner to walk the final blocks to the *Britannia.* But in the window of Lawton's Jewelry, something caught his eye. He had almost missed it, but its familiarity drew him back, and he stopped and stared. There in the window was a small silver cross with a circle surrounding its crossbar. Alec thought of Will.

Forever *dóchas.* Alec remembered Will's Irish word for

hope. He knew his mum would like the cross. With the money he made on the *Britannia,* he could buy it for her birthday. She could wear it to church.

He pulled himself away from the window and ran toward the docks, hoping his brief stop at the store had not lasted too long. But when he arrived, the captain and Douglas were just pulling up lines to set off toward Folkestone.

"Can you give us a hand with that line? Toss it to me as you come onboard."

"Aye, Captain. Anything else?"

"Well, Douglas made tea, but it's terrible stuff. Go below and brew us up a fresh mug. He spent too many shillings at the pub. He'll need a strong drink to make it through the morning."

"Me mates at the White Horse, they kept me drinkin' too late," Douglas grumbled, and turned away. Alec was relieved that Douglas wanted to be left alone. He'd already argued with his father; he didn't need another row with Douglas.

The engine chugged as the *Britannia* pulled out of the harbor and made for the Channel and Folkestone. Alec watched as the shore slipped away behind them; then he went below to brew the tea. Turning the white cliffs and the tunnels and the Celtic cross over in his mind, he had trouble holding to one thought. He was brought back by the captain's voice.

"With Churchill taking the post now and commanding the troops, things are going to get better."

"Aah think yer wrong, Cap'n," Douglas argued. "So do all me mates. It's the talk that we've got trouble in France. That 'itler's army is movin' fast, rollin' their tanks through new villages every day. The blokes at the White Horse say we'll lose all our troops if we cannit do somethin'."

"If we were in deep trouble, the BBC would tell us. We'd read it in the *Daily Mail*. Can't keep news like that quiet long. We've got too many men over there to not hear if things have gone rotten. No, my trust is in Churchill. He won't let anything happen to our boys."

"'ave it your way, Cap'n. Think what ye want," Douglas answered. "But aah'm sayin' things are goin' to get worse. That's the word I'm hearin' from that bloke at the pub. Some of 'is Majesty's finest right here in Dover, 'e says— takin' charge of the troops. Cannit believe it meself, but somethin' doesn't feel right."

Alec made himself think about the information he'd read in the lieutenant's papers. Could it be that Will and his demolition group had gone to France to destroy their own artillery? Could it mean the British were in retreat?

"Sonny—lad—have you fallen asleep? We're looking for our tea!" Captain Cairns called down.

"Have a seat over on the locker box there," the captain said when Alec came up with the mugs of tea. "You look as bad as Douglas. Too many pints for you last night as well?"

Alec did as the captain said. He watched as the ship moved on through the Channel toward Folkestone. To his right, the white cliffs rose above the water, a sharp contrast to the blue sea. On top of the cliffs, he could see patches of green where grass covered the hills. Sometimes, when the cliffs dipped down and he could see farther inland, he caught a glimpse of sheep roaming the green hillsides. Settled far back, away from the edge, cottages with their slate roofs dotted the landscape. Though he often wondered what it would be like to be away from the coast and his home, he was glad he didn't live far from the fishing harbors. As much as he grumbled about the Shaftbury, he could not imagine living outside Dover.

For now, he needed to think about his plan. Douglas had said the stout man came most nights and always on payday. Alec didn't have enough time to wait until Thursday. Although he couldn't go every night, he didn't want to miss the man.

The water was calm and the trip smooth, but Alec thought the journey to Folkestone was slow. Then the harbor was busy, and they had to wait to dock. When they were finally ready to unload, the boom arm wouldn't swing out over the cargo hold. Douglas went after it with his wrench and other tools, but by the time it was working again and they were finally unloaded, they had spent an extra hour in port before shoving off for home.

Back in Dover, Alec heard the seagulls squawking around the rubbish bins as he worked quickly to secure the lines and swab the deck before running off to the bakery for Aga. By the time he arrived at the inn, he was in a foul mood—his head stuffed from the barrage of words from his father that morning and Douglas that afternoon. It seemed foolish to be following the same routine day after day when war hovered so close to them now. He didn't want to do the inn work anymore. He had to force himself to keep going—setting the table and running errands as though nothing out of the ordinary were happening. Inside the hotel, they seemed nearly untouched by the ravages of war. And in the midst of his work, his father always was nearby.

"Alec, Aga," his father barked. "We've got to be prompt with supper. It's important to keep the guests happy." He left the kitchen before either one of them could answer.

"He's just getting worse, not better," Alec sighed, placing all the silver and dishes on the tray. "There's no pleasing him. I don't know how Mum stands it."

"Now, Alec. Lad, I can't let you be blasting your father so. It isn't respectful."

"He deserves it. You know that. Never happy about what I do. Forever telling me how much trouble I cause. Always shouting about something or grumbling about the war and Churchill. Aye, there's no pleasing him."

"Oh, Alec," Aga said. "I know that you and your father have had hard times these last few months since—" Aga stopped.

"Since what, Aga?" he said. "Since Georgie died because of me?"

Alec couldn't believe his own words. He couldn't remember when he'd ever shouted at Aga. But here he was, just like his father, bellowing like a bull at his one true friend.

Aga fell silent. Turning back to the cooker, she stirred the kettle.

"Oh, Aga. I'm sorry. I don't mean to take it out on you. This is between Father and me. It's not your fault."

"I know, Alec, that you don't mean to hurt me. But you shouldn't be trying to hurt your father, either. He's a bit ornery these days, I'll grant you that, and even a trifle demanding, but he's got lots on his mind. He doesn't mean to sound so hateful. He's just worried about the times. We're living in bad times, you know."

Just thinking about his father made Alec want to quit—to gather his things and go off on his own. But he snatched up the tray and started for the dining room. "I'll not let him turn me into someone like him; I'll leave before that happens! I'm not like him." The words had spilled out of him. Knowing he was too late to take them back, he charged toward the table. But Aga was too quick.

"Wait a moment there, Alec boy. What do you mean you'll leave? What plans are you making?"

"I . . . I was . . . oh, Aga." Alec stumbled over his words. "I was just being silly."

But Aga was not fooled. "Alec lad—this is your friend, Aga. I know that look; I've seen it when you snuck off to fish in the Channel with Georgie or when the two of you came back from clambering around the cliffs. Just what are you planning to do? Go off to war?"

Her words caught Alec off guard. She'd said aloud what he'd been afraid to imagine. Had she known him so long that he had no secrets? Struggling for what to say next, Alec heard Aga's words again.

"Alec. Alec, I'm speaking to you. Tell me now. You won't be leaving me wondering all night about your doings."

Slowly, Alec answered. "It's just that I've heard some rumors about the war, about the troops in France, and I'm planning to find out what I can about Will and Thomas. Nothing plucky, Aga. Just snooping a bit. I didn't mean I was going away or anything"—he lied again—"just planning to do a little night sleuthing up near the cliffs."

"The cliffs? Alec, you know Mr. Frank has forbidden you to go near the cliffs. And what could you possibly find out there about the war?"

He had told her too much already. Aga could keep her mouth shut. She'd covered for him many times before. But if she thought he was in danger, she'd tell his folks to keep him from getting hurt. No, he wasn't going to let anything else out.

"There's a chap in Dover who says he can get a message to Will. I just have to meet him at the base of the cliffs one night. He'll post something to Will and bring me word back of how he's doing. That's all. But he needs to meet me at night so the officers won't catch him. I told him I'd come next week."

Aga looked doubtful. But before she could say more, Alec's mum appeared. "Your father's wondering about the table, Alec."

This time, Alec was grateful for his father's demands. *That was too close,* he thought. Aga wouldn't be put off so easily the next time. He had to go back to the White Horse soon.

The rest of the evening Alec moved about the dining room, waiting on guests and serving tea. When he could, he sneaked a look at Aga, but she was occupied. He hoped she would forget their conversation.

Later, stacking the dirty dishes into the wash tub, Alec plotted his next step. The White Horse and the cliffs had been a part of this city from the time he was born. He had roamed among them many days after school, yet he had never imagined they would consume so much of his attention. He could think of nothing else. By the time Aga came in, he had washed every dish.

"Why, Alec. You've taken my job. What's moved you to do such a lovely thing? If you think this will make me forget about your sleuthing, don't be so sure."

"No, Aga. Nothing else to do since the curfew's on."

"Aye, the curfew's a good thing right now. Keeps lads off the streets and home where they should be."

"You're right, Aga. That and the blackouts give little chance for lads to do anything but stay home."

He offered her his arm. "So shall we keep our date with the radio?"

"If it will prevent you from sneaking out, I'll sit here every night and listen to that silly box," she said, taking his arm as they strolled into the drawing room, where Alec's mum sat alone, her face white with fear.

"Germany has invaded France," she said.

13
LOST GIRL

THE NEXT MORNING, ALEC WOKE THINKING ABOUT THE news on the radio. The BBC said German panzers had crossed into France. He remembered Aunt Lucy's words to the lieutenant. She had been right after all; the war news had been hidden from them.

He took his time going to the docks. He had left a few minutes early, thinking his father would never allow him to leave, given the BBC report from the night before. So, having done his chores and stirred the fires, he slipped out before anyone else was up.

But even though he was moving slowly, he nearly tripped over the girl. He hadn't seen her before, and he wasn't sure why she was standing there now—in front of the inn. In the early light, he was struck by her odd appearance. Her dress hung nearly to her ankles; it was not the dress of a common English girl. He could see that, though worn, the fabric had once been elegant, made for special occasions. Her hair drooped in stringy clumps over her eyes. But the eyes were what held his attention. They showed no emotion. Just dark spots gazing directly at him, they never shifted from his face. She made him uncomfortable.

He guessed her age to be about the same as his, though her sagging shoulders told him her life had been hard. He wondered what she needed. Why was she there? She looked so hopeless; he couldn't pass without saying something.

"Do you need some help?"

The girl only stood there, staring blankly at him. She made no movement to speak or run.

"Are you lost?" Alec asked.

Still she only stared. Then she moved backward, as if she was going to leave. But she didn't.

Finally, slowly, she spoke. "*Ich*—I—am lost." Alec barely understood her. "I live nearby. *Meine Tante*—my aunt—she sent me to get milk. From the man. I can't get back home."

She had a definite accent—though he'd never heard one like it, certainly not in Dover.

"What street are you looking for?" Alec spoke slowly.

"*Die Strasse,* the street *ist*—is—Market. Market Street. Am I close?"

"Yes," Alec answered. "It's the next lane over; you need only to step down to the end of the block and then turn right. One block over and you'll find yourself on Market."

She didn't understand his words. He spoke again and pointed this time so that she could follow his directions. "Just go down that way and turn right," Alec said, swinging his arm wide, "and you'll be on Market. Once you're there, can you find your aunt's house?"

This time, she seemed to understand him, and she turned to move away. "Be sure to stay right," Alec repeated. "The left will take you to the docks. You won't be needing to go there."

He watched her go. She looked out of place. And her accent . . . What a strange girl. But knowing he would be left behind if he didn't hurry, Alec moved on to the docks, eager to be back on the boat.

The sky was bright and the day looked unusually clear for their trip down the coast. He was not going to spend a day like today worrying about his father. So he skipped into a run and, slinging his pack over his shoulder, hurried on.

All the way to the docks, Alec kept thinking about the girl. Her eyes held her story. He was haunted by her look, and he wondered if he would ever see her again.

Running along York Street past the jewelry store, he paused only a moment to gaze again at the cross in the window. Tomorrow, he would finish his work early and hurry back to Lawton's before it closed. His mum would like that it was from him, but she would like it even more for what it meant. She was always needing hope.

Alec raced from the store to the docks just in time to hear the captain say, "Now, where's that lad today? Seems like we're waiting for him more and more."

"Aye, Captain," Alec said. "Sorry I'm a bit late. I ran into someone outside the inn. She needed help. I won't be late again. I promise."

"*She* needed 'elp? So yer 'elpin' a fair maiden in distress,

I suppose?" Douglas snickered. "Well, what was the lass's problem?"

Alec felt himself blushing at Douglas's remarks. He wished he had thought a moment before giving his excuse. Now he would be chided the whole trip about the girl. Trying to pretend he hadn't heard Douglas, Alec moved to untie the moorings and toss the ropes onto the *Britannia*.

"Did ye not hear me, lad?" Douglas challenged. "Aah said she must 'ave been in great trouble for ye to stop and offer yer 'and. What's the story?"

Alec climbed aboard and pulled at the ropes. "All I know is that she said she was lost," he muttered. "I couldn't really understand her that well. She had a strange accent. She acted as if she didn't understand everything. Said something about her aunt's home on Market Street. So I showed her the way and came here."

"Strange accent?" Douglas asked, turning more serious. "What did it sound like? Was she from up north, or even Irish, maybe? What did ye think, lad?"

"I don't think she was northern, and I'm sure she wasn't Irish. No, she's not from anywhere near us."

"Aye, just as aah thought. She's one of those orphans sent here from Germany. Jewish children shipped off to escape the Nazis. Docks 'ave been full of stories about children comin' to England without their folks—probably to never return."

"From Germany?" Alec questioned. "How could she have come to Dover from Germany? Who would do such a thing?"

"Well, Alec, you ought not to be so surprised," the captain said as he maneuvered the *Britannia* through the harbor and toward open water. "You've heard that Dover parents are sending their children north to escape the bombing by the Jerries. So why would you not think the German parents would do the same for their young ones?"

"But Germany? That's such a long way away. How could they ever hope to find all the children again?"

"Some would have relatives and friends. Others have been taken in by English families eager to do their part to fight the Germans. We don't know if your young lass is really German, but if she is, she's no doubt Jewish as well." As he finished, the captain turned his eyes away from Alec and toward the water.

Alec scooped up the lines that lay about the ship, coiling each one and placing it near stern or bow. Then, rubbing his hands together to clean them of dirt, he turned to go below to boil water for tea. Just as his foot reached the top of the step, he felt someone grab his arm. It was Douglas.

As Alec faced the first mate, he smelled Douglas's hot breath. "Aah don't care what the cap'n thinks about those German orphans," Douglas hissed. "They don't belong 'ere. It'll just make the Nazis angrier by us 'arborin' the lot of them. We've trouble enough of our own without takin' on Jewish scum. Tell yer little friend that. An' tell 'er there's even more like me in Dover what think the same."

"She's not my friend." Alec squirmed free of Douglas's grasp. Then, glancing at the captain, who was preoccupied with steering the *Britannia,* he said, "She's just a young girl. How could you hate her so?"

"Aah 'ate everythin' that is pullin' us into this bloody war. We've no fight with the Germans, an' now our troops are backed up in France an' are goin' to die. An' we're 'arborin' runaways."

"What do you mean 'backed up in France'?"

Douglas stepped away from Alec and moved to his post. But Alec wasn't finished. It was his turn to be forceful. Grabbing Douglas's sleeve, he asked again, "What do you know, Douglas?"

"What do aah know?" Douglas snapped. "Aah'm only sayin' what the blokes at the White Horse are sayin'. We've got trouble in France. Me friends—they say our lads are being forced back to the coast. That we can't get enough 'elp to them, an' the Jerries are pushin' 'ard with their tanks." Douglas paused. "But don't be worryin' about somethin' ye can do nothin' about. An' stop this badgerin' an' brew us some tea."

Alec stumbled below and slapped a pot on the cooker. He felt helpless as he replayed Douglas's words and thought about the man at the White Horse. He had little time left. He couldn't wait until Thursday. Tomorrow, he would have to try again. He had to know what was going on.

When the water was hot, Alec set the tea to brew and pulled some mugs from the cupboard. Returning topside, he gave Douglas and the captain their tea. He looked about at the water surrounding the ship. It lapped lazily against them as they motored along near the shore. Most days, their trips along the coast were filled with overcast skies and strong breezes. Alec welcomed this sunny change.

Once the ship was under way, he lay back on the steel locker and waited for orders from the captain or Douglas. The sun warmed his face, and he remembered how he and Georgie had battled choppy seas and dreary skies, how they had longed for a day like this one to cast their lines into the Channel and search for mackerel or halibut or snapper.

Then his thoughts turned to the German girl. She couldn't be the trouble Douglas claimed she was. And it wasn't her fault that she had been sent away. Why was he thinking about her now? She wasn't a lovely sight. But something about her made him feel jumpy inside.

He rolled onto his side, steadying himself on one elbow, and peered across the Channel. There, beyond the smooth waters, Calais, France, shimmered in the distance. He resented never having ridden the ferry across the Channel to Calais, but his father would not take the time away from the inn. Now, with the war at its edges, the city was even more beyond his reach.

As he peered at the distant shore, something above the water caught his eye. Moving slowly along the horizon were two tiny specks. He glanced toward the captain, and wondered if he saw them, too. But Captain Cairns was looking at Douglas, no doubt listening to the first mate still muttering about the girl Alec had met.

Turning back to his left, Alec looked for the specks. This time, they were not hard to see. They had grown larger as they moved across the sky toward the English coast. Not sure whether to say anything, Alec watched as they drew near. They approached in neat formation. Then Alec heard the noise.

Because the day was so calm, the plane engines roared above the sound of the *Britannia*. Alec was worried now. Turning again toward his shipmates, he saw that the captain and Douglas had also noticed the planes as they swooped toward the shore.

"Sonny, come here, lad," Captain Cairns called.

Bounding from the locker, Alec hurried to the captain and Douglas.

"I'm guessing those are Jerries headed our way," the captain said. "Alec, I want you to get out of sight. Douglas, you need to go below and grab the rifles. They won't do us any good, I'm sure, but I feel better having them above deck. I'll do my best to steer toward the coast. We're not far from Ramsgate, and I don't think they are interested in a tiny ship, but we need to be ready."

Douglas took three quick strides and was at the door to the galley. Alec didn't move. Though the captain had given an order, he didn't want to hide. He could not take his eyes off the planes. He examined the curved wings as they nearly skimmed the water and drew closer to the ship.

The captain spoke again. "Alec lad, you heard my order. Get yourself out of sight and do it now." With that, the captain turned the wheel to guide the *Britannia* closer to shore.

This time, Alec obeyed. Scrambling around the deck, he looked for a place to hide and spotted the steel locker.

The planes' engines were roaring now. Alec lifted the locker's heavy lid and grabbed the canvas cover stored inside. Tossing it out on the deck, he hoisted himself up and over the locker's edge, sinking down into the dark space. Just before closing the lid, he looked once more at the planes and spied the black cross spread across the Stukas' tails. Then, with his knees scrunched to his chest, he waited—he wasn't sure what for. A bomb to drop? Fire from the gunnery?

He could hear the muffled voice of the captain as he called to Douglas. Alec worried that the ship would be spotted, but he pushed the thought out of his mind. It was hot inside the hot locker, and his shirt was soaked through. *What are Captain Cairns and Douglas doing? Will we be bombed?* The dull roar of the planes grew weaker.

Hidden in the locker, Alec felt as though hours had passed, but then he heard a crunch and squinted as light stole into his hiding place. From his dark hole, Alec saw Douglas holding the lid aloft as he waited for him to climb out.

"Aah think the danger's passed, boy. Ye can come out. It's safe now."

"What happened?"

"We don't know, lad," the captain answered. "We didn't see anything except that iron cross. Jerries for sure. The dailies reported that Stukas have been seen along the coast, photographing the harbors, no doubt. I'm sure the chaps in Ramsgate saw them, too. We'll ask when we get there. But we're wasting no time unloading this wire. If your folks discover we were out in the Channel when those Jerries flew over, your days on the *Britannia* could be done."

Alec nodded. He was not going to tell his folks or even Aga about this scare. He knew what his father would say, and he could only imagine his mother weeping and begging him to leave the shipping to the other men. No, this news was not leaving the *Britannia*.

In a few minutes, the ship glided into port, and Alec helped Douglas and the captain carry the wire and stack it near the docks. They scrambled to finish quickly and be on their way home. When some dockhands from Ramsgate stepped up to help, the captain asked them about the fighters.

"Aye, mate. We saw them. Thought for sure they were coming to drop a load on our docks here. But they just flew on over and turned back for France. Don't know what to expect now."

"I'll wager they're scouting the coast. Looking for a good place to clear a landing for their German ships," Captain Cairns said.

"Well, if that be the case, then your town of Dover is more likely to get the drop. You folks need to be on your guard. Hitler will take all of England if he gets into Dover."

Alec listened. The Germans were getting bolder every day—flying scouting missions in broad daylight. How could England protect itself when most of the British troops were across the Channel? What were they going to do?

Though the day continued bright and clear as they made their way home, Alec could no longer enjoy it. Once they cast off, he sat back on the locker and peered at the horizon, fearful that the Germans might return. But the sky remained empty.

Back in Dover, the crew finished their chores in silence before Alec picked up his rucksack to start for home. But as he turned to leave, a hand once again caught his arm. Douglas stood over him.

"Boy," he said sharply. "The cap'n's wrong. Yer folks should know about today. They should know about the girl, too. This war is comin' our way, an' it's not going to pass ye by. Keep yerself close to 'ome, an' don't be takin' up with some German girl."

Alec didn't have the strength to wrestle himself away from Douglas, but he didn't have to. Douglas released his arm and stepped back. Perhaps he expected Alec to say something, but Alec didn't. Douglas was a man out for himself. He cared little for others. Alec wasn't that way.

Weaving in and out among the fishermen on the docks, he rushed toward home. He would have trouble for sure if he was late getting back to help Aga. Pulling his pack over his shoulder, he turned toward the Shaftbury. He climbed the hill and was almost home when something familiar caught his attention. Moving up the street in front of him was the girl from that morning. Even from the back, Alec recognized her—her scraggly hair and shabby dress were unchanged.

What was she doing there again? Alec wondered.

Just then, the girl turned. She slowed her pace and waited for Alec to catch up. But he didn't want to stop. Aga needed him. Still, the girl was already by him.

"Hello," Alec said. "Are you lost again? Market Street is just around the corner, remember?"

"*Nein*—no, no, I am not lost," she answered. "I—I was hoping to see you. To say *danke*—thank you—for your help. My aunt—she's grateful, too."

Alec listened for the accent. It was definitely there, but her English was better. She was calmer, not so flustered with her words. He began to think Douglas was wrong. Though she was not English, Alec didn't believe she was German. Yet he couldn't be sure.

"I am visiting my aunt," she continued. "I know no one but her. What is your name?"

Alec hesitated before answering, remembering the first mate's severe warning.

"Alec," he said. "My name is Alec. What about yours?"

"Eva. I'm *vierzehn*—fourteen," she volunteered. "How many *Jahre*—years do you have?"

Alec didn't want to tell her he was her age. He didn't want to tell her anything more. She clearly wasn't in the hurry he was, and he had no time for anyone right now. "I hope you'll like Dover, Eva. I'll see you another time. I'm late for supper."

He kept himself from turning around until he reached the rear stairway. Then he glanced back down the street, expecting Eva to still be there. But she had gone.

He was glad. Things were getting too muddled. He didn't need another person taking up his time. Especially some silly girl.

14
TROUBLE IN FRANCE

THOUGH HE WAS NEARLY BURSTING TO TELL SOMEONE about how he had stowed away in the locker while enemy planes flew overhead, he knew both his mum and his father would keep him back the next trip. So he said nothing.

As the night went on, Alec learned more about the growing threat of war. One of the guests, a Mr. Sharpley, had arrived that day from London. With his booming voice and his precious news about the war, Mr. Sharpley was difficult to ignore. "The news in London is grim," he began. "Rumor is that the Germans have our boys boxed in, forcing them up into northern France." He belched loudly as he reached across the table for the potatoes. "Churchill's got trouble for sure. Word is that the Royal Air Force can provide some bombing cover for our boys, but they can't get them out of France."

"But how do we know what's even going on?" Alec's father shot back. "The BBC just keeps saying the same thing. They say our boys are moving through France toward Belgium, trying to push the Germans back across the borders. I don't understand it. If what you're saying is true, why don't we know?"

"Aye, that's what I say," the man agreed. "But if the rumors are true, our boys are going to be facing dark days in the next few weeks. We've got most of the British army sitting over there in France. England is defenseless without them. We could be next; everything rests with Churchill."

At the mention of the prime minister, Alec's father's chair creaked as he pushed back from the table. "You're saying England's survival rests with Churchill? I've no faith in him. He's made too many blunders in the past, and now he controls our boys and our fate. I don't like any of it."

Alec watched his mum as she picked at her supper. Occasionally, she stole a look at Alec while he cleared the table and refilled the teapot. And he saw her squirm at the harshness in her husband's voice and the reality of Mr. Sharpley's news. For weeks, Alec had seen her fears increasing. But the children being sent away and the news about the stranded troops were before them all now. Alec knew that his mum was worried most about him. He felt guilty now for having mocked the Anderson shelter. She had wanted it for his protection. He didn't want to hurt her with his plans to snoop around the castle and uncover news about Thomas and the others. In her sad face, he saw surrender.

Alec tried to look busy, but Mr. Sharpley's words captured his attention. Though the dailies and the BBC were not saying so, Douglas and Mr. Sharpley had declared the same news: The British army was in trouble in France.

While he cleared the table and washed the dishes, Alec

tried to stay calm, but the silver and teacups clinked as his unsteady hands stored things in their places. The news about France made him want to sprint up to the castle that moment. Yet he was helpless to do anything with his mum and his father only a few feet away. Still, he would stick to his plan and return to the White Horse the next night. He didn't know whether he'd have any more success than the first time, but he had to try.

He worked steadily, filling the larder with tins of salmon and peaches that he had collected the day before with their ration cards. Aga had moved to the large table in the kitchen, scrubbing its bleached and scarred surface. With a sigh, she sat in a chair and rested her feet on the bottom rail of the table.

As he moved around the kitchen, Alec hoped Aga would not start up again with her topic from the night before. If he said any more, she would badger him until he told her everything. He wanted no row with her, and he was tired of lying. But he could not ignore her sniffling and sighing as she sat waiting for him to finish.

"What's wrong, Aga? Are you ill?" Alec whispered.

"No, Alec boy." Aga sniffled. "I'm not ill. I'm just so worried about the news tonight. Makes me think of the Great War. Makes me worry about all those lads and about your cousin Thomas."

Alec couldn't comfort her. He'd seen Aga sad before, but never so weepy. Even when he had teased her that day while wearing the gas mask, he had eventually been able to pull a brief smile from her. But tonight was different. The darkness from outside had crept into the kitchen.

"Do you think they know the trouble they're in, Aga?"

"Alec, that's the thought that bothers me most. That they might be sitting there in France, thinking they're sure to rout the Jerries, and they don't know they're actually trapped."

Alec pushed the thought out of his mind. If he allowed himself to worry, he would not keep a clear head for his mission tomorrow. No, he had to finish up his chores and ignore Aga's words.

Later, in his room, he pulled his chair near the fireplace and set his journal on his lap. He needed to write about the German fighters, but he fixed his eyes on the burning embers. Then he sketched the German cross he'd seen on the planes and quickly scratched through Hitler's mark.

He scribbled some notes about his day. He wanted to remember the flyover. But afraid his parents might sneak a look, he wrote in code—*2GF over the EC May 15, no bbs.* That was enough to remind him what had happened—two German fighters over the English Channel, no bombs. Then he thought of Eva: *A silly girl named Eva crossed my path twice today. She's nice, but too pushy. I have no time for her now.* He closed the book, stuffed it back into its new hiding place in the closet, and stretched out on his bed to think through his plan once again.

Alec found the *Britannia* deserted the next morning. Believing he was just early, he sat down on the wooden planks and stared out into the Channel. Unlike the day before, this day was cloudy; he could see only a few yards beyond the pier.

No chance to spot planes today. He dangled his feet over the edge of the dock and gazed at the *Britannia's* bow. The smell below him was a mixture of rust and rotting seaweed and old wood. "Even the docks smell like death," he said aloud.

"What's that ye say?" Douglas bellowed as he stepped up behind Alec. "Ye wouldn't be talkin' to yerself, now, would ye, boy? Yesterday's scare make ye a bit addled?"

"No, no," Alec stammered, caught off guard by Douglas's sudden arrival. "No, I was just thinking about this sea life. Thinking about how one day I want to be a first mate like you, and then later own my own ship like Captain Cairns."

"Ye, lad?" Douglas roared. "Ye be a skipper? Now, that's cheeky of ye, boy. Thinkin' a lad like yerself with fair skin and smooth 'ands could one day skipper a ship. Ye don't 'ave what it takes to fight the sea, boy. Ye might 'ave the desire, but ye don't have the 'ardness that the sea demands. Yer too tied to the land and your family up the hill. Ye've got to be willin' to give that up, to live lonely most of the days. That's not ye, boy."

"But I could do it," Alec argued. "I know I'm still young, but I'm learning from you and the captain. I want to be free of that other life. I want to live like you."

Douglas turned away. Then he put his rough hand on Alec's shoulder and spoke Alec's name for the first time. "No, Alec," Douglas argued, "ye don't ever want to be like me. Aah'm a worthless shipmate who drinks too much and cares nothin' for no one else. Aah spend every night alone, and aah squander everythin' aah earn. This life of mine is wasted. Go 'ome to yer family and make somethin' better of yerself."

Alec had not seen this side of Douglas before. Looking at him now, Alec wondered about Douglas and his home. How had he never thought about where Douglas went when he left the pub at night? Where did he go? Alec leaned over and slipped one of ropes from around its mooring stake. "So, where is home for you?"

"Home? That's where we all should be today," the voice said, but it belonged to the captain, not Douglas. Douglas stood up and straightened his shoulders as if to say to Alec, "We're not speaking of this again." Then he snatched up his rucksack and waited for the captain's orders.

"We're not going out today," Captain Cairns announced. "After yesterday's brush with the Jerries, I want to stay docked and sit tight today. Not sure what to expect, but we need to keep close to shore until we get news about what we should do. Some say the war's turning against us. Not safe to head out. So you both are free to go. Come back in the morning and we'll run a load of wire to Ramsgate if things are clear."

Douglas grumbled as he stepped off the boat and started toward town. "Can't be doin' this often, Cap'n. Work's too light as it is. Aah need steady work."

"Aye, Douglas," the captain agreed. "I don't want to think we're done because of this rotten war, but those roaming

Jerries made everyone nervous. We've got to wait for more news before we carry on. Come back tomorrow."

Douglas strode up the dock and onto shore. Alec remained, watching the ripples in the water.

"Sonny, lad, did you not hear me? We're docked today. Run on home."

"Aye, I heard you, Captain. I just don't want to go home yet. I've nothing to do but help Aga at the inn and listen to my dad complain about Churchill and the war. So I'd rather wait a bit."

"He's being a father, lad," the captain said as he sat down next to Alec, who was still holding the loose rope. "He's afraid for you and for England. We all are. The Jerries are moving fast through Europe."

"But they're bad for everyone—for you, too. And you don't act like him. You're worried, too, but you don't go on about Churchill. I'm tired of that. I won't stay with it long. I'm done with school, and I can pick my own life."

The captain was silent for several minutes. "He's no different than any father with a lad he doesn't want to lose. He's afraid for you, Alec. Don't mistake his fear for hate. He cares only about you and your mum and your safety. He just doesn't know how to say it. But when you get older, you'll understand better."

Alec wanted to believe the captain. He knew his father was worse now because of the war. Maybe his father did deserve another chance. Maybe the next move was for Alec to talk to him, tell him that he respected him. But it wouldn't help. His father would just grunt and walk away.

As if reading Alec's thoughts, the captain spoke again. "He's had a rough time himself, you know, that father of yours. His hatred of Churchill goes far back—to the Great War in 1916. He has reason to be angry."

Alec was confused. "How do you know?"

"I was there. . . . We were there together. In the Dardanelles—during the Great War. I was there when your dad—when sonny—finished his time, when they brought most of his men back in bags or on stretchers. Your father, he was angry at the foolishness that killed his men . . . wept over each lad. Couldn't even talk about what had happened, though the rest of us already knew."

"Knew what? What are you telling me, Captain? That my father was an officer? Under Churchill's command?"

"Churchill's plan," the captain continued, "was for the Brits to forge through the Dardanelles passage, cut off one of the prime shipping routes. Then we'd be in a better position to fight the Turks and Russians. Except the planning was poor, and execution worse. The Turks were waiting. Many of our lads were cut down before they got thirty yards in. Your father was a sergeant in charge of one division. He could only watch as his boys fell, sprawled all over the beach. He came home angry and blamed Churchill. So did others. After that blunder, Churchill was relieved of his command. But many, like your father, still think he has not paid. Seeing Churchill now as prime minister stirs up some painful memories."

His father? A sergeant? Weeping for his men? Alec had never even seen him cry; he didn't think his father could.

Alec tried to imagine him different from the father he had known over the years.

Slapping Alec on the back, the captain stood up and took the mooring line from him.

"Here, I'll give you a hand," Alec volunteered.

"No, lad. I'm just going to poke around the ship a bit and then head on up myself. Go along and enjoy the day. We've not many quiet ones left, what with the war so close."

"Do you think we're close, Captain? A guest at the inn last night was going on about our troops in northern France. He says they're trapped, that the German panzers are pushing them toward the sea. Says we'll lose them all if England doesn't do something."

The captain hesitated. "Aye, I've heard the same myself. We sent our lads over to help France and Belgium, and both countries are in trouble. Some blokes say that without help from outside, our boys will be lost to the Jerries. Don't know what to think, but I know I'd do anything to help those boys. The problem's the Channel. It's rough waters out there, and they say there's well over two hundred thousand lads stranded in France. Impossible odds, I'd say. Impossible."

"Two hundred thousand? What will they do? What can we do?"

"I don't know, sonny. But Churchill's been through war. I just hope he's up to the charge."

"Aye," Alec said. "I hope so, too. Will and the others, and my cousin Thomas, are all over there. My aunt and uncle couldn't bear to lose Thomas. Not after losing—"

Alec stopped short of using Georgie's name. Although the captain knew of the drowning, Alec didn't want to say more. "But," he continued, "we can't just sit here and wait for the Jerries to overrun our army. We need to do something."

"And we will, Alec. I know we will. I just don't know the plan. For now, all we can do is wait—and pray for a miracle, I suppose."

"A miracle," Alec scoffed. "Who believes in miracles?" Alec was thinking again about Georgie. He had wanted a miracle in the water that night with Georgie. And when Georgie was gone, he had wanted to be gone, too. But no miracles had come for him.

"Miracles come carefully, Alec boy," the captain reflected. "They are delicate and unexpected, and they come when absolutely nothing else can make the matter right. That's what makes them miracles."

"You talk as if you've seen one, Captain," Alec said.

"Aye, I saw one—saw it in the Dardanelles. I know your father had a different experience, but I saw something else in that battle in 1916. A bunch of us were stranded. Hunkered down in trenches and bombarded by enemy fire. We thought we'd been abandoned. Then—miraculously—these lads from Australia, of all places, fought their way through to us and saved every one of us British blokes left in our division. Even carried our wounded to safety. A miracle. It was nothing less than that for me. That's why I believe in them. And you, lad, you need to believe, too. Otherwise, when it comes, you'll miss the miracle. And no one's promised even one, much less more."

The captain stood still, his pipe steaming in the morning air, and he looked beyond the ship to the water. Alec was silent. Then the captain stepped back, twisting the rope around its mooring and tugging hard to tighten it.

Alec would have liked to stay. The captain's words had calmed him—unlike the talk at the inn or the post office. But Captain Cairns had ordered him home once already, and he needed to obey. He stood up on the dock and grabbed his gear, and snapping a quick salute, he called out, "Tomorrow, Captain," and started up the hill.

He hesitated at the corner where he would turn for home. His family would never know that he was not working the docks today. He could wander about Dover—take some time for himself. But Aga had been pretty upset by Mr. Sharpley's words the night before. She could use his help. So he hurried on and entered the kitchen just as Aga plopped down on her stool.

"No work today with the captain, Alec boy?" Aga asked, startled by the sound of the back door.

"No, no work today. Or at least, no work at the docks. Captain said I could have the day off. So I'll be around if you need me."

"Oh, Alec," Aga answered. "Why don't you just enjoy the day? A lad your age needs his own time. I have a few errands you can do, but I'll not look for you before supper."

"Give me the list and I'll do the errands now," Alec said, and waited while Aga scribbled a few lines, handed him the ration cards, and sent him on his way.

Relieved that he had something to do near the shops,

Alec scurried out the door before his father caught him home and gave him more chores. He had his own errands to run today. In fact, his first stop after the post office would be Lawton's Jewelry, where he'd seen the cross. The captain had been generous with his last pay, so Alec had the money to buy the gift for his mum. Aga wanted him to stop at the market as well, and he thought he would go back to the newsagent's stand and pick up that *Beano* comic if it was still there. The farther he walked, the lighter he felt. A day to himself—he needed it. Besides, he still had some thinking to do. He hadn't forgotten about the White Horse. He already knew the route the man would take. This time, he would be ready.

Alec ambled along the sidewalk as he headed toward the heart of the town. The day was still cloudy, but he didn't care. All he wanted today was time to himself. He had earned it, and he wasn't going to feel guilty about avoiding his father. If Aga didn't tell him, Alec could be gone all day with his father thinking he was off on the ship. Yes, the day was just what he needed. He had plenty of time.

And then he turned the corner and saw the girl, Eva.

15
ICH BIN SO EINE

THIS TIME, SHE WAS NOT ALONE. WALKING WITH HER was an older woman—an English woman whom Alec had seen before at the market. He slowed his step to keep from catching up. Eva and the woman moved silently, looking straight ahead. Then, almost as if someone had tapped her on the shoulder, the girl turned and spotted Alec. Grabbing the sleeve of the woman, Eva pointed back toward him, and the woman spun around. Together, they waited as Alec approached. He didn't hurry.

"My lass tells me you are the kind lad who helped her out yesterday," the woman said. "She's not been in Dover long, and her English is still a bit weak. I'm sorry she troubled you."

"She wasn't far from where she needed to be," Alec said. "I just pointed her in the right direction."

"She was grateful regardless. She's been afraid to go out much, so she was happy to find someone friendly to her."

"It was a small thing," Alec said. "I was on my way to the docks anyway."

The woman clearly wanted to talk more, but Alec didn't care to spend his free day chatting with someone's aunt on a street corner in Dover. Yet the girl interested him; his disappointment slipped away as he stared at her. She was different—better—than before. She had exchanged her ratty dress for a new one. Its plaid fabric made her look like an English girl. Her tired boots had been replaced by flat shoes like those Alec's mum wore. Around her trimmed and combed hair she wore a ribbon the same plaid as her dress. Alec liked the difference the clothing made. He searched for something else to say.

"His name," the girl said, "his name *ist* Alec."

"*Is,* Eva, *is*—not *ist,*" her aunt corrected her. "His name *is* Alec." Then, turning to him, she asked, "Where's your home?"

"The Shaftbury Inn," Alec said. "I live with my mum and father there. We own it. That's where I saw Eva, outside our place when I was going off to the docks."

"Oh, I know the Shaftbury," the woman said. "Your cook, Elizabeth Greshem, she comes to market to shop. She's a grand woman."

"Aye," Alec said, impatient to move on.

"And are you on your way to market today, Alec?" the woman asked. "Might Eva step along?"

Earlier, he would have said no. But Eva seemed so different today—happier. It had been a long time since he had roamed about with someone young. Besides, Aga's grocery sack over his shoulder betrayed him.

"I told Aga that I'd collect some packages for her, and

I've got stops to make besides, but if you don't mind if we take some time, she's welcome to come."

"Oh, that would be lovely," the woman answered. "Eva needs to get a better look at the town. She'll be staying with us for some time, and I'll want her to run errands. So walking about with you can help both of us. You really don't mind?"

"I'll take a longer route," Alec said, "and show her some of Dover. We'll be a bit."

"We've nothing pressing," the lady responded, juggling the parcels in her arms. "Eva is safe with you, I'm sure. And you can help her with her English. She doesn't like to be alone, so don't let her off on her own."

"Aye," Alec said, realizing the errands would now be harder than he thought. "We'll be careful. But she'll be able to find your home when we're done?" Alec asked. He couldn't let anything interfere with his plans for later.

"Get her to Market Street and she'll do fine," the woman answered. "Thanks, lad."

Alec turned to face Eva. "Well," he began, "we're not far from Dover Priory. Let's walk there; it's near Lawton's Jewelry. Then you can see where the train station and the jeweler are."

As they started out, Alec felt odd. He'd never walked around Dover with a girl before. He'd always been alone or with Aga or his mum. He wasn't sure why he should feel any different, but for some reason, he did.

Eva walked slower than he did, noticing everything along the way. Scones cooled in a bakery window, and she pressed her face against the glass, as if trying to smell them. The newsagent, Mr. Kelly, saw them pass by and winked at Alec. Alec picked up his pace—but Eva didn't stay with him.

"What's wrong, Eva?" he asked, turning to face her. "Don't you want to go along?"

"*Meine Tante*—my aunt. She tries to help me," Eva said, moving to him.

"I can walk slower if you'd like," Alec said. "I don't have to hurry." He was confused. He didn't want to be too close to Eva, yet the space between them now seemed awkward. It was a strange feeling—wanting to be rid of her, yet wanting to be with her at the same time. He thought about taking her hand so they could keep the same pace as they walked. He was just about to reach for it when they turned the corner near Dover Priory and came upon a scene that made both of them stop and stare.

Groups of people were milling about outside the station. The hissing of the train's engine could barely be heard above the cries of children as they pleaded with their parents not to leave them.

Then a queue began to form, and people slowly made their way toward the doors of the station. Eva and Alec moved closer. Parents shuffled their children along, clutching packages and small suitcases. Alec stared at the crowd. Though he'd heard about it for days, he had not imagined that the children would actually be shipped out like parcels.

Eva edged closer still, and Alec followed. All the children had papers pinned to their clothing. There were *Lester Donovan, Dover* and *Callie Everett, Ramsgate*. One little lass wore a pink tag and a matching bonnet. The tag read *Sarah Nelson, Dover.* In the thickness of the crowd, the smell of sweat and urine burned Alec's eyes as small children, bundled in wool coats for weather to come, queued up to find a spot.

Alec and Eva moved to the side of the station where they could see the train waiting for its passengers. They saw fathers and mothers picking up their little ones and placing them on the top step of the train. Thrusting a bag or suitcase at them, the parents hurried away, unable to bear the sight of their children crying for them.

"Mum! Dad! Mum, don't leave!" Lester Donovan cried. But then someone from within the train car reached through the doorway and gently led him inside. As Alec watched, the scene replayed itself over and over again—weeping parents handing off their weeping children to strangers.

Swallowing hard, Alec turned to Eva and saw her eyes flash from the children to him and then again to the children. She backed away.

Alec reached for her hand. "Eva," he said to her. "Eva, it's all right. They're being sent to safety. They'll come back. Eva, what's wrong?"

But Eva didn't answer. Instead, she broke through the crowd and ran from the station.

"Eva!" Alec called. "Eva, wait. Wait!" he called again, chasing her down the narrow lane. "Eva, stop!"

He raced after her, the grocery sack flapping behind him. Turning a corner, he reached her just as she stopped for a bakery lorry coming down the lane.

"Eva," Alec gasped, trying to catch his breath. "Eva, where are you going?"

"*Weg*," Eva said. *"Ich musste*—I had—I had to run. I had to get away from them—from *die Kinder*," she said, almost in a whisper.

"I know it's sad to see, Eva. But the children need to be safe. Their parents are sending them inland to be away if the war comes to England. They'll be back," Alec explained.

"*Nein*, Alec," Eva said angrily. *"Es ist auf immer*—it is forever. They will never get back. I know. They won't come back. They are like me. *Ich bin so eine*—I am one like them."

"I know," Alec said. "But you're safe here. You have your aunt. She'll take care of you until—"

"She's not my aunt. Frau Miller—she's *meine Freundin*, my parents' friend. They thought I was in danger. In Deutschland. So they put me on a train—like *die Kinder* back there—and sent me away. Then I got a boat—for London. *Ich*—I—I stayed in an orphanage until *meine Tan*—Frau Miller sent me train fare to Dover. I've been with her since."

Alec watched Eva's face. The empty eyes he'd noticed the first time he saw her—the story explained her eyes. The lines creasing her forehead were not the lines of a fourteen-year-old. "She has been kind," Eva continued, picking every word carefully, "teaching me English . . . and keeping me safe. But *Ich*—I don't want to be safe, I want to be home."

"But you need to be safe," Alec assured her. "And you'll get back home. Your parents will see to that." As he spoke, he doubted his own words. The dark feeling from the night before was hovering again.

"*Meine* aunt—she wants me to make this my home. She thinks if I learn about Dover, I'll feel safer. But *Ich bin*—but I am—I am a Jew. I am not safe even here. I've heard the others. They think Hitler will strike England because we are here. They want us to leave."

Alec thought about Douglas. Quickly, he changed the subject. "Come with me," he said. "It's my mum's birthday soon, and I have a gift to pick up at the jeweler's. Come along. We'll go to market first and then to Lawton's."

For a moment, Eva looked as though she wouldn't go. Then Alec took her hand, and she didn't resist.

He looked again at Eva. She had lost her home. He wanted to protect her. He was sure Douglas wasn't the only Brit ready to toss the Jews out of England. In fact, just a few days earlier, his father had complained about the Jewish orphans.

"We've no room for Jews here," his father had said. "We've rationed our food and fuel—why should we feed those who aren't like us?"

Now Eva walked next to Alec, hundreds of miles from her home, running from Hitler just as the British army was doing in France. The captain was right—war touched everyone.

As they walked hand in hand, Alec recognized shop owners and seamen from the area. Charlie from the docks turned up Snargate Street, but not before he gave Alec a big wave. Dr. Henchley sauntered by, his medical kit in his hand, and slapped Alec on the back.

"G'day, laddie. Who's your pretty lass?" he said.

"Her name's Eva," Alec called back, and kept walking. But if they were suspicious of Eva, Alec couldn't tell. He decided that they thought she was just a guest at the inn. He felt good being with her. How long had it been since he had felt so necessary? So valued? He found himself wishing the day would pass slowly.

Eva spoke quietly. As she grew calmer, her English improved. "*Mein* papa—he *ist* a lawyer, a criminal lawyer in Magdeburg," Eva said. "He has a good business; we have nice things and many *Freunde*. They like us and our *Haus*. We had many guests. *Meine Mutter,* she is a kind lady and she helped me with my school studies. I wore fine dresses and did well in school. I was happy."

Alec didn't interrupt. Eva needed to talk, to tell someone that she was part of a real family. She picked at her dress as if to say that this was not what she was used to, that this was not what she had left behind.

"We didn't do anything wrong. You must believe me," Eva pleaded. "One day I was attending *die Schule*, and then the next day Papa told me I could not go back. When I asked why, he said that all Jewish students had been refused *die Schule*. It was a sad day. I loved *meine* studies, and then suddenly I could never go again."

"Without notice?" Alec asked.

"They didn't care what happened. They just didn't want us in *die Schule*. So *mein Mutter und meine Tante* gathered books and taught us. But soon, the Nazis ordered all books destroyed. It was *das Ende*—the end."

"And then what happened?" They had stopped walking and stood facing each other on the lane.

"*Meine Mutter* bought me a nice dress and coat and packed a bag. And one night, she and Papa took me to the *Bahnhof*—to the railway station. They said I would be in an orphanage at first, and then their friend would call for me from Dover."

Alec could barely hear Eva now. He stepped toward her and bent down to listen.

"I was crying when Papa lifted me off the platform and put me on the *Zug*. *Mutter* was trying not to cry, too. I begged them to come with me. To not make me go alone. But they said they couldn't; the Nazis had taken their papers. They said they would come soon and get me. *Ein Jahr*. That was one year ago. I've heard nothing since. . . . *Ein Mädchen*—one girl—she was sitting near the door. I saw her *Mutter* on the platform. And then, just before the *Zug* started to move . . . her *Mutter*—she ran onto *der Zug*, picked up her girl, and carried her off. Through the window, I saw the girl's arms around her *Mutter's* neck. She wouldn't let her go. I wish *mein* papa had saved me like that."

Alec watched as Eva kicked a stone on the walk. Her head was down, and though she wasn't crying, Alec feared she might. He didn't know what to say to her. How many times had he wished to be free of his home? And his young friend was aching to find hers. None of it made sense to him anymore. Not his father, not the war, not even Eva. What was she supposed to do if her parents never came? Could she stay with her "aunt" forever?

"Perhaps he did save you, Eva," Alec whispered. "You just may not know it yet."

Eva tugged the front of her dress and then looked at Alec. She was ready to move on.

Listening to her, Alec felt again the dark power of war. Eva had been in England a year, and in that time Hitler and his Nazis had moved quickly through Europe. Now they were threatening to ruin England. Alec feared they could. If they treated their own people as Eva had said, the Nazis would not turn from France or beyond. And if Mr. Sharpley was right, England had been left unprotected. Alec wanted to forget about errands and go home. Anything he did now seemed unimportant compared to what was happening a few miles across the Channel.

Walking along with Eva at his side, he thought again about his plans for the White Horse. There was no time left; he would go that night.

At the market, Alec was careful to keep Eva close by. The place was in chaos. In the center, greengrocers peddled potatoes and turnips and squash. Near the outside, bakers held their loaves aloft and shouted to the crowd, "Hot buns for sale here, mate. Get some for your supper while they're fresh!"

One butcher, trying hard to earn his wage, called out, "Lovely meat! Lovely meat! The same what the nobility eats—lovely meat!"

"Aye, the nobility," the baker shouted back, "the nobility gets all the bread and meat it wants. They're not pinched for ration cards and pork. They get what they want, they do—and we just see our rations get smaller and smaller. Why, I cannit get flour for my bakin' most days. Never know until tomorrow if I'll even 'ave 'ot bread to sell."

After collecting their cabbage and potatoes and bread for the evening's supper, Alec led the way as they moved up Larkin Street toward Lawton's Jewelry. Neither spoke. Then Alec broke the silence. "It's a Celtic cross I'm buying. Mum will like it, I'm sure. My friend Will showed me one before he shipped out. His grandda had given it to him when he was my age. Will is never without it. He believes it brings him hope."

"Everyone wants hope," Eva sighed. "I'm sure your *Mutter* will like it."

Later, holding the cross in his hand, Alec felt proud to have earned enough to buy his mother a gift. "You know that silver's a rare find now, lad?" the shopkeeper had said. "Like everything else, the war's taking all the fine metals from us. You're lucky I had this one. Guard it well."

Alec had promised him that the cross would be well taken care of. He could hardly wait to give it his mum.

For the rest of the day, Alec and Eva moved about Dover, visiting the post office and wandering along Castle Hill Road, and York and even Snargate streets—though Alec warned Eva against going into the pub district alone. By the time they were done, they had only a few minutes to stop at Cooper's Sweets before hurrying home for supper.

"When will we meet again?" she asked.

"I'm not sure," he answered, feeling his face flushing red. "I've—I've got to go out on the *Britannia* tomorrow, and after that, I don't know."

"*Ja?* I can come to your inn tomorrow afternoon, then?"

Alec didn't answer. He certainly didn't want her snarling things up that night. But he didn't want to make her angry, either, and not see her again. He had liked being with her—had liked having her walking next to him through the town. But right now, he had other plans. So he stood quietly at the corner of her street and waited for her to speak again. She didn't.

"Maybe on a day when the *Britannia*'s docked," Alec finally said. "Maybe then I could come by for a visit."

She looked defeated and turned quickly toward her aunt's house.

He thought about going after her, maybe to set a specific day to meet, but she was out of sight before he could make up his mind. So he swung around toward the Shaftbury, where he was certain Aga was waiting for her packages.

That odd sadness crept over him again. He wondered where it came from. He'd been fine before Eva. He didn't need her. Still, he couldn't make himself hurry away. Why was he so confused? She was only a girl. She wasn't like the sea. The sea held adventure. And it didn't talk back. He could make a good wage roaming the sea. A girl would only take the money he'd make. Why waste his time?

16
SECRET PASSAGE

JUST AS ALEC HAD FEARED, NEWS HAD GOTTEN BACK to his folks about the German planes. Again, Mrs. Tanner was to blame. As she had done when Badger was hurt, Mrs. Tanner marched into the Shaftbury and gossiped about the Jerries. Alec stayed near the kitchen, trying to avoid his father.

"Oh, Alec boy, we've got trouble, you know. Those German planes prove how bold the enemy has become."

"We'll be all right, Aga. The Jerries were just out taking a few photographs, the captain said. Nothing happened."

"But it will, lad," Aga argued. "I know the signs of war. And we're seeing them for certain now."

He couldn't talk to Aga when she was so anxious. But then he remembered the necklace and pushed his hand deep into his pocket to pull out the tiny box. "Aga, I nearly forgot. Look what I've bought Mum for her birthday. Isn't it grand?"

At first, Aga only glanced at the box; then she looked again. "Why, Alec, that's like the cross Will wore. He showed it to me one day. It's a fine gift, lad."

"I know it's early, but I want her to have it now. So I'll give it to her after supper tonight."

"It's a gorgeous thing," Aga assured him. "And special since it's from you."

Together, they stood looking at the shiny cross nestled in its box. Then Aga threw her hands up and hurried toward the cooker.

"Oh, my, lad. We've got to get this supper on or we'll be late for the guests. Come help me."

Alec was relieved to get past the war talk. After his time with Eva, he would never tease Aga again about overreacting. But within minutes, he wished he had stayed longer with Eva, as the swinging door slapped against the wall and his father charged in.

"Alec, where have you been? Captain Cairns said you left the *Britannia* early this morning. What have you been doing all day? And what about those German planes? Your mother is nearly sick with worry."

"To market, Mr. Frank," Aga stepped in. "I sent him off on errands. Told him to take his time."

"I'm asking you again." Alec's father directed his words to Alec. "Why are you holding back news? You always—"

"That's what I'm doing," Alec shouted. "I'm holding back—staying out of your way so I don't have to listen to what a rotten son I am. If I tell you news, you fly off. If I hold the news back, you toss me off. I can't do anything that pleases you, and I'm sick of trying!"

Alec's father curled his hand and swung hard at Alec's face, catching him just below the eye and knocking him back against the larder. "You wretched boy. What can I do to make you understand?"

"Understand what?" Alec said, holding his face. "That you hate everything I do? That you will never accept I'm not like you? I will never be like you!" He darted past his father and hurried to his room.

Alec took a deep breath and vowed that his father would not see him cry. Slamming his door and falling back against it, he touched his cheek where his father had struck him. Already, the spot felt tender and puffy. His father had never hit him before. He now knew for sure that it was not going to work for him to live at the inn. His mum was hoping that he would take over the inn someday, but he was fearful that if he stayed, he would become as bitter as his father.

"Alec." The gentle tap at the door interrupted his thoughts.

"Come in, Mum," he answered as he brushed his wet face with his hand.

The door opened just a crack, and his mother's face peered around the edge. "Have you got room for me, Alec?"

"Always room for you; you know that, Mum. Sorry, it's not made," he said, straightening his bed so she could sit.

His mum reached out to touch his face, but Alec pulled back.

"It's okay. He didn't hurt me," Alec snapped. Then, seeing his mother's sadness, he patted her hand. "It's okay, really, Mum. I'm fine. I probably had it coming for not telling you and Dad about the planes. But I thought if you knew, you would worry more."

"Oh, it's not the planes, Alec. It's the whole war. Your father's worried about you."

"No, Mum," Alec argued. "He's not worried so much for me as for his precious inn and the business. Ever since I've gone to the *Britannia*, he's looked for reasons to make me quit. He wants me here, at the Shaftbury, doing his work. Well, I'm not made for that, Mum. I'm a seaman."

"I know, Alec. I know you love the sea. You always have. But the Shaftbury needs you, and you'd be safe."

"It doesn't need me, Mum. You can carry on without me. . . . I'm sorry, Mum. I hate to see you caught in the middle."

"I've gotten used to the middle, Alec. It's a place I fell into years ago. I've let myself get too comfortable there." She paused, looking at her son. "When *did* you grow up so? Just like your father—always having to make your own path. Well, Alec, I can no longer ask you to stay and work for your father. I would rather have you go away and be happy than be like this." She touched his cheek. "Someday, your father will want that, too."

Alec stared at her, looking at the weariness in her face and wondering how she put up with her husband's bitterness. Then he remembered the gift in his pocket, and he handed her the box.

"For you." He grinned. "An early birthday gift. I've been saving my wages from the *Britannia*. The first time I saw it, I knew I wanted to get it. Something to give you hope."

"It's not my birthday yet," she argued.

"You can't enjoy it if you keep it all wrapped up."

"All right," she relented. "But if it cost every pound you've earned, I'll make you—" She didn't finish. She had the box open. The Celtic cross sparkled. "Alec! It's lovely!"

Alec smiled, pleased that he had made the right choice. "Will had one, you know. Thought it gave him hope—forever, he said. I wanted you to have one, too. You can wear it to church."

"Oh, I do like it, Alec. It's a real treasure. Thank you, love."

For a moment, they were silent, and then they heard his father's voice just outside the door.

"Gwen!" he called "We have guests who need to eat. Are you coming?"

"Yes, I'm here," she answered, and rose slowly from the bed. Touching her hair lightly and adjusting her apron, she turned to look once more at Alec. "Why don't you just rest for a bit, Alec? I can help Aga . . . and I'll tend to your father."

Alec nodded, not wanting to face his father again..

Fingering the cross, she whispered, "It's a special gift, Alec. I'll think of you whenever I touch it."

Then she slipped out the door and was gone, leaving Alec alone to think about all that had just happened. He didn't know when, but he would make a choice soon as to where he would live.

He didn't go to supper. Aga brought him some cabbage and bread, and he waited for night to come and for his parents and Aga to retire to their rooms. He wrote about his day with Eva, about her running away at the Priory Station, about her new clothes. He recounted how at first he had not wanted her with him, and then how much he had enjoyed the day. Her attention had made him blush. *Walking down the pavement with her, I felt important—like her protector,* he wrote in his journal. *It was good to be needed— to just be myself and have someone want to be with me.*

He scribbled these thoughts quickly and returned the journal to its spot. Then he grabbed a pile of clothes and stuffed them under his bedcovers. If anyone opened his door to check, he wanted it to look as if he was sleeping.

He listened for any noise that would tell him Aga was still up. Hearing nothing, he stepped into the hallway, went past the dining room and through the kitchen. The whole place was dark.

In seconds, he was outside and leaping off the back steps. Coming out of the alley behind the Shaftbury, he hurried down the street and turned right onto Market, heading toward the pub section of town. He was out before curfew, so he wasn't worried about the constable— though after being chased the last time, he was always wondering who else might be lurking in the dark. It would be harder to keep hidden tonight. The half-moon gave some light to the blacked-out streets. He raced the two blocks down Market, but as he turned the corner, someone called his name.

"Alec!" the voice said. "Alec. Wait!" He recognized Eva's accent. She was a short distance back and racing toward him. He waited for her to catch up.

"Eva, what are you doing here? Where's your aunt?" He glanced around to see if anyone else was nearby. "Why are you following me?"

"*Was ist los*—what—what is the matter? I was in the alley. *Mit*—with the rubbish *und* I saw you run by. Something *ist* bad, *ja?*"

"Nothing's wrong. At least, nothing more than usual. My father heard about the German planes. We had a terrible row," Alec confessed. "I'm done with him."

Eva was silent as they stood together on the curb. He thought she was feeling sorry for him. Then she turned toward him. "Be sure, Alec. Your papa and *Mutter?* They may not always be near."

Eva was looking at him, expecting him to say something. But he turned away, convinced that she didn't understand. "You need to get back," he snapped. "I've got something to do."

"*Was?* What? *Was ist*—what is it?" Eva asked. Then she saw him glance toward the pubs. "*Nein,* Alec. You told me *nein*—you said stay away from there."

Alec needed to leave. He didn't have time to argue with Eva. "I've just got something to do. It won't take long, but I need to do it now. So please, Eva, go home. I don't want to worry about you tonight."

"Worry? *Ich*—I don't need your worry."

"That's not what I meant," Alec answered, wondering why she was so angry. "I've just got to do something."

"Then wait," Eva pleaded. "I want to help. I'll tell

meine Tante. If I'm with you, she will say yes. Wait here, *bitte*—please?"

"No, Eva. I won't wait, because you can't come. I need to do this alone or the man will—" He stopped himself.

Eva looked puzzled. "I will go with you. *Bitte,* Alec, don't send me off. I can help."

Alec was speechless. He had never expected this from quiet Eva. What had happened to change her? But he couldn't have her wandering around the pub area; he had to wait for her. So he nodded, and she gave him a rare smile before she dashed off.

In a few minutes, she was back, sliding her arms into the sleeves of her sweater. They made their way quietly down the street and turned into the alley across from the White Horse. There, they squatted against the wall and peeked around the corner, watching the door. The street was filled with little pubs wedged next to each other. In the moonlight, Alec could see the pub shingles dangling above the pavement, announcing their brews. Alec had never been inside a pub, but Aga had told him they were noisy and grim. "Not much good happens in there," she had said.

He heard Eva breathing next to him. In the dim light, she held even more mystery for him. His stomach felt tight; his palms were damp. Although he thought his mission would go best if done alone, he remembered how lonely it had been the first night when he was sprawled out in the dirt behind the rubbish bin, waiting for the man in the white hat. With Eva next to him, he wasn't wondering about the time or thinking about the cold.

"*Auf was warten wir?* For what are we waiting?" Eva wrapped her sweater tighter around her.

"A man in a white sailor hat," Alec whispered. "But keep back; he can't spot us or we won't be able to follow him."

As he talked, three chaps wandered out of the pub; none of them wore a hat.

"And this man? He *ist* there *heute abend*—tonight?"

"I don't know for sure. But Douglas says he comes often. So I'm hoping he's here and he'll lead us to the castle."

"The castle?" Eva said. "*In der Nacht?*—at night?"

"Shh," Alec whispered. "It has to be at night; we'd be seen during the day. I followed him before. But I lost him. Tonight I'm going to find out how he gets in and out. There are secrets there. Secrets about the war, about our boys. I've got to know."

Eva sat quietly, trying to understand all that Alec had said. She did understand that she had made things worse.

"I'll help you, Alec," she offered.

Looking at Eva's face, Alec could not help thinking about Georgie. He had always wanted to be a part of Alec's plans. Georgie was like a puppy, nipping at Alec's heels, begging to go along. Alec would never forget the price he had paid for not being more insistent that Georgie stay home. Now, looking at Eva, he had the same fears. But something was different with her. She'd already fought her own battles, and she had not given up.

"Eva, promise me you'll do only what I say. I know the area around the castle. It can be dangerous."

"*Ja,* Alec." Eva nodded. "*Ich verspreche*—I promise."

Turning back to watch the door, Alec decided that something about Eva made him stronger. It was that she wanted to come, that she liked being with him. Maybe, he thought, she would help. Just then, the pub door swung open wide, and out stepped the man in the white hat.

Alec nudged Eva and pointed toward the pub. Rising from their hiding spot, they waited for the man to move up the street; then they strolled behind him.

As before, the man sauntered along the pavement. Doffing his hat at two blokes heading the other way, he continued. Alec and Eva walked slowly, their heads down as they kept a safe distance from the man.

They'd only gone a few yards when the man suddenly stopped and turned. Impulsively, Alec grabbed Eva's hand and turned her to face him, wrapping his arms around her and drawing her close.

"Shh," Alec whispered in her ear. "He's watching us. Just pretend we're a couple out for a stroll."

Alec could feel Eva's heart pounding. Her rapid breathing told him she was afraid. Then the man continued, and Alec pulled her along as they kept after him.

Soon the man turned and started up Castle Hill Road. Alec could see the lane winding its way toward the castle, silhouetted high above them.

"We've got to stay close," Alec whispered to Eva. "I lost him the last time after that bend up there." Eva nodded.

Alec led the way, lengthening his stride as he kept the man in view. Eva was close behind—so close that when Alec stopped suddenly, she bumped into him.

"Wait," Alec whispered. "He's resting on the rock like before. I'm going to keep moving up. You stay off to the side here and watch for my signal. Then come on up once I tell you it's safe."

Alec moved farther up the path and turned briefly to see Eva huddle behind a hedge. Insects sang around him. The wind ruffled the nearby trees. On the street below, someone called out to a mate. Still watching, Alec saw the man rise to his feet and continue his climb. But almost as soon as he had stood, the man stepped to his right, pushed back a large pine bough, and disappeared into the thick shrubbery.

So that's how I lost him, Alec thought. *He didn't take the normal path. He's got some secret passage on the side of the cliffs.*

Alec waited a moment and then tunneled through the shrubbery near the castle. He stayed back far enough to not be found out, but the man's quickness told Alec the path was a familiar one. As the man neared the spot where the castle path narrowed and hung above the Channel, he slowed. He clung to the rocks on his left and made his way around the bluff. Just to his right, the cliff dropped three hundred feet into the Channel. The man paused and looked up.

Alec ducked behind a rock as the man glanced casually around before stepping onto a small boulder. Looking around again, he climbed even higher, to a narrow ledge that hung out over the Channel.

Where was he going? Alec strained to see in the darkness. The castle and white cliffs stood as a backdrop against the man's black clothing. Then Alec saw an opening about waist high on the side of the castle wall, just to the left of the man. Hunching his shoulders and leaning out a bit more from behind the rock, Alec looked again. The opening was square, and big enough to spot even in the dark. As Alec watched, the man shuffled along the ledge until he stood next to the opening. Then, as smooth and silent as a thief, the man removed something from the opening and slipped easily through the space. Alec watched as the man fit the cover back into place and disappeared within the wall.

"So that's it," Alec breathed aloud. *All the time Georgie and I spent scrambling over these rocks, we never saw that window. It was a well-kept secret.* He wondered how the man had not been caught.

Alec retraced his steps on the path, climbed through the shrubbery, and waved for Eva to come to him. Taking her hand once again, he led her through the shrubbery and out to the castle wall where the man had disappeared.

"*Wo ist er*—where is he?" Eva asked.

"Inside. He climbed through that small window above the ledge. You wait here. In the bushes. I'll duck in the same way."

"You're going in? *Jetzt*—now?"

"Yes" Alec answered. "And I'm going alone."

17
A Yellow Line

THEY SAT DOWN TO GIVE THE MAN TIME TO MOVE AWAY from the opening.

"I hope that window doesn't land me in a place where someone will spot me right off," Alec said to Eva.

"*Der Mann*—for him it worked. He has done so before, *ja?*" Eva said. "Maybe a closet or secret room? In our *Haus* in Magdeburg, we made a secret room—for hiding silver, other things."

Alec nodded. "It's time," he said softly. "Wait for me. But if I take too long—if I don't come back— go home to your aunt. I'll hurry. But I don't know what I'll find. Stay away from the cliffs there," he said, pointing to the white rocks. "And promise me you won't follow me inside."

"*Nein*. I cannot follow," Eva agreed.

"Aye," Alec said. "If I'm going to do this, it must be now."

Rising to his feet, he walked the last few yards to the rocks and, swift as a goat, scrambled up and rested quietly on top of the ledge. Following the man's lead, he moved to his left and ran his finger around the edge of the window cover. He tugged lightly on it, and it pulled away from the window. Then he put one leg into the opening and searched for something to rest his foot on. He felt a hard surface and placed his foot there. Then, backing into the window opening, the cover still in his hand, he drew his other leg in and stood up. Since he knew he might need to make a quick escape, he left the window covering off. Then, peering into the darkness, he laughed nervously. The hiding place was a lavatory, and he was standing in the sink.

Stepping down from his perch, he moved to a door in front of him. Light was creeping in near the floor. He listened for any sounds and then tried the doorknob. The door creaked as he pulled it open and peeked around its edge. To his right, as far as he could see, was a dimly lit tunnel. For just a moment, he wanted to turn around and go back to Eva. But he waited for his eyes to adjust, and then he looked again. No one was in sight. He knew he couldn't stay in the lavatory, but his feet wouldn't move. His mind was telling him to scramble back through the window—to go home.

He stood there, hearing only the sound of his own breathing. Then Margaret's familiar voice seemed to whisper, "You've come this far, Alec. You can do the rest as well."

Sliding past the door and into the hallway, Alec turned to his right. Several openings branched off from the tunnel before him. Creeping along, he listened for the sound of footsteps. No one was coming. He was relieved that his soft shoes let him move without a sound.

Slowly, he made his way down the corridor. Single

bulbs burned dimly in the ceiling. The tunnel smelled damp and moldy. Passing each side opening, he noticed that the hallways were marked by colored lines. To his right, he saw a blue line leading away from him. Up farther to his left, a red line trailed off. At his feet, he saw a yellow stripe. He started straight ahead along the yellow line until it angled to his right. Then he paused.

Ting, ting. A sound rang out from his right. *Ting, ting.* It sounded again. He turned toward it. Two right turns—he needed to remember.

Hunched down and staying close to the wall, he passed several more hallways on his right and left. Each was marked with a colored line.

Ting, ting. The sound grew louder as he continued. *Ting, ting, ting.* He was nearly upon it. It was metal against metal, ringing out from a room up on the left.

He felt that he was being sucked deeper and deeper into the castle. He looked around the long hallway, expecting to be caught any minute. Then the sound was right next to him, and he ducked into an opening in the wall. *Ting, ting.* It rang out again. Crouching lower, he saw that he was not in a hallway this time, but a large entrance leading into a room. A curtain separated him from what was inside.

Taking a breath, he stood halfway up. The *ting*ing began again, and he realized it was just on the other side of the curtain. He crept toward the curtain and nudged it aside. The stronger light made him blink. As his eyes adjusted, he stared in disbelief at the sight before him. There, arranged neatly in three rows, were several hospital gurneys. All of them were empty but for one patient tucked over in the corner. A nurse, with her back to Alec, was stacking metal basins on a shelf near the patient. Alec wasted no time. He crawled into the room and ducked behind a gurney near the doorway. The long sheet draped over it kept him hidden. The patient moaned, saying something to the nurse.

"Why, yer going to be all right, mate. Don't give it no mind," the nurse said. "I seen worse, I 'ave. Aye, ye've 'ad a bad time of it. But I'm takin' good care to 'elp you. And soon we'll get you 'ome to yer mum and dad. And that bloody swine, 'itler, 'e'll get 'is."

The man on the gurney moaned again and let the attendant check his wounds. From where he was hiding, Alec could see that the man had a bandage covering the end of his left arm where his hand should have been. Wrapped around the man's head was another white bandage showing a spot of red blood seeping through. Alec knew it was the color of war.

"Yer not the first to be lyin' in 'ere," the nurse continued. "Cripes! We've 'ad others like you come from France! This bloomin' war, it'll bring us plenty before it's done. And, Churchill, God bless 'im, 'e's got a full-blown row to manage."

Listening to the nurse, Alec knew he didn't have much time. He looked around and waited for the right moment to escape. He needed to find someplace or something that could tell him more than he was hearing in this room. But where was he to look? Or to go? He started to move, then ducked down again as he heard the clicking of heels on the concrete floor outside the room. Someone was coming down the hall.

Squeezing in tighter between the gurney's sheet and the wall, he froze as two British soldiers pushed aside the curtain. Standing not six feet from Alec, they stared at the man in the corner.

"This is only the beginning, mate," the one closer to Alec said.

"I know. But we've no other plan. With Belgium gone and France to follow, we've no choice but to heed the vice admiral's orders. Aye, we've men stranded on that coast. England needs them home. The navy alone can't do it; we've got to ask for help."

"But civilians?" the first soldier argued. "The risk to their lives? Can we bear those losses? Blast them—the Jerries have already sunk two of our ships, and the Luftwaffe has been flying over northern France for hours, bombing our lads. What are we thinking, asking civilians to cross the Channel?"

"If we don't do something, we'll lose them all," the second responded. "And then what will the people say? They'll say they would have helped if they'd known. . . . We'll have a bloody mess either way, that's for sure. And we'll see every hospital in England filled. But we'll see every lad dead if we can't get to them soon. . . . Aye, we need the little ships. If it's seaworthy and can make it across, it will be put to use. The call has gone out tonight only to the docks, but by supper tomorrow, all of

England will know. In the next few days, the prime minister and the archbishop will implore all of England to pray."

The soliders' words echoed in Alec's head. Though he had heard the rumors for days, he now knew he was hearing the truth. England really was in trouble. Thomas and Will and the others were stranded in France. The entire army could die. They were calling for help—they were calling for his help.

He had to get out of the castle. But the soldiers lingered, watching silently as the attendant moved around the room. They were dressed much like Will and the others had been: brown trousers and shirts, and gray socks tucked tightly into their boots. But the boots caught his attention. Clean and smooth against the concrete floor, they revealed that the men had spent little time outside the castle. Oddly, tied to their thick black belts were gas masks, which Alec had once thought so amusing. Now, seeing the masks dangling from the soliders' waists, Alec found them frightening.

Then, as if he had ordered it, a bell rang in the corridor beyond. The soliders looked at each other, turned, and moved down the hallway. Alec heard their heels striking the scrubbed concrete, and the sound soon died away.

He waited a minute and then looked again at the patient on the gurney. The man had lost his hand. Alec tried to imagine what he would do if he woke up to find his hand missing. It was the part of war Aga had been trying to tell him about. Now he understood.

When the attendant turned her back, Alec slid out

from behind the gurney and scrambled down the long hall. As he hurried back the way he'd come, someone shouted from far behind him. "Stop. Stop now!" Without looking back, Alec broke into a run. Frantic, he raced down the corridor searching for his escape. Then he stopped. He looked down. A red line ran along the floor beneath him.

"The yellow line!" he gasped. "Where's the yellow line?" Turning full circle, he heard the voices growing nearer. "The yellow line," he said again. "Where's the—" Then he saw it: another hallway, just a short way back. Turning, he retraced his steps and dashed down the long corridor marked in yellow. The small light outside the lav door kept him from missing his exit a second time. The shouting behind him grew louder now. "Stop!" the voice called from down the hall. He didn't dare turn to look; he was out of time.

He tried the handle and was relieved when it turned. Back in the lavatory, he flipped the lock on the door and stepped quickly onto the sink. He reached toward the window, but his hand bounced back. Someone had replaced the covering! He clawed at the edges of the board and, prying it loose, slapped it away from the opening. The shouts of people outside the door nearly froze him. But he thrust one leg, then the other, through the opening and dropped to the ledge below and ran back down to Eva.

He pulled her along as, together, they raced through the shrubbery. They stumbled down the rocky path until they reached the street below and ducked into a nearby alley. Fearing the soldiers might still be after them, Alec led Eva through the alley and out the other end, stepping over rubbish as they ran. Soon they were on the street just above the docks.

Breathless, Alec and Eva ran around the back of the dockmaster's shack and crumpled to the ground.

"Alec," Eva whispered. "What happened?"

Holding her hand tight against his heaving chest, Alec whispered, "They're trapped, Eva. The lads in France. They're trapped. I'll tell you the rest later. For now, we need to get back."

Perhaps because she was too tired to protest, or maybe because she did not want to think about being chased again, Eva followed as Alec led her home. By now, curfew had begun, so they stayed in the shadows and reached Market Street without anyone spotting them.

At her stoop, Alec let go of Eva's hand and said, "I don't know when I'll be back. This news will muddle our cargo plans for the *Britannia* tomorrow. But I'll find a way to come by as soon as I can."

Eva nodded and turned away. He waited until she was inside and then headed to the Shaftbury. His mind still reeling from what he had heard, he crept through the back door and down the hallway to his room. Everything was quiet as death.

He closed his door and stared into the darkness that surrounded him. It was more than the darkness of night.

It was the darkness of fear. A darkness that would not go away with the dawn.

His mind couldn't rest. He knew what the captain would do. He knew what his father would say. He knew his own path was set.

18
LITTLE SHIPS

BY THE TIME LIGHT SHONE AROUND HIS DRAPES, ALEC had already started to fill his kit. He knew they would call for the little ships that day. The captain would agree to go; Alec was sure of that. He would need to pack lightly; there wouldn't be much room.

Stuffing a jersey and an extra pair of trousers into his pack, he looked around for his knife and his cap. He stepped to his closet and pulled out his journal. Then he stopped. What was he doing? This would be no holiday; there'd be no time for writing on the ship. So he opened its pages and scribbled a few lines:

25 May 1940. Today I'll find out what war is really like. Already I know that it's worse than I ever thought. The injured man in the castle proved that. But I have needed this day to come. It will be my chance to do something right. Father doesn't want to believe I can do it. But Will and Thomas are in trouble. Other blokes, too. They need our help. I've got to go. I've got to make it right for Georgie. I'm a seaman now. The captain will want my help.

Closing his journal, he started to return it to his closet. Then he realized that if he didn't come back, his mum would need to know why. So he opened the nightstand drawer and placed it inside. With a bit of searching, she would find it.

Looking around his room, he wondered about the days to come. The uncertainty almost kept him from going. But then he thought of Thomas and Will and knew that his choice had already been made.

Aga didn't see him stash his kit just outside the back door. Stepping up next to her, he patted her arm. "Good morning, Aga," he said, trying to hide his eagerness to leave. "Same as always?"

"Aye, Alec boy. Set the table as usual. Be sure to put the jellies and jams out. We've got toast today, with eggs and beans."

"Aye, Aga. I'll do it now."

"It's a good lad who is so eager to go to his work. The captain must be proud to have such a loyal mate."

Alec laughed. "I don't know about that, but he does like the tea I brew."

Working quietly, Alec acted as if nothing unusual was going on. Thankfully, his father did not join the other guests that morning. Alec was hoping to get away before he had to face him again. As quickly as he could, he finished his chores—and left for the docks.

He was still uneasy as he made his way to the *Britannia*. Though he wanted to help with the rescue, he was haunted by the soldiers' words about the relentless bombing by the Luftwaffe. Not that he was afraid for himself. He worried about the soldiers. His hands shook as he carried his kit to the ship. He couldn't stop thinking about the injured man in the castle, his stump resting on his chest. Alec was afraid he would be sick—the Channel was squally this time of the year. And the death he knew he'd see—he thought it would be too much for him. He might freeze up and not be able to help anyone. Yet he was more afraid of staying behind and doing nothing. He just needed to get on with it.

At the docks, he saw that the call for ships had already gone out. Sailors bustled about, storing jugs of water and food. Blankets were piled on the docks, waiting to be loaded. Drums of petrol were being pushed along the planks. The seamen worked furiously. No one noticed Alec as he walked to where the *Britannia* was moored. The ship looked deserted at first. Then he saw the captain coming up from the galley with two long guns in his hands. He stopped when he spotted Alec.

"Aye, sonny. We won't be doing much hauling for the next few days. We've got a special assignment that Douglas and I will handle alone."

"What assignment?" Alec asked.

"It's no job for a young boy, that's for sure."

Alec stood on the dock, wondering what to do. The captain darted about the ship, stashing chunks of dried meat and jugs of water. He didn't seem to notice that Alec was still standing there, staring at him.

"I've been good to have on the ship," Alec protested.

"You've told me so. Who is going to fix the tea—and scrub the deck?"

"We'll worry about scrubbing it down when we're back. Go on home, lad. Go home to your folks. They thought it was too rough when Badger broke his leg. They won't want you along on *this* trip."

Alec lowered his head and stared through the planks at the water rolling under the dock. He had not planned on this setback. He had believed that the captain and Douglas would need his help.

The docks were alive with activity now as each captain went to work readying his ship for its journey. Alec was frustrated watching the other sailors scramble over ropes and on and off decks, storing blankets and water, unloading anything that wouldn't be needed for crossing the Channel. Fishing poles and lines, nets and oyster bins were discarded on the docks to wait until they could be used again. Stacks and stacks of ropes and food stood waiting to be loaded on any ship that could store them. This was the moment he had waited for—the moment he could finally do something to help Thomas and Will. And the captain was sending him away like one of the children. It wasn't fair.

But it was no use arguing with Captain Cairns. And when Douglas arrived, Alec knew it would be no better. Douglas had told him before that he didn't think Alec was a seaman. Even now, he felt himself pushed aside by the other sailors as they scurried to be part of the fleet of ships.

Letting his kit drag at his feet, Alec turned slowly and started home. He wanted to protest more, but the captain was set on keeping the news from him. So if Alec slipped and let on that he knew about the little ships, he could be in trouble. Everyone would want to know how he had found out. No one, especially not a kid, needed to be sneaking around, taking risks that could endanger the soldiers. Alec couldn't know before the rest of Dover, and the crews of the little ships were not saying anything.

He had gone two blocks toward home when he thought about Eva. The night before, he had told her he would let her know what he'd discovered in the castle. Certain that no one was expecting him back at the Shaftbury just yet, he walked down Eva's street and climbed her steps.

Her aunt surprised him by opening the door before he knocked.

"Why, Alec!" She smiled. "What are you doing standing on my stoop so early?"

"I've come to see Eva for a minute. Is she awake?"

"Yes, yes. Come in. She's out in the kitchen. Go on back. I'm off to market for a quick bit of shopping."

Alec ducked through the dark hallway, passed the drawing and dining rooms, and entered the kitchen just as Eva was sitting down to breakfast.

"Alec, so early—you're here so early? *Was ist los?* You are tired, *ja?*"

"Tired, yes. And upset. That's why I've come. To tell you what I found out last night."

"What? What is it? They are coming, aren't they?"

"There's a hospital in the castle, Eva. I saw an injured man there being cared for by a nurse. And while I was spying, two soldiers came into the room and started talking—

about the war, about France. The Nazis have taken over France, Eva. They're pushing our boys to the sea."

Eva's face turned pale. "Oh, Alec, I told you. *Ja,* just like *mein Haus* and Germany and Poland. The Nazis—they'll destroy us. We cannot win. They are too powerful. They took the business of *mein* Papa. They took *meine Familie.* They will ruin you, too."

"No, Eva. I've just come from the docks. All the captains in Dover, anyone with an able ship, they're all making ready to cross the Channel and rescue the British army. The call has gone out up and down the coast to vessels everywhere. Other towns are doing the same. We're not beaten. We must believe there's hope. For the lads left over there, we must believe the little ships can help.

"I only wish I could go along." Alec sat down. "But they've got too much to do. They've no time for a boy."

The two friends remained silent. They were out of schemes, and they both were in places where they didn't want to be. One longed to be with family again, to have things as they were before. The other couldn't wait to be on his own, finding his own way, leaving his past behind.

Just then, the front door flew open, and Eva's aunt rushed into the kitchen. "There's terrible news at market," she gasped. "The British army, all of our lads, they're stranded on the coast of France, up by Dunkirk. Hitler has them trapped. We've not enough navy ships to get them off. The Admiralty in London, they want every ship that can, to go over. To rescue the lads. They're to leave before midnight."

Alec and Eva tried to act surprised as Eva kept her aunt talking. "The soldiers—for how long will the ships go?"

"I don't know, Eva." Her aunt moaned. "Oh, we're in for a terrible time."

Alec sat quietly, only half listening to them. He was thinking of something Eva's aunt had said. "They're to leave before midnight."

That night. After dark.

"I've got to run," Alec said, jumping up and snatching his pack.

"So soon, lad?" Eva's aunt asked. "I thought you and Eva might go back out—to the post office. You'll find more news there, don't you think?"

"Oh—I mustn't just now," Alec stammered. "Mum—Mum will be beside herself with the news. I need to be going."

Eva frowned. "Alec, you'll be here. For market?"

"Yes, yes, maybe market—tomorrow. I'll stop by when I go."

"I'll walk to the door *mit*—with you," Eva said, following him.

At the door, she turned to him. "If *Ich*—I—if I could have helped *meine Mutter und mein* papa, I would have. You, Alec, you have a chance to help someone, *ja?* You must do what you can."

Alec nodded and squeezed her hand before hurrying out the door and down the steps. He could hardly keep himself from running home, but he needed to think. If all of Dover was now finding out about the evacuation, then his parents would know as well. If he didn't go home, they would look for him at the *Britannia* and be sure to keep him home. Somehow, he had to get on that ship.

At the inn, he found Aga weeping, her head buried in her apron.

"Lad, have you heard the news? The Admiralty—they've called for ships—as many as can go—to be off to France and lift our troops from the coast. These are bad times, lad. Bad times indeed."

"Yes, I heard the news on the way from the docks," he said, twisting the truth a bit. "Where did you hear?"

"The BBC. Your father had the radio on this morning, and the news broke then. Oh, what will we do if Hitler captures our lads? Or worse, kills them all? It's a grim day for England, lad."

"Hitler won't win, Aga. I've been down by the docks. Hundreds of ships of every kind, from ferries to pleasure boats to tugs—they're all making ready to leave. We've got a chance. We can't give up."

Just then, his mum pushed through the swinging door and found Alec standing there. "Oh, Alec," she said. "I was so afraid you'd gone off. When we heard it on the radio, I was sure you'd already left with the *Britannia*. Thank goodness you're here," she said, hugging him close.

Feeling his mother's arms around him, he knew he could not look at her, or he would break from his plan. So he patted her shoulder and turned quickly toward the larder. "The best plan for us is to keep doing what we've been doing. Hitler would like to have everyone stop for him. But we won't."

"Alec." His mother stepped between him and the larder. "Tell me that you will not go with them."

"Captain Cairns made that decision for me, Mum." He was careful to use the captain's words to avoid a lie. "He said it's no job for a lad like me. He sent me home."

"I know you don't agree, Alec, but the captain's right. You shouldn't go this time." She placed her hand lightly on his cheek and then stepped back, leaving him to his work.

Except for meals, Alec worked the rest of the day away from the others. He stumbled around upstairs in the guest rooms, knowing what he had to do. If the captain would not give him permission to go, he would find another way. This was not just an adventure; it was his chance to do something that mattered. He imagined Will and Thomas calling for help from across the Channel, just as Georgie had pleaded for someone to save him. The sound was deafening. He wanted to shout, "We're coming! Have hope. . . . I'm coming."

19
STOWAWAY

THOUGH HE HAD SNEAKED OUT MANY NIGHTS BEFORE, tonight would be his most difficult escape. He doubted his courage. His mum, Aga, Eva, the captain—he didn't want to disappoint them. And what about the boys in France? What if he got there and then ran away in fear?

When everyone had gone to bed and the rooms were empty, he walked through the downstairs. He slipped into the drawing room and saw the radio resting silently on the mantel above the fireplace. He ran his hand along the mantel's edge, thinking about the nightly gatherings for the BBC.

He moved back into the lobby. A peg on the hat stand held the slicker he had been wearing the day Badger broke his leg. And in the dining room, the sideboard held stacks of dishes and cups, ready for breakfast. Back in the kitchen, he pushed the larder door shut and then paused at the back door. The lingering scent of Aga's pot roast tempted him to give up and go to his room.

He had thought so often of leaving the inn—of launching out on his own, of making his own path. But he had never thought about not coming back. Through all his planning and wishing, he had known that, should he need to, he could return. But the path he was setting out on now could not promise a safe return. He was going into battle— a battle that could take his life. But he was going to help others whose lives were lost for sure if the ships didn't go. The answer for him was clear; he'd known it since the discovery inside the castle. He was sorry for the way he had deceived his mum, but he'd been given no choice. His path was across the sea. He shook off his doubts and went on his way.

He knew he would need some great luck to board the *Britannia* without being seen. If the docks weren't busy, he would certainly be spotted. He hoped that something would distract the captain and Douglas, so he could scurry onboard.

But he didn't need a distraction. The docks were nearly deserted. He could hear some blokes talking far down the planks, but at the *Britannia,* everything was quiet.

"Aye, as soon as the rest of them are back from their final pint at the pubs, we'll shove off," Alec heard one seaman call out.

He looked around the *Britannia* and noticed that the ship had been outfitted for a long journey. Jugs of water were strapped to the inside rails. Dozens of blankets had been folded and packed tightly in the open hold.

He moved to the locker and lifted its lid. It was filled with bread. Grabbing as many loaves as he could, he scrambled down the galley steps and stowed the bread under the bench. Then, two more times, he climbed back up on deck, and carried all but a few loaves to the galley, storing them anywhere he could find room. He hoped the captain and Douglas would each think the other had moved the supplies.

Back on deck, he pulled the tarp from the bottom of the locker, stuffed his pack into the corner, and climbed in. He lay down and pulled the tarp up to his chest. Then, with one hand, he spread the remaining loaves on top of the tarp and ducked beneath it. The space was tight, but he could manage.

He no sooner was tucked inside than he heard noises on the dock. The sailors were boarding their vessels. He kept still, waiting to hear the captain's or Douglas's voice. His heart was pounding; his palms were wet as they gripped the tarp. Then he heard the thud of feet as the two men climbed onboard. The locker muffled the crew's actions, but he could tell they were unlashing the lines and preparing to shove off.

Alec could hear himself breathing—quick, raspy sounds. He feared the men on deck would hear him, too, so he slid deeper into his hiding place and waited. He wasn't sure when he would make himself known. He had to be careful to allow enough time for the ship to be too far out in the Channel to return. Again, he felt guilty. What would the captain say? He'd be angry, no doubt. But once they were gone, what could anyone do to him? He'd stowed away: that was the truth. He'd take each blow as it came.

He heard other boats start their engines and motor away from the dock. Then he felt the *Britannia* shudder and lurch forward as its engine powered it out into the Channel. He imagined the captain in the wheelhouse, his pipe between his teeth, helping the *Britannia* to queue up with the other little ships.

After a while, he heard less noise. The steady *swish-slap* of the waves as they beat against the bow nearly lulled him to sleep. He roused himself. A good shipmate was always alert, he remembered. He had to follow seamen's rules if he wanted to prove himself. So he sat up as best he could and waited. He didn't know how long they'd been gone, but he knew the sea was rough by the groaning of the ship and by the way he had to steady himself inside the locker.

Alec lifted the lid of the locker just in time to hear the captain order Douglas to go below for a rest before taking his turn at the helm. Feeling confident that they had sailed too far to turn back, Alec dared to lift the lid a little higher. From his hiding place, he could see the captain staring straight ahead, guiding the *Britannia* toward France.

Alec dreaded his next move. He didn't want to see the look on the captain's face when he appeared on deck. But he couldn't stay hidden forever. He had come to help, not to hide in a box and miss all the action. So he climbed out of the locker and dropped the lid. It clanged as it fell, and the noise caught the captain's attention. In an instant, the captain knew what Alec had done.

"Come here to me, sonny," the captain shouted from

the open door of the wheelhouse. "Come now if you don't want to be thrown overboard!"

Alec crept toward his boss, keeping his head down.

"What do you think you're doing, lad, stowing away on my very own ship? In all my years of sailing, I've never had a stowaway—till now. And it's a lad I trusted with all my heart. What have you got to say for yourself? Come on, speak up!"

"I had to come," Alec said. "I've been to sea enough to know what to do. And my friends are stranded there in Dunkirk. I couldn't stay any more than you could. I'm a seaman, just like you. I couldn't be left behind."

"Aye, Alec. I know you're wanting to be the hero and save everybody. But war is not so easy a place to shine. The report when we left was that the Germans had stopped their tanks ten miles from Dunkirk. Said they were just going to hold there and keep our boys up against the Channel so that the Luftwaffe could destroy them from above. It will be hellish—not like anything you've ever seen."

"I'm not afraid, and I have to go. Please, Captain, don't be angry."

"There'll be thousands of lads sprawling on that coast. What makes you think you'll ever find your friends? And we're not on holiday, you know. This is war."

"I'll do anything you ask. Let me stay and work with you."

"As if I have any other choice now! You've managed to come out of hiding when we're well under way, though we've a long way to go. The Germans have mined the

Channel, and we're having to take the north route. It's going to be a long journey and an even longer night, Alec. Now be off with you. Go down below with Douglas and get some rest. I'll mind the helm."

Alec wasn't ready to meet Douglas yet. "Can I just stay here? Near the locker? I can lie back on the tarp inside. That way I'm close if you need anything."

"All right, lad. I'm thinking Douglas would thrash you if I did send you below. So sit back in the locker, and from now on, follow orders. Get some rest. No one knows what we're in for when we get there."

Alec was weary. He heeded the captain's words and settled back on the tarp. The sky was unusually clear, no hint of clouds. He gazed at the stars and thought of his mum. She would be sad to discover he'd left after all. He remembered the soldiers in the castle saying the prime minister would call for England to pray. He knew his mum would go to church. This time, if he had been there, he would not have let her go alone. He also thought of Eva. She had understood. She recognized his need to do something to help. He hoped he wouldn't disappoint her. As he drifted off to sleep, he realized that if ever he needed to do right, this was the time.

He woke to thunder, or so he supposed. It was after dawn; Alec could not see a hundred yards beyond the bow. It wasn't the usual Channel haze, though. Instead, the air was cloudy and smelled odd—like something burning. The odor of petrol stung his nose. Then he remembered where he was. He jumped up from the locker and caught Douglas's stare. Sometime during the night, Douglas and the captain had switched places, and now the first mate sneered at Alec.

"Lot of good ye'll be to us, boy, if all ye do is sleep and eat. What a bloody fool ye are to have stowed away. Ye've no idea what ye've done to yerself. Well, aah won't be your nursemaid."

"I want to help," Alec shot back.

"Don't talk tripe, boy. Ye'll suck food and water that should be saved for the other blokes. Ye'll be little 'elp. Just keep yerself out of the way an' don't be sobbin' when the bombers drop their loads."

Off in the distance, the thunder roared again, and Alec heard a faint whine. It sounded like a motor that was struggling to charge. Then he remembered he'd heard the sound before—the day the Jerries were scouting the coast. Straining now to see, he scanned the horizon and saw the black smoke curling toward the sky.

"Yer right, boy. That's the Jerries poundin' the coast. The same coast where the Brits are sittin', waitin' for us to 'elp. We're in for it, that's for sure. We'll need all the luck we can get to make this trip work."

By this time, the captain had come up from below deck and was standing next to Douglas, watching the sky as well. As they drew closer to shore, the sounds grew louder.

Wheee, wheee, kaboom! Wheee, wheee, kaboom! The Stukas screamed as they dropped their bombs on the French coast. The air was clearing a bit, and Alec could now see other ships trailing along with them. In front and behind, ships of all sizes and designs were making their way toward the Dunkirk coast. "There must be a thousand of them," he said to Douglas. But the first mate only grunted and kept his eyes fixed on the bow.

Ahead of them, Alec recognized one of the paddlewheel boats he'd seen on the Thames when his mum had taken him to London. To their left was a tugboat chugging to keep up. The *Britannia* kept its course, following the lead of the vessels in front. Within minutes, Alec could see the coast. Dark, heavy smoke seemed to rise from every inch of the shore.

Boom, boom, boom. Alec watched as British destroyers took aim at the planes overhead. Puffs of smoke hovered in the skies above them as the ships fired round after round from their antiaircraft guns.

Overhead, the German planes shrieked *Wheee, wheee, wheee,* then dropped lower to release their bombs before rising again out of range of the British guns. Alec saw fountains spray up where the Jerries had sent their bombs into the Channel.

He had never imagined anything so horrible. They were near enough now to see the Dunkirk coast, littered with disabled tanks and lorries. A jetty stuck out into the Channel, but as Alec looked closer, he saw that the jetty was made up of sunken boats, lorries, and abandoned equipment lying end to end and settled into the shallow waters near the shore. About a mile beyond the jetty, several large navy vessels were anchored. Other ships lay burning in the water, victims of the Stukas' shelling. The whole place looked like a ship graveyard.

What most alarmed Alec were the queues of men that snaked along the shore and into the water. Thousands of men, their bodies blackened with spilled oil, stood chest deep in water. Hoisting their rifles above their heads, the men waited for their turn to board the little ships.

"There are so many," Alec said to no one in particular.

"What's that, lad?" the captain called.

"There're so many of them," Alec said again. "How can we ever make enough trips to get them home?"

"We won't be making trips home. See those destroyers out there? It's too shallow here for the lot of them. So we're to pick up the men and take them to those ships. It'll be tricky work, though." The captain spoke quickly now, as they were getting closer to their target. "These men will be cold and starving. Our biggest problem will be to keep them queued up so they don't rush our boat and swamp us. Then we'll come back and do it again."

As Alec looked around, he saw the war that Aga so hated. Lads, some barely older than Alec, shivered in the water. They pushed to move closer to the small vessel edging toward them. The Channel was up to their necks. Others were screaming to their mates, "Keep back! Don't push! Stay in your queue!"

Some of the smaller ships were already starting to load soldiers. Alec watched as crew members beat back the few who broke ranks and stormed one boat. Within minutes, the boat was filled and moving toward the larger vessels out in the Channel.

The *Britannia* was next. Rather than work from the water, the captain turned toward the jetty and pulled up alongside. Like the other parts of the shore, the jetty held long rows of British soldiers. But these queues were reserved for the wounded. As the *Britannia* edged toward the shore, Alec saw hundreds of soldiers, their faces, arms, and legs wrapped with bandages. Some men, their heads covered in white gauze, were led by fellow soldiers. Others lay helplessly on the makeshift dock, unable to stand. Many were simply staring out to sea. Unlike the thousands of men in the water, the wounded waited patiently, even quietly.

The *Britannia* bumped noisily against the jetty, and Alec jumped off to tie up. Slowly, he helped the bandaged warriors climb aboard one by one. The captain and Douglas then settled each man into a spot. When the *Britannia* could take no more, Alec untied it from the jetty and jumped on deck. As the ship pulled into the Channel, Alec rushed about offering bread and water to anyone who could eat. If he had stopped to gaze at the men, he would have been useless. Their injuries were gruesome. Blood drenched many of the bandages, and several of the men drooled and vomited when he tried to help them drink. Still, Alec moved along from man to man.

Alec counted thirty men on the ship's main deck, pushed together like bags of grain. And except for a few moans from those most severely injured, the ship was quiet. For now, the enemy planes had disappeared, so the roaring overhead was gone. But the shouting of those onshore and in the water reminded Alec of what a big job lay before them.

When they reached the destroyer, Alec stood out of the way as men from the larger ship dropped a rope ladder over the side. Then two sailors hurried down the ladder and boarded the *Britannia*.

"First we'll take those who can climb on their own," one of them ordered.

Alec watched as the ones who were able got to their feet to board the big ship. The sailors stood at the bottom of the ladder, each holding a side as the first man made his way up. The ladder swayed in and out with the weight of the man, but soon he was helped onboard by those on the larger ship. Then went the next man and the next, until all who were able to climb on their own were aboard.

The sailors then called for a gurney, which was lowered by ropes over the side and placed on the *Britannia*'s deck. Douglas helped a soldier slide onto it. A sailor secured the straps that would hold the injured soldier, and then the sailor signaled for those on deck to crank the hoist and raise the gurney skyward. Alec held his breath as the gurney spun in half circles while it was lifted to the deck of the destroyer, but the soldier was soon unloaded and the gurney was again dropped over the side. The process was repeated until the *Britannia*'s deck was empty except for its crew.

When the last man had been lifted off the *Britannia*, the captain ordered Douglas to turn around and head back to the jetty. As they neared the dock again, Alec noticed that the queue looked even longer than it had before. It looked to him as if they'd made no progress.

But they did what they had come to do. They ferried load after load from the jetty to the destroyer. The hours passed into late afternoon, and the queue moved slowly forward. Occasionally, a brash soldier from another group would try to muscle his way in among the wounded, but Douglas needed only to snarl at him to turn the lad around and send him scurrying.

It was difficult work. Just when Alec thought he had gotten used to the sight of blood, he would turn to face a young soldier with a gash on his face that had nearly severed his nose. Or he would touch the arm of an injured soldier and feel the man's hot breath as he cried out in pain.

Each load brought more injured. And Alec searched every face. He didn't know if Thomas or Will was hurt, or if they were even in this spot. But something told him they were, and he wasn't going to miss them. When the ship was full and they had set off for the destroyer, he walked about looking at each soldier, asking if he'd seen a Thomas Spencer or a Will Sweeney. When the *Britannia* passed close to the other queues, he scanned them for familiar faces.

The planes didn't return until late in the day. Perhaps blinded by the smoke from the burning equipment onshore and in the water, the Jerries chose certain times to swing down and drop their bombs. At the first hint of their whining engines, those men not in queues jumped behind abandoned equipment on the beach. Others ducked into pillboxes built by the French. Anyplace they could find cover, the British troops hid, and the planes buzzed overhead, aiming for the massive ships at sea.

Alec and the others could only watch helplessly as a Stuka lowered its left wing and broke from the others. Racing toward a trawler packed with soldiers, the Stuka leveled off just above the crowded ship and let loose with its bombs.

Wheee, wheee, wheee! The bombs screamed, all of them hitting their mark. Men cried out as the ship split in two and rolled onto its side, spilling its cargo into the Channel.

"Let's go to them, Captain!" Alec cried out. "They need our help." But Douglas and the captain shot a look at each other and shook their heads.

"We can't, sonny," the captain called back. "There'll be only bodies left to pick up. I'm sorry, lad, but our orders are to help the living."

Alec stared at the sinking vessel, nearly gone from sight. Nothing moved in the water. The captain was right; they were all dead. Turning his eyes away, Alec watched as the men in his queue waited. More fearful of losing their place than of being hit by bombs, they stood firm. Alec, too, grew more used to the whistling of the bombs. Though he couldn't ignore them altogether, he was grateful for the *thud, thud* he would hear when the bombs fell useless on the beach, their power smothered by the sand.

The raids lasted only a few minutes at a time, but they delayed the evacuations. Sometimes, the little ships had to move away from the coast when the Jerries came, and then it took time to return to shore and start loading the queues again. The effort was painfully slow.

"We'll never be able to keep this up if those planes stay in the air," the captain said.

Douglas agreed. He was ready to leave. "Aah say we fill the *Britannia* with as many as it can 'old an' make our way back to Dover. Wait until after dark an' just slip into the night. No one will miss us; there's so many little ships 'ere. Aye, we've done our part to bring some 'ome."

"We didn't volunteer to bring just *some* of them home," the captain retorted. "We came to do all that we can to help. Running away before the job is finished isn't what we do."

"Aah say it is!" Douglas shouted. "Why, we've barely moved two hundred men. An' there are thousands 'ere. We cannit 'elp them all. Aah say we go while we can— before the Jerries find *our* ship with one of those bombs."

"And I'm the captain of this ship, and I say we stay another day. We'll work through the night. Do whatever we can when the Jerries aren't flying. Every man off the shore is another man on his way home. That's what we're here to do."

Douglas looked at the captain and then at Alec. Alec knew Douglas was a rough sailor, crude at times, used to getting his way. But he wouldn't mutiny—though he was ready to thrash someone.

"Aah won't be likin' what yer sayin' I must do, Cap'n, but aah won't be quittin', either. Look at this place! We'll never be finished. But aah'm 'ere until my captain says to go."

With that, Douglas stormed across the deck and jumped down to the galley. Something made Alec want to follow—to tell Douglas he understood. The job did seem useless. But Alec knew Douglas's ways; he knew Douglas did not want anyone's help—especially the help of a galley boy.

When they docked again for another load of men, Douglas was back up top, barking out orders and pointing people to their places on the ship. Alec was sure that Douglas wasn't done with the fight, and he admired the first mate for pushing on.

When he had time, Alec spoke to some of the soldiers who were willing to talk. Many of them hailed from London; none was from Dover, and none knew Thomas or Will.

"Is there a hospital nearby?" Alec asked one of them. "You've been bandaged up." He was remembering the feeling that had nagged him for several days now, a feeling that somebody—Thomas or Will—needed his help, that someone was not able to help himself.

"Aye," the soldier answered. "There's an infirmary where the worst are taken. We were treated and sent on. But some are on gurneys. I don't know how they'll get off. One bloke—he came in while I was there—he was one of those poor chaps who came behind us, blastin' all the equipment we had to abandon. He was bad. Torn up and too weak to even walk on his own."

"What?" Alec questioned, startling the young soldier.

"What did you say about blasting equipment? Do you mean the demolitions unit? Is that what he was?"

"Aye, that's what his friends said when they brought him in. I didn't see him after that. They took him away from the rest of us."

Alec listened as the soldier told him where to find the infirmary. Located about a thousand yards back from the jetty, it was one of the few spots protected by a solid roof, the soldier said.

"The infirmary unit," the soldier continued, "they took over a church. Set up a hospital right there. It's suffered some damage from the panzer shelling, but the Jerries have backed off. So the doctors and nurses are making do for now."

Alec didn't want anyone to suspect what he was thinking. If Douglas had any hint that Alec might leave the *Britannia,* he would tie Alec to the helm and hold him until they were back in Dover. But Alec also knew that if he did sneak away, the captain would not leave him behind. The skipper could never face Alec's parents and tell them he'd left their boy on the beach at Dunkirk.

Alec knew what he had to do. He also knew it was mad. But he could not go back to Dover without having tried his hardest to save Thomas and Will. And something else was pushing him to get off the ship. Was it Margaret? Could he hear her voice even here? In Dunkirk? He thought again of the hospital in the castle and the lone soldier lying injured on the gurney. He didn't want that for his friends. From the beginning, he had felt he had to get onshore. Now, the news from the rescued soldier confirmed his fears. One of the men from the Shaftbury needed his help.

Turning to the other wounded, he wrapped blankets around them and then sat on the locker to wait for the *Britannia* to reach the destroyer. His mind was not on this trip. Instead, he wondered how he was going to get off to find the hospital without Douglas or the captain or one of the soldiers snatching him. He needed a bit of luck, but luck was nowhere on the beaches of Dunkirk.

20
FOREVER *DÓCHAS*

ALEC HAD LOST TRACK OF THE NUMBER OF TRIPS THEY had made. Empty once more, the *Britannia* found its way through the flotilla of other crafts and turned again toward the jetty. Back and forth, back and forth throughout the night the little ships had shuttled, working as quickly as they could to make the queues of men disappear. But they needed more time and cloudy skies. Unlike most days on the Channel, the skies were clear, making it easy for the Jerries not only to fly but also to spot the navy destroyers below them.

Alec imagined that with skies so clear, a plane could find a dinghy in the middle of the ocean. They needed a bit of luck—or that miracle Captain Cairns had talked about—to get all the lads back to England. And with Douglas so intent on weighing anchor and going home, Alec was running out of time. He wanted a chance to get onshore, to get to the infirmary.

As they pulled up once again and Alec started to jump out, he was knocked to the deck by a sudden jolt from underneath the boat. *Whack.* The sound echoed as it rose from the stern.

"What in the king's name has happened now?" Douglas shouted.

The captain shook his head. With all the sunken and broken ships littering the shore, they were fortunate to have avoided obstacles this long. "I think we've struck something with the propeller. I can't get the engine to turn."

"Blast it! Aah knew somethin' would happen if we stayed too long. Now what are we supposed to do?" Douglas demanded.

"I expect you'll have to go below and find out what the problem is. You're the first mate," the captain said.

Douglas stood glaring at Captain Cairns. Then he strode toward the steps and jumped down the hold to the engine. Alec waited, hoping the others would forget he was there. After a few minutes, Douglas called to the captain, and he, too, went below deck.

It was the moment Alec had been waiting for; he wouldn't get another. He bounded over the side, turned in the direction of the shore, and looked down the jetty to see men crowding its entire length. But he had already made his move; he was not going to give up now.

"Sorry, mate; yes, sorry. I've got to get through," he muttered, keeping his head down as he pushed through the soldiers. Realizing Alec must be from one of the little ships, the soldiers let him pass, and soon his feet touched the sandy shore. He scrambled up the beach—and then he stopped and stared.

Before him, covering nearly every inch of ground, were soldiers waiting to be rescued. Some of them hovered near the queues that snaked out to sea. Others were just sitting, waiting until the last moment before they had to stand. Some lay motionless on the sand. As Alec drew closer, he realized those were corpses.

He saw hundreds of men who had been struck down while waiting to be rescued. Too many to count, they lay as they had fallen, faces contorted, arms and legs bent awkwardly beneath them. The smell was sickening. Decaying flesh and old blood tainted the air. Alec covered his mouth and nose with his hand to avoid gagging as he walked among the dead toward the infirmary.

He also saw burned-out carcasses of lorries and tanks and ambulances. All of them were useless, rotting in the sand, waiting for another bomb to finish them off. Seeing the mangled mess reminded Alec of the soldiers' orders at the inn. "Demolition experts," he said aloud. "Sent to destroy their own artillery." The thought made him push harder toward the infirmary.

He shook off the fear that surrounded him. So many men. Thomas and Will could be among them and he wouldn't even know it. But that feeling from before, telling him they weren't dead, telling him they needed him—that feeling pushed him forward. He kept on. If he was wrong, then he was holding up the captain for nothing. If he was right, he would do what he could to get them out.

He stopped by a group of soldiers who had settled in

the sand near the end of a queue. They looked surprised to see such a young boy. "That bandage," Alec said to a soldier with a white cloth around his hand. "Were you at the infirmary? Can you direct me to it?"

"Aye," the soldier said. "Crest that hill and look to yer left. Ye'll see the church steeple. That's the place."

Alec nodded and started up the hill. When he came to the top, he saw the damaged steeple. Moving quickly toward the door, he worried about what he would find. Some men on the jetty had been badly injured, yet they had been sent on. He could only imagine what those inside looked like.

At the church, he pushed through the door and entered the sanctuary. It smelled of blood and urine and sweat. A nurse in a red-stained smock moved quietly from gurney to gurney. She leaned over a soldier whose chest was wrapped tightly in bandages. He was trying to tell her something, and she leaned closer to hear. She smiled, patted his hand, and moved on. She spotted Alec and stared at him, then motioned for him to come to her.

He couldn't move. Most of the wounded were lying on their backs, staring at the broken ceiling. One soldier called out, "Mum, Mum. Why don't ye come to me? . . . God help me."

This is what death looks like, Alec thought. *This is what Aga was remembering—what the captain meant when he talked about my father.* He gagged and choked back the thickness in his throat.

The nurse came over. "What is it, lad? What are you

doing here?" she whispered. "Have you come from the little ships?"

"Aye, I'm Alec, Alec Curtis—I'm here with my captain, helping with the evacuation. But I—I thought," he stammered, "I hoped to find my cousin here. His name's Thomas Spencer."

The nurse thought a minute and then shook her head. "No, we've only a half-dozen patients left. Not many, as you can see. But we've got no Thomas."

"I didn't know . . . that is, he could be dead," Alec admitted, though he didn't want to believe that Thomas might be one of those lying back on the Dunkirk beach. He had risked too much, and that feeling still nagged at him—that Thomas needed him.

Now, looking again at the nurse, he mentioned Will. "There is another soldier, a friend I met in Dover. He's young, not even twen—" But he didn't finish. An open medical case on a nearby gurney caught his attention. A few pieces of silver jewelry lay on its cover.

"Do you think . . . ," he started to ask. "Do you think I might have a look in that case? My friend . . . "

"Yes, yes. That would be okay," the nurse said quietly. "Though I'm sure there's nothing there to help you. Those are the personal items we have from the patients. Often the jewelry gets in the way, and we have to remove it."

Alec barely heard her. He was already at the case, digging through the silver pieces lying there. And in among the silver, he spotted a Celtic cross.

"Do you know where you got this? Was it from someone

who came here, to this infirmary?" he asked, dangling the cross in front of her.

The nurse looked at him oddly. Fingering the cross, she hesitated before answering. "Well, yes, yes, it was. A young soldier gave it to me. He wanted me to keep it for him. He was afraid that someone would take it, and he wanted it returned to his family."

Alec slumped against the gurney. Will was gone.

The nurse watched as Alec fingered the piece of silver. Anxious to get back to her patients, she fussed with a blanket on a nearby cot.

"He was my friend," Alec said. "I knew him from Dover, before he came here. Before he died."

"But he's not dead," she whispered. "The soldier with that cross? He's not dead, though he's in a very bad way. He was Special Forces, you know. He and his mates came behind the infantry as they retreated to the coast. They set charges to destroy equipment so the Germans couldn't use it. He was hit in the chest when a bomb went off early. Aye, he was very serious when his mates brought him in. I made them move out, though they didn't want to leave him. I didn't think he would survive a day, but he's still alive. We've put him in a room behind the sanctuary. I'll take—"

But Alec was already ahead of her, weaving around gurneys and instrument tables while he made his way to the rear of the church. He pushed open the door and was instantly reminded of the scene in the castle tunnel. On a stretcher tucked away in a corner was Will. Alec thought again of the wounded soldier in the castle. He was right to have come.

The nurse moved to one side and passed her hand across Will's forehead. Smiling slightly, Will opened his eyes and stared at her. He didn't speak, but Alec could tell that he was used to her touch. She continued rubbing his face and arm and then leaned down to whisper something to him. He turned toward Alec. His eyes brightened to see his friend, and he motioned for Alec to step up.

Wrapped in bandages that were red from his seeping wound, Will looked much older than his eighteen years. His face was gray and his lips were dry. Alec wanted to scoop him up and carry him back to the *Britannia,* to Dover, to safety. But his bandages told Alec that Will would not leave this place.

"Will," Alec finally whispered. "I've been waiting for you to come home."

Will offered a weak smile.

"I spotted the cross in the medical case," Alec went on. "Knew there weren't many like that one. I was sure it was yours."

Will tried to speak, but no sound came. Then he looked at the nurse, who grabbed a spare blanket and propped it under his head, raising him to face Alec.

"I'm hurt, Alec," Will gasped. "I got meself injured bad."

"I know, Will," Alec whispered back. "But the nurse said you've done better than she thought. She said you're strong," Alec lied.

Will lifted his head and looked at Alec. His smile was gone, and his tired face told Alec what he had already guessed.

"I won't be coming back, Alec," Will answered. "I made my choice and it cost me. Now I must pay the price. I've been a fool."

Alec watched as he settled back, exhausted from the few words. "Will, Will—you did what you needed to do." Alec took his hand. "You came because you thought you should."

"Aye," Will said softly. "I did what I wanted to do. I wish I had waited until my family had wanted it, too. I wish I'd done more to make it easier at home. Now it will be harder yet for them."

Alec wanted to argue with Will, to tell him it was okay, that his family would understand. But he could only stand there, holding Will's hand and watching him struggle for breath, watching the wound in his chest seeping more blood.

"We would've been the best of mates," Alec said.

In a few minutes, Will dozed off, and the nurse motioned for Alec to follow her. Back in the sanctuary, death hovered. Even the church walls could not keep it out. It hung there, waiting to snatch another victim. To take Will.

"He can't go with you, you realize that, Alec," the nurse whispered. "He would never survive the trip to the water, much less the boat ride to England. He wants to stay here. He wants his spot to go to someone else, someone who will live."

Alec knew she was right. He had known it the minute he saw Will lying on that gurney. But he had come so far, given up so much, to be—to be what? A hero? Was that all he wanted? He knew it wasn't that; he had wanted to find Will and make things better. He had wanted to believe that Will had been right to follow his own path. Now Will had said just the opposite; Will had said he'd been wrong.

"You need to go," the nurse said. "Your crew is waiting for you. There's nothing you can do here. I hope you find your cousin."

"Aye—Thomas—Thomas Spencer," Alec murmured, his mind still on Will.

"I'm not remembering the name, but we have a ledger—a record of those we've treated. I'll check it," she said, turning to a large notebook on the table behind her.

As she thumbed through the pages, Alec fingered the Celtic cross. By now, his mum would know he had gone. He pictured her at the Church of St. Mary, touching her cross and thinking of him.

The nurse turned again to him. "I have some news. A T. Spencer was here—two days ago. Suffered an arm wound. Not serious, but enough to bandage. We put it in a sling and sent him off with the others. I'm sorry," she said. "You've missed him. . . . Now you really should go."

"What's to happen to these men—and to you?"

"Most of these soldiers will not survive the night. Their wounds are too severe. We've got orders to stay as long as we can. We'll be one of the last boats out. By that time, I expect my work here will be done. The doctors are already gathering what supplies they can find to help the wounded on the return ships. The bigger concern," she said, pausing, "the bigger concern is the soldiers on the beach. We need to get them out of France. That will take a miracle."

"Miracle." Alec smirked. "I've been on the little ships for more than twenty-four hours, and it *will* take a miracle to rescue all the men stranded on those beaches."

"We'll all do what we can," the nurse continued. "Now you need to move along. God only knows how worried your family must be. Get yourself back home. Give yourself time to grow up. I'll take care of Will. He won't be alone."

Grow up? Alec turned to go, but the nurse stopped him. "Wait," she said. "Will asked that I notify his parents when I got back to England. He wanted them to get more than a telegram. I told him I would, but it would be better if they heard it from a friend. Will you let them know? And keep the cross," she added. "He would want you to have it. Guard it well."

Alec held the cross and looked at the nurse. Then he gave her a quick hug and disappeared through the door. Stumbling at first as he swiped at his eyes, he wanted to sink into the sand and not go on. Then he thought about Will, who was never going to leave Dunkirk, and he took off running toward the jetty.

Cresting the hill, he looked down to see the men plodding along in their queues. He doubted they would ever get away. There were just too many. But some blokes were so far back, they couldn't see how hopeless it was.

The men didn't speak as Alec passed them. Like cattle waiting to be fed, they followed one another—helplessly wedged between the German army and the English Channel.

He hurried on, certain that Douglas was ready to leave without him. Moving down the jetty, past the wounded soldiers, he glanced quickly at those who waited. Now they all looked the same: dirty faces and matted hair, their shoulders stooped from all the standing.

An arm wound, the nurse had said. An arm in a sling—two days ago . . . Could he be in the queue for the wounded? Alec searched each man's face as he passed. But then he remembered that Thomas stood a good head taller than Alec's father. He would be bigger than most of the others in the queue. Alec needed to be looking higher.

Nearing the ship, he could hear Douglas cursing his name. "Bloody little swine!" the first mate bellowed. "Aah'll give him a thrashing he'll not forget!" But Alec didn't care anymore.

He was nearly at the *Britannia,* and stretched to try to catch a glimpse of Douglas. He looked past the injured and saw just ahead of him a bandaged arm hanging in a sling, and above it, a face he had last seen on the platform at the Dover Priory.

"Thomas!" Alec called out, pushing his way into the crowd on the jetty. "Thomas, it's me, Alec!"

For a moment, no one paid any attention. The lapping of the waves on the jetty and the shuffling of boots and rifles as the soldiers scraped along the surface drowned out his voice.

"Thomas Spencer! Thomas, it's me! Please, please!" Alec was shouting now. "Please look this way!"

In that moment, the sea of men parted, and Alec lunged for his cousin. Clinging to him like a life raft, Alec couldn't speak. Then he pulled back and looked up.

"Alec," Thomas gasped. "What . . . what in the name of . . . What are you doing here?"

"I stowed away on the *Britannia*," Alec confessed. "I came to help you. I've been looking for you since we got here."

Thomas stood there, staring at Alec and shaking his head. "I can't . . . I can't believe it's you. Here in France. In this mess. My dad always said you could cut a path where one couldn't be found. No matter, you're a good sight to behold."

Alec brushed at his hair and looked around, embarrassed now by the stares of those nearby.

"Come on, Thomas," Alec said, grabbing his cousin's hand. "Let's go on up. We've got to get you out of here."

But Thomas didn't move. "Alec . . . mate, I can't just leave this queue and come with you. Those blokes ahead of me have been waiting longer than I have. They're not going to let me move on past them."

Alec stood a moment, looking at Thomas. He glanced at the others around him. He felt too tired to go on. Then, somewhere inside, he started to get angry. He wasn't angry with Thomas or even with the other men. He was angry that nothing had gone as he'd hoped—until now. And he was not going to leave his cousin behind.

"Just grab your stuff and come with me," Alec ordered. "I'll lead you there."

Thomas looked at Alec and then the other men. Still hesitant, he adjusted his rucksack and watched as Alec pushed through the soliders and moved up the jetty toward the *Britannia*. In a second, Thomas was right behind him. As they maneuvered their way through the crowd, some soldiers grabbed at them, shouting for them to go back.

"Hey, mate! What do ye think yer doin'? Get in yer queue!"

"Aye!" another screamed. "We've no spot for ye here! Get back where ye were."

Finally, Alec couldn't take any more. He was almost to the ship. He turned, planted his feet, and looked into those faces around him.

"Listen to me, all of you," Alec ordered. "I'm Alec Curtis, galley boy on the *Britannia*. That's the ship that's docked right there waiting to ferry you out to the destroyer. Now, my captain's been missing me." He pointed to the captain. "And he wants me back soon. If any of you hold me here, I'll remember your faces, and the captain's first mate—he's about as strong as any you'll meet—he will be eager to help you wait for another ship. So stand in my way or get out of it. My cousin Thomas is coming through."

The men stood still for a moment, and then slowly they stepped aside and let Alec and Thomas walk the last few steps without trouble. Climbing over the gunwale, Alec took Thomas's rucksack and helped him find a place to sit. He handed Thomas the blanket he had set aside in hopes he would find his cousin. Then he turned to Douglas.

Glancing from Alec to Thomas and back to Alec, Douglas shook his head. "The lad's right, Captain, we best keep moving. Aah'm ready to make a few more trips if you are. Aah guess it's safer to wait until dark to 'ead 'ome anyway."

The captain stuck his pipe in his mouth and started the engine.

"I see you got it going again," Alec remarked. "Shall I start loading the next bunch?"

"Aye, aye, Alec Curtis, galley boy. You can start anytime," the captain answered. "And let that first mate know if any bloke gives you a hard time."

21
FINDING AND LOSING

ALEC AND THOMAS SPENT THE REST OF THE MORNING and early afternoon on the *Britannia*. Though Thomas should have boarded the destroyer, he and Alec did not want to be separated again, so the captain allowed him to sit below in the galley. The morning had been discouraging; German planes had strafed the beaches again and again. Alec had watched as one of the larger rescue vessels exploded from a German hit, spewing all the men into the Channel.

Wheee, wheee, wheee. The German fighters shrieked as they dove through the clear skies to strike the beaches. The wailing of the planes and men made Alec want to scream himself.

"When will it stop?" he called to Thomas.

"It's been like this since I came," Thomas called back.

Because of his injury, Thomas sat as Alec, the captain, and Douglas worked steadily, helping the injured to board and then shuttling them out to sea where they were lifted to the deck of the waiting destroyer. Several of the large ships had already departed, moving toward the ports of England to deliver the men before returning for more. The Channel grew even more crowded as ships moved in and out of each other's paths, zigzagging to avoid floating debris and the steady bombing.

Their crews were exhausted. Though the ships had brought extra fuel, some captains knew they would have to return home soon to replenish supplies. And then there were the waves. They had kicked up in the early afternoon, slapping against the boats and slowing progress.

But in the late afternoon, the skies changed. After two days of clear weather and shrieking Stukas, the heavens were now filled with a thick mass of dark clouds. Though no rain came, the clouds, together with the black smoke from burning vessels and tanks, obscured the shore. Almost at the same time, the men on the jetty and onshore realized what had happened. The sky had grown eerily quiet. Down the queues the word was passed.

"Aye!" one soldier shouted. "The bloody Jerries can't see. They've gone home to hide!"

Alec watched as each soldier's face turned skyward, and then he listened as, one by one, the men passed the news: "They can't fly," the soldiers repeated. "The clouds are grounding them."

"'Tis a miracle for England, 'tis," another said, and Alec smiled, remembering the captain's words back in Dover: "You need to believe. . . . Otherwise, when it comes, you'll miss the miracle."

"We've bought some time with this cloud cover," the

captain said to Douglas. "Let's work as fast as we can. We'll do two more trips to the jetty and then take what soldiers we can and make for Dover for more supplies. We've been out of blankets and food since this morning. We need petrol as well."

"Captain. Aah'm feeling stronger," Douglas said, looking at Alec. "We can make more passes than that, don't ye think?"

"We best not, mate," Cairns answered. "But we'll be home and back again—if you're willing."

"Aye," Douglas answered. "Just get me a pint or two, and aah'm fit."

It was after dark when the second load was onboard the destroyer, and the *Britannia,* filled with wounded soldiers, turned toward Dover.

"Douglas," Captain Cairns yelled. "Shift some lads to the port side and give us some balance for the trip."

"Aye, Captain," Douglas answered, helping two young soldiers to their feet. Then the boat turned slowly toward the center of the Channel. Thomas had come back on deck to be with the others. Alec was too tired to talk, and with no soldiers to load and deliver, he had some time to rest and think. He thought of Will and touched the cross hanging around his neck. He had lost three friends to death now. But this time, he knew he had done all he could to prevent it. Will had said it himself: "I made my choice." Still, Alec felt empty as he let the cross fall against his chest.

The ship bounced through the waves, rocking side to side and lurching when it slapped down in the frothy water. They had gone at such a hectic pace for so long that now the captain and Douglas could do little more than sit at their posts and stare into the blackness ahead. Many of the soldiers slept, relieved to be on their way home.

Thomas sat on the locker that had been Alec's hiding place, his wounded arm still resting in a sling. Alec moved among the men, checking to see that they were as comfortable as the crowded space would allow.

Douglas was at the wheel. The darkness prevented him from seeing more than a short distance beyond the bow. Alec watched as he peered into the night, listening for any sound that would signal disaster. But the waves and the weariness were taking their toll—Alec knew that Douglas was struggling to stay awake. Then a blaring foghorn brought them all to attention.

There, directly in front of them, not a hundred yards away, a large ship, one of the barges from the Thames, was moving slowly through the water. The *Britannia* was at full throttle, bearing down on the barge like one of the German planes. Though the barge had tried to warn him, Douglas did not have enough time to avoid a collision unless he pulled hard to the leeward side. With no other choice, he spun the wheel and shouted to the passengers, "Hold on, mates. We're sure to roll a bit!"

The *Britannia* turned sharply into the brunt of the waves, shifting sideways as it did. Anything not tied down hurtled toward the passengers, who tried to shield themselves from the flying cargo. In the chaos, Alec saw Thomas slip off the locker. With one arm in a sling,

Thomas used his good hand to slap away a barrel that was rolling toward him. Then, too fast for Alec to grab him, he lost his balance, slid across the deck, and flipped over the rail into the Channel. Alec spun around just in time to watch him fall.

"Thomas!" Alec screamed, charging to the rail. "Thomas!" he called as the ship righted itself in the waves. Glancing portside at the barge drifting out of their path, Alec turned again toward the black water, straining to see his cousin. "Thomas!" Alec called again. "Answer me!"

Someone grabbed his arm. It was Douglas. "Do ye see 'im, Alec? Can ye see 'im anywhere?"

"I can't," Alec shouted. "It's too dark."

Then Alec heard a splash. Douglas had jumped into the sea. Alec saw him clawing at the water as he spun around searching. Just beyond him, Alec suddenly spotted Thomas struggling to stay afloat.

"There!" Alec cried. "There, Douglas, to your left. There he is!"

Lunging toward Thomas, Douglas caught him by his shirt and pulled him back to the boat. Then he whirled about and pushed Thomas to Alec, who stretched over the rail and grabbed his cousin's good hand. Aided by two of the soldiers, Alec dragged Thomas up and over the gunwale, and he flopped onto the deck, gasping for breath.

"Now Douglas," Alec called to the others, and turned to the water. Hanging far over the rail, he reached out his hand for the first mate. The sea churned around them. But Douglas was nowhere in sight.

"Douglas!" Alec cried into the wind. "Douglas, where are you?" There was no answer. Alec ran to the other side and called out, but the sea and sky blended together as blackness hid any sign of life. "Douglas!" Alec called again and again, and then stopped to listen. The sea and the wind were all he heard.

Leaving the wheel to one of the soldiers, the captain rushed over to Alec. "Can you see him, lad?"

"No. No, I can't see him! He's not where he was when he helped Thomas."

They were both at the side now, calling and looking into the dark water. "Douglas!" Alec cried. "Douglas, answer me!" Back and forth Alec ran, crying out for Douglas—until the captain caught him.

"He's gone, Alec," the captain said, his voice breaking. "It's too dark. We can't see him. I'm sorry, lad. There's nothing more to be done."

"But how?" Alec called out. "How could he do that? Douglas, you silly fool; you can't even swim."

"He did it for Thomas," the captain said, swiping at his eyes. "He saved Thomas through sheer strength and guts. And he did it for you. You're the one that gave him a purpose today—made him feel needed. But as you said, he was no swimmer, especially in these seas."

Alec sat down hard on the locker. He couldn't believe Douglas was gone. "Then what was he thinking? Jumping in like that?"

"He was Douglas, Alec. You know that. He would stare anything down, including his fears. His toughness was all he had."

Alec shook his head at the senselessness of it all. What had made Douglas do that? Just jump right in without a thought? He had told Alec once that he lived only for himself; no one else mattered. But in Dunkirk, Douglas had changed. He'd gone from grumbling about the soldiers to carrying onboard those who couldn't get on alone. The captain was right; he'd saved Thomas for Alec.

"He did what needed to be done. Be glad for that," the captain said, moving slowly to the wheelhouse.

Alec slid off the locker and pulled a blanket around Thomas, who was shaking from the drenching. Neither boy spoke. Sitting next to his cousin, Alec leaned his head back and stared up into the sky. It was time to go home.

22
AN EXTRA PLATE

ALEC COULD SEE THAT DOCKING THE *BRITANNIA* WAS going to take some time. Other little ships had come in before them, and the pier was crowded with people waiting to help the soldiers. Some men came off carrying nothing, while others clung to their rifles. "Keep back!" one soldier shouted when someone tried to take his gun. "My lieutenant said to stay close to my weapon. I'm to give it to no one." But after some coaxing from an officer nearby, he relented and handed the weapon to the ship's captain. "Only until I have use for it again," the soldier said.

It was chaos at the landing. Families were hanging around, hoping for a glimpse of a loved one. Women from local churches held out sandwiches and mugs of tea. The soldiers grabbed greedily at anything offered, some not having eaten for days.

Everyone wanted to know what had happened. Questions flew over Alec's head as he finally drew close enough to lash the *Britannia* to its stakes. Almost before he had tied up, people from the town were climbing aboard, helping the wounded from the ship. The women wrapped blankets around the soldiers, gently leading them toward waiting ambulances and autos.

Alec was tired. He had spent the past two days scrambling from ship to dock to ship again, and though he was happy to be back, he didn't want to talk. But then he remembered Thomas.

"Aunt Lucy and Uncle Jack," Alec called to Thomas. "They'll be looking for you. They haven't heard anything in weeks. Come on, let me help you get up."

But Thomas wasn't listening to Alec. His eyes looked past his cousin to something on the docks. Alec turned to see Aunt Lucy gazing at the *Britannia* and her son standing on its deck.

Uncle Jack was fighting his way through the crowd. People swarmed around each ship, looking among the soldiers for a son or father as the injured were being helped off. Finally, Uncle Jack was able to climb onboard and hug his son. Then, noticing the sling, he stepped back and mumbled, "Oh, Thomas . . . I'm sorry, son. I didn't see . . . I didn't know you'd been hurt."

"I'm okay, Dad. Just glad to be home. To be back with you and Mum. We thought we wouldn't see England again."

Aunt Lucy watched as the men stepped off the ship and came toward her. Then the three of them stood there, encircled in each other's arms, as Alec had seen them do the day Thomas had shipped out.

He should have felt happy. Standing there, watching

this family come together. He should have been relieved to be home. But something was missing. He turned back toward the ship just as Aunt Lucy spoke his name. She was standing next to him.

"Thank you, Alec," she said. "Thank you for finding Thomas. I know you shouldn't have gone. And I would have stopped you myself if I'd known your plan. But thank you for bringing our son to us." She smiled and hurried away, joining her men once more.

It's over, Alec thought. *I found Thomas and Will. I didn't foul things up. So why don't I feel better?* He realized that the little ships had made a difference for Aunt Lucy and Uncle Jack. And the trip had proved that he could tend a ship and follow a plan. But inside, that dark feeling crept in again. He knew what was wrong.

"I wish I'd done more to make it easier at home," Will had said. Alec knew that he himself could have said the same. He had heard the words in his head all the way home. He had tried to ignore them—and that nagging, but it was there again. Something was still pushing him to act.

Ever since Georgie's death, Alec had struggled to find his way. Now he realized that the captain had told him what he needed to do. So had Eva. And Will had really meant the same thing: Value what you have now. There will be time later to make your choices. But for now, look around at what you have and do what you can to keep it going.

It was family that mattered, Alec realized. Eva had lost hers. And Will—Will's family had lost him. But Alec had time yet. Time to grow up with his family. He wouldn't be so foolish as to throw that away.

He finished winding up the rope and checked the knots on the moorings to be sure they were secure. Captain Cairns, his pipe in his hand, was busy talking with one of the officers, filling him in on what they'd seen at Dunkirk. As Alec passed them, he heard the captain remark, "And the weather—why, it just turned, mate. In a matter of hours, we had cloud cover and smoke so thick a seagull couldn't see to fly. Gave us the break we needed from those Jerries, it did."

Alec smiled. "Aye, Captain," he said. "There's your second miracle. Not too many lucky enough to have seen that."

"Aye, you're right, sonny," the captain said. "You keep that for yourself as well. Miracles are few," he said, tipping his hat.

"I won't be joining you on the next trip across the Channel," Alec said.

"Aye," the captain said. "I'm not surprised, lad. You've got business here. It'll be tough, but I'll manage with a new crew until you're ready to join me again."

Alec nodded and moved on down the dock. A familiar voice was barking out orders, just as Alec had heard it do a hundred times. He'd know that voice even among the milling crowd that now surrounded him. It was his father's.

Alec wasn't ready for his father, and he searched for a spot to hide until he could think what to do next. Crouching behind a tall stack of blankets and water jugs waiting to be carried on the next ship across the Channel, he drew his collar up around his face. He couldn't be found out—not yet. He was hopeful his father had not seen him.

He watched as soldiers were gathered up and driven to hospitals or lodging. Some, like Thomas, had minor wounds that would keep them in Dover only a few days before they could catch the train back to London. Others couldn't move without help. Alec thought about his visit to the castle and wondered if the more seriously injured might end up in the tunnel infirmary. It was the night he'd entered that tunnel that had pushed him to Dunkirk, and to the dock where he now stood.

"We've got beds enough for six at the inn," Alec's father called to the women handing out food. "So if any of these lads need a room, ring us up and we'll be down to get them. They'll get a good meal and a warm place to sleep. We'll make sure of that."

Something in the voice made Alec look again in his father's direction. What had happened? His father was different. Then Alec, too curious to hide any longer, stepped silently past the crowd and edged down the pier toward a lorry waiting at the end.

Slamming the door and waving the lorry on, his father turned and faced him. Neither said anything at first. Then Alec spoke. "Dad, I heard your voice. . . . I'm sorry I left—"

"Don't, Alec," his father snapped, stepping toward him. "Don't apologize to me," he said, nearly whispering now, "not before I have a chance to say I'm sorry. I'm sorry for pushing you so hard, lad, so hard that you could do nothing except push back. I have wronged you, son. It's me who needs to be asking for forgiveness," he said as he wrapped his arms around Alec and held him tight.

"No need to talk now, lad," Alec's father continued. "We'll have plenty of time at the inn. You've had some hard days—most of them *before* you crossed the Channel. We'll talk soon. For now, it's enough to see you're safe. Your mum has been lost since you left."

"Lost?" his mother shouted, grabbing Alec's jacket and spinning him around. "*Lost* is not the word, love. Weeping day and night. That's what I've been doing. And praying God would bring you to me. And He has. Thank God, He has!"

Alec wilted in her embrace, burying his face in her shoulder. He wanted to tell her he'd changed. He wanted to confess he'd been wrong about a lot of things.

For a few minutes, they all stood there—Alec, his dad, his mum. Then his dad nodded toward the lorry. Alec saw Eva huddled there, looking as lost as when he'd first seen her. She didn't move.

"Eva," Alec called.

She walked slowly toward the family, not wanting to intrude. But Alec reached out and caught her by the arm, giving her a quick hug. His parents watched quietly.

"Well," his father said, breaking the silence. "The lorry's full. I guess we've got no choice but to walk. Okay with you, Gwen? Eva?"

"Aye," Alec's mother said. "We've not walked from the shore together in a long time. I think the walk is just what we need."

"But we best be quick. We can't be too far behind that lorry or Aga will start emptying the larder, fussing that she has nothing to feed those lads."

They all laughed at the thought of Aga opening the door to six soldiers covered in oil and dirt, and her muttering, "Not a soul around to give me a bit of help!"

Still holding him by the arm, Alec's mum let their pace slow, allowing his father and Eva to get several feet in front of them. "Your father's changed, Alec. I hope you can see that."

"Aye, Mum. When I heard him at the docks—and then when I saw him with the soldiers—I wondered what had come about."

His mother smiled. "Believe it or not, Alec, it was Mr. Churchill *and* your journal that made the difference. When I found your bed empty two nights ago, I searched for a note, anything that you might have left. Then I found your journal. It was too late to stop you—the ships had long sailed. So I read about you and Georgie and your dreams of being a seaman. And then I read the part about Eva. I wished you could have told us about her."

"We'd only just met. And you know what Dad said about the German orphans. He wouldn't have liked it."

"I know, Alec. . . . Then yesterday, the prime minister and archbishop called all of England together for a day of prayer. Your father wouldn't go, so I went to Eva's home and asked her to join me at St. Mary's.

"But Dad?" Alec asked.

"At first he wanted to hear nothing about Eva, but then,

at church, I turned to see him standing near the back. When I motioned him over, he sat down in the pew until we were finished. On our way to the inn from Eva's, Mrs. Tanner told us that soldiers were on their way home." She paused. "Your father couldn't get to the docks early enough this morning."

"Aye. I can see the change. And I've changed, too. I saw Will, Mum, before he died. He told me to come home."

They continued for a several steps and soon found themselves opposite Mrs. Tanner's Fifty Shilling Tailor Shop—just as she emerged, broom in hand. Alec stopped, then went right up to her.

"My cousin Thomas, Mrs. Tanner. He's home and safe. Will you tell whomever you see, Mrs. Tanner? He's safe."

Mrs. Tanner stared at Alec, her mouth open, as she watched the family go on their way home.

Stopping at the front steps, Alec looked up at the inn. *It'll have to be painted once this war's over,* he thought. He took the front steps two at a time and held the door for the others. *Plenty of work and plenty of time,* he said to himself. For now, he had a table to set, with an extra plate for Eva.

The next two days kept them all busy as they shuffled soldiers in and out of the inn. Alec's dad had promised hearty meals and warm lodging, so Aga spent her hours in the kitchen, while Alec kept the fireplaces clean of ashes and filled with cozy embers. The damp weather continued into June as soldiers spilled onto the Dover docks for several days before the evacuation was over.

"I wouldn't have believed that Churchill could do what he's done at Dunkirk," Alec's father said one night at supper. "This time—this time he did what was right. Brought those boys home. Saved England, that's for sure."

"Aye, 'e did," one of the soldiers answered. "'e's a tough old bird, 'e is. We'd be sittin' there still, methinks, if Churchill 'ad been as weak as 'itler 'ad thought 'im to be. Thank God, 'itler was wrong. Aye. Thank God."

"But France," another joined in, "France. . . . She's not so lucky. Those lads that got left at Dunkirk, they're probably in the Jerries' hands right now."

Alec listened quietly. The war talk no longer set his heart racing. Rather, he felt more like Aga. The war he'd seen, the queues of men, the shrieking Stukas, the thundering guns—he wanted to leave all of it and its darkness back at Dunkirk. For the first few days, he even avoided the drawing room and the nightly BBC reports. "I've lived it," he said to Aga. "I don't want to hear about it ever again."

But one night he sat down by his mother to hear the prime minister's special broadcast. Alec found himself holding his breath as Churchill's words rang from the radio and filled the room: "We shall defend our island, whatever the cost may be, we shall fight on the beaches, we shall fight on the landing grounds . . . and in the streets . . . we shall never surrender!"

The next morning, Alec helped Aga with breakfast before going off to the market with Eva. Using their ration cards, they picked up some bread and beans. Alec's dad had also given him a few shillings to buy three red roses. After dropping their packages at the inn, Eva and Alec walked up the hill to the cemetery near the church and placed a flower on Margaret's and Georgie's stones. Then they headed to the docks.

"Never surrender," Alec said to Eva as they walked along the Channel to where the *Britannia* was moored. "We shall never surrender. That's what Churchill promised. It was Dunkirk, you know—that made the difference. We will not give up!"

"*Ja*—yes, yes. I heard you, Alec; you've said it over and over now. Herr Churchill; he saved England. He saved us."

"Aye, he did. And I can't explain it, Eva. I can't tell you why I'm sure. But one day we'll fish the Channel, you and I. On a clear day, when we can see France, and the fish are hungry. It will happen, Eva. It will. And we'll talk—about your family and mine and about Georgie and Will."

He stepped onto the deck of the *Britannia* and helped Eva onboard. Then the two of them walked to the bow, and Eva watched as Alec leaned far over the gunwale and flung the final rose into the Channel. "That's for Douglas," Alec announced. "We'll be talking about him for some time. Aye, I'll never forget my mates."